THE SAGITTARIUS MEN
Joseph Dickerson
© Copyright 2022

ONE

Cold north wind blowing squally showers across a series of small hills.
Some were green, many were just mud, and one was a kaleidoscope of gaudy plastic bagged rubbish.
Two ploughs, their engines belching black smoke, pushed the bags upwards to form the next hill.
Men laying black plastic piping into and on the hills, away from the ploughs.
To one side a series of Nissen huts and a weighbridge.
Muddy roads. No trees.
A car park three quarters full.
A high steel wire fence encircled the entire area.
A pungent smell of rotten waste was everywhere, carried by the wind.

"Right. Listen up."
Bernard Jones strode to the front of the small room.
Cold concrete floor. One window.
Along the back wall were three dummy gas points.
Behind Jones was an overhead projector and a white dry wipe board.

Six men sat on chairs facing him.
They each had an old school type wooden desk, with a sloping lid. All had seen better days.
"My name is Bernard Jones, but you's can call me *Mister* Jones. I shall be teaching you's the basics of being a Gasman. I were sitting where you's are some years ago. With hard work, I've worked meself up to me present position. We're recruiting you's cos the field is expandin' and we has to have more monitors. I sacked two men three weeks ago cos them was lazy bastards."
He looked at the faces one by one.
His eyes stopped on Hamilton Veene.
'Oh, I say, a blackie, not many of thems around 'ere, not in Norfolk there ain't. Ah well, he can do the D Section, any weekends and any shit late night call outs he can eat.'
He smiled.
Hamilton felt uneasy in his seat.
'Good mix that, a blackie workin' in shitty D section.'
"Anyone ever done this sort of technical monitoring before?"
Nobody moved or spoke.
He shouted.
"Hello! Anyone there?"
The six men shuffled in their seats.

Each mumbled, "No," or shook their heads.
"Right. So you's all are virgins. That's how I like them."
Bernard Jones was a newly promoted, junior site manager for Thorne's Gas Systems. He'd been with the company for seven years. Previously he'd been a not very successful carpet salesman, knocking on doors, although he never admitted to that.
"At the end of these two weeks I will have taught you's all you's need to know about our gas fields, and how you's can monitor 'em, service 'em, an' make reports on 'em for *senior* management like me to analyse."
He moved his head rotationally to ease his neck stiffness.
"War wound."
Bernard Jones had never been to war, never been in *any* armed forces, but he told anyone who would listen that he was an Iraq veteran.
He was six feet tall. Had a very big and hooked nose that had a permanent reddish tint to it and walked with a hunched over posture.
With small eyes he often squinted, and his sallow complexion made him appear ill. He had a scant amount of straggly black and grey hair on his head.
Hamilton Veene, from Brixton, who was a fourth generation Jamaican, proclaimed to his

new colleagues at their first coffee break that Jones looked like Fagin. They agreed.

The six new recruits sat looking glumly at Bernard as he gave them the make-up of a gas field.

He squinted along the line of new recruits.

He stopped at Danny Bentley, who was wearing John Lennon sun glasses.

"You's got bad eyes, chap?"

"No."

"Why you's wearin' sun glasses indoors, you's blind, or somethin' then?

Danny shrugged.

"No. Just like to, that's all. Habit."

"Is it a disguise? You wanted by the law? Or, 'as you punctured some tarts baby button, an' you is hidin' from her Daddy?"

He looked around for laughter. None came.

"No. None of those, I just like to wear them, no other reason."

Jones shook his head.

"Right. Here's how it works. I'll keep it simple for you's. First a huge bit of land what has all its aggregate, sand, or gravel, extractedated from it. That do leave large valleys of nothin', well, not *nothin'* exactly, but well, um, empty fuckin' big holes. We lay thick clay down an' then gets the councils to come along and drop their household shit in the valley on top of it.

When the valley is full and a ginormous hill has been formed, we gets heavy vehicles to compact it before we does lay thick clay on top of all the shit. We does then drill big plastic pipes through the layers of clay and into the rubbish, right to the bottom nearly. The pipes have filters on 'em at the bottom what keeps out any shit. The council shite eventually does produce a gas what is called methane, see? We then suck the fuckin' methane along a pipeline and into runnin' our massive fuck off generator engines, what you's can see in the compound behind this classroom, an' them produces electricity, what we then flogs off to the National Grid. That's how the company make their dosh."

He looked along the line of men searching for suitable expressions of wonderment.

"Simple eh? But fuggin' clever. Of course, there's a shit load of technology that do gets the system to work. You Gasmen don't need to know nothing of this, leave that worry to engineers and high management people like me."

He squinted at the row of men.

"Any questions so far?"

"Does it ever blow up?" asked Nigel Infine.

Jones nodded.

"Bloody good question. That's where you's lot comes in. You's monitor the pressures see, an' tell senior management like me if the pressure gets too much, an' then I tells you to reduce the pressure so it don't blow up the whole fuckin' field."

He squinted at the new employees in turn.

"Now, does you all understand the basic mechanemism of a gas field?"

Ham smiled at Oliver.

They all nodded.

"Good."

He turned to a dry wipe board.

Oliver Wilson spoke out of the corner of his mouth to the bespeckled Danny Bentley sitting on his left.

"Wonder why we don't just turn the pressures down ourselves, if we see it getting dangerously high?"

Jones wheeled around.

"Who'se talking? Come on, who'se got summat to say. Share it, come on!"

Oliver held his hand up.

"I was just wondering why *we* can't turn the pressure down ourselves, as soon as we see it's high."

Jones sneered at him.

"*Why?* Cos you's ain't senior management, that's fuggin' *why.*"

"Yes, but it would save valuable time, if *we* did it."

"Been here five fuckin' minutes, an' think you's better than the rest of us already, does you?"

"No, I just thought…"

Jones shook his head.

"That's the trouble, you didn't think. Only senior managers like me, *think,* an' *know* when it's safe or not, cos we 'as experience. You's know bugger all. Even the engineers what service the engines look up to me. They know me 'as experience see? You lot are just '*Monitors*', you's don't need much brain to be a fuggin' M*onitor.* The engineers look down on you's."

"What if the pressure is too low?"

Jones squinted at Ollie.

"Then I'll tell you's to turn the fuggin' pressure *up*. Obvious ain't it?"

Oliver shrugged, and thought to himself that Jones was confusing him with someone who cared.

Hamilton thought he'd done a first-class job at motivating his new staff.

Bernard Jones spent the next two hours showing the new men the basic lay out of a gas field, and the different types of fittings that they used.

He looked over his shoulder at them as he wiped the board clean.

"You's will all get precis to take home with you's, so don't worry about taking no notes. There is an hexam at the end of the two weeks, or when me thinks. If you fail it, you fugg off. No job, sacked!"

He turned to face his students.

"Right. Anyone 'ere good at repairin' cars?"

Nobody spoke.

Nobody moved.

Jones sighed.

"Right. Coffee break now, back here for half ten. The canteen is that ruin over there, it has a greasy spick running it. Don't get poisoned, an' don't be late back. Off you's go."

The coffee bar was a very large old static portable Nissen hut type building. It was dilapidated and shabby.

The ceiling was hard plaster board nailed on to wooden beams. Many large stains on it showed where rain had come in at one time or another.

A wooden counter was at the far end across the width of the building, and on it was a large glass cabinet that contained food. Behind the counter was a tall refrigerator, a wooden table where more food items were displayed, a grill, and a big water heating urn. Drinking mugs were piled up next to tins that contained tea bags, coffee, and a glass milk jug.

Alex Emil, a young man of nineteen, was the server, the tea boy.

On the walls of the cafe, stuck on with cellotape, were nude pictures of young ladies taken from men's soft porn magazines and a large picture of Wayne Rooney that had numerous insulting captions written on it in felt tip and biro.

Alex was of medium height, ruggedly good looking with strong dark wavy hair.

He'd been taken on as the tea boy at five pounds an hour and he could keep any profits he made from the café. He paid an accountant friend of the family to ensure he paid the correct tax and other necessary contributions to the state.

He took his job very seriously, he felt it was a good opportunity for him.

He'd learned English at his school in Romania, and after three years in the UK he spoke like a native, albeit a Norfolk native.

His little empire did well. He made a small profit and most of the sixty workmen on the site liked his wares and used his canteen. Others came from surrounding companies. Alex gave Jones ten pounds a month to turn a blind eye to non-company people using the café on the Sagittarius End complex.

His first major purchase had been a second-hand TV, placed high on the wall atop a shelf. He had the TV permanently tuned to the BBC News channel for the benefit of his customers.

Teas and coffees were made to the liking of his clientele, and over time he had brought in bacon butties, pies, pasties, sandwiches, toasties, crisps, fizzy drinks and various chocolate bars to sell.

With his cheerful demeanour, he was popular with most of the men, but there were one or two, like Bernard Jones, who thought he was making a fortune. He wasn't. His prices were good, and not inflated.

Many thought this was very reasonable. He rose early in the mornings to collect and ensure his produce was fresh each day.

He hummed and sang. He was a happy young man in his adopted country.

The six new men ordered, then sat down with their coffees and teas on one of four long benches that had four long plastic tables in front on which the customers could place their mugs.

"Fucking boring was that," said Danny Bentley, shaking his head and making his long shoulder length bleached blond hair move back and fro across his shoulders.

"Hardest bit was staying awake."

"He's a racist *bastard*, and the art of lifting morale is totally lost on him," said Oliver.

The others agreed with the ex-guitarist, and Oliver, except for Nigel who thought he was okay really.

"What a prick. He really thinks he's God almighty, don't he?" observed Hamilton Veene.

"Yeah. There's more gas coming from his frigging gob than there ever was coming out of the gas field," said Jim Mortimer.

"That's true. He's like a nappy, always on your arse, and full of shit."

Oliver got talking to Steve Skipmore, who lived in Norwich and was a bricklayers' labourer in his previous life.

Steve was bald on top and his side hair had been shaved. He was muscular and knew it. A white tee shirt with a tiger's head on the front showed off his impressive physique.

"Cheap prices in here," said Oliver.

"Yeah, can't remember the time when I only paid thirty-five pence for a cuppa."

Oliver agreed.

"Indeed. Think I'll not bother with doing my own lunch pack tomorrow, his food is cheap too."

"Do you prefer people to call you Oliver, or Ollie?"

"Either. Most people call me Ollie. I don't mind, as long as they don't call me fanny-face."

Steve laughed.

"Okay, Ollie it is. Where do you live, Ollie?"

"Attleborough."

"Where's that?"

"In the country on the A11, sort of halfway between Norwich and Thetford."

"Oh yes, I know it. Shit hole, isn't it?" said Steve.

"It's not too bad. The people who live there like it."

"Many decent women there?"

Ollie smiled.

"There's decent women everywhere Steve, its finding them, there being a mutual attraction, and them being single that's the hard part."

Steve shrugged.

"It don't worry me if them are single or not. I got the sack from me last job cos she weren't single. Husband caught us, he just happened to be my boss as well. Bugger gave me a clout *and* binned me. This is my first job since."

"But you look as if you could take care of yourself. With your physique, you must work out surely?"

"Yeah, but I don't fight. Don't like it. I worked out to make meself look good. They used to take the piss out of me on the building sites because I was skinny, and a bit timid."

"You need to get yourself a decent woman Steve, then you won't stray," said Oliver.

"Got one of those, been married nearly two years. Not looking any more. I'm happy with what I've got."

On the television, a man was on the news saying he was going to challenge Jeremy Corbyn for the Labour Party leadership.

In the background, they heard Alex singing. Good voice, strong and clear. Apparently, someone called 'Smiley' was popular in Romania. Alex liked his songs.

Oliver walked back to the classroom with Jim Mortimer.

Jim was neatly turned out in blue jeans, a white tee shirt, and brown leather cowboy boots. He had a small Freddie Mercury type moustache, and a severe crew cut.

"So, you were in the Royal Navy, eh?" said Oliver.

"I was. Who told you that?"

"Saw it on your site booking in sheet under 'Previous Employment'."

"Oh, right. Nosey bugger, aren't you?"

"Couldn't miss it. You write big and your bit was right above mine."

"I probably could've stayed on in the Navy if I'd wanted, if I'd pushed it, in spite of all the trouble I had."

"Oh, really?"

Jim Mortimer sighed.

"Told my CPO I was gay after he caught me reading a gay magazine on watch one night. He tried it on with me, so I suppose he was too, even though he had a wife. Didn't like him, I told him to clear off."

"Good for you."

"Yeah, well, then he gave me so much flipping grief, shit jobs, never satisfied with what I did, and all that malarkey. I got pissed up ashore in Gib one day and saw him in a bar. I finished up punching his lights out. Got three months in the Colchester services nick and choice of reduced seniority or leaving. I decided to leave."

Ollie nodded.

"So, is this your first job since leaving then?"

"Yeah, I tried for one or two others. Jock strap fitter. Ollie Murs, Elton John's and Cliff Richard's personal dresser, cross dressing

correspondent for The Daily Mail, resident homosexual at the Theatre Royal, but no one would take me on."
Ollie smiled.
"Not very good money here, is it?" said Ollie, changing the subject.
"Nah. Shite. Seven twenty an hour. Slave labour. After tax and National Insurance, I reckon I'll be lucky to take home nine hundred a frigging month."
Ollie agreed.
"Like all of us new guys, I guess I'm just working here until I can find something better. Trouble is, what with this Brexit shite no one is hiring at the moment, except for companies like this, who want you for nothing, or zero hours. Lot of unemployed guys walking around, looking."
"But they say unemployment is going down," said Steve.
"Registered unemployed is, but those that were registered unemployed before have been made to do zero hours, go part time, and have to do jobs that pay below the minimum wage. They're worse off, but the government don't care. Their figures sound and look good and ordinary people out there believe everything they're told by the media, and the media of

course repeat the bullshit, especially the BBC, unfortunately."

"Yeah, I get it. Are they a big company? This lot?"

"God yes. I looked them up on line. They turned over way past one hundred million last year and declared profits of nearly fifty million."

"Jesus H!" said Jim, "All out of sticking pipes into rubbish. But they still pay us a bloody pittance."

"Yep. They can well afford to pay us a decent wage but prefer not to. That's capitalism for you. Minimise outgoings and maximise profits, no matter what."

Nigel Infine had caught them up and was listening.

"We're lucky they've given us a job," said Nigel, "Plenty of others don't have one. We don't have no experience neither. I'd say we should be grateful to them."

Ollie looked askance at Nigel.

"Perhaps we should ask for a pay *cut* and work extra *unpaid* hours to show the rich bosses just *how* grateful we are."

"I wouldn't go that far, just saying we're lucky that's all," said Nigel, shrugging his shoulders.

"I'd say *they* are the lucky ones. *We* make the money for them," said Ollie.

Nigel fell back behind them, his slim tall frame cutting a lonely figure.
'Friggin' commie he is.'
Nigel hadn't told them he had been dismissed the service for four cases of theft from other airmen.

When they got back Bernard Jones was waiting.
"Right. Sit down."
The six took their seats.
"I'm now goin' to put on an 'elf an' safety film. It's manda, mandar, mandra….it's compulsory. You 'as to see it. Friggin' EU says so. Frogs, Eyeties and German gits tellin' us what to do. You 'as to answer some questions at the end. If you ask me it's a load of bollocks. If UKIP was the government this 'elf an' safety bullshit wouldn't need to be worried about."
He rolled the film. It covered the workplace safety procedures and essential first aid.
When the film was finished, Jones read the set questions from a file he held. He asked questions of each of them in turn and if anyone was stuck he gave them the answers. A sheet was passed around and each man signed it.
"You all is signing that you 'as seen, an' understands the 'elf and safety film what you

'as just seen. I also signs it to say you's passed the test what you had to take. Bloody stupid I calls it. We didn't have no 'elf and safety in Iraq, and we got through all right."
Ollie bristled.
"A lot of our soldiers didn't get through it all right, they died in Iraq, others lost limbs and their minds, and so did hundreds of thousands of innocent Iraqis, including children, so I think it was a pity we even went there, never mind any Health and Safety regulations." "Oh, here we go, another fuckin' Corbynista tellin' us how bad war is. We 'is a proud warrior nation we is, and no fuckin' wogs is going to push us around, we freed them people, they 'as democracy now, even if a load of the buggers is dead," said Jones.
"Sorry, but Iraq has been *ruined*. A million dead, including some of our own brave soldiers, their entire infrastructure has been destroyed, their gold and oil assets have been stolen and spirited away to God knows where. The Iraqi people have absolutely no hope in a totally lawless society, *and,* there were *no* weapons of mass destruction found, even *if* that *was* a valid reason to bomb, and invade a sovereign state, which it wasn't."
"Yeah, but them is Arabs, so who fucking cares? We showed 'em what *real* soldiers is."

Ollie shook his head but said nothing more.

Jones handed out the various precis for the gas field and the Health and Safety information.

"Probably won't need any of this bollocks when we leave the fuckin' EU. We can start being *men* again, instead of floozies, worrying about this rule an' that rule. Interferes with profits, that's what it does. We're turning into a load of friggin' Nancie's."

At lunch in the hut the men talked about the morning's 'lessons'.

"I haven't changed my opinion of Jones. He's just reinforced it. First class flaming idiot," said Hamilton Veene.

Steven Skipmore agreed.

"Likes the sound of his own bloody voice does that one. How on earth he finished up as a boss is beyond me."

Nigel butted in.

"He's alright, but ain't had no management training, you's can tell that. In the RAF, you couldn't get promoted unless you'd done a management course. Prepares you for the big decisions you see. He's had none, obvious."

"What rank was you in the RAF then, Nigel?" said Danny Bentley.

"Well, I was a member of Logistics see. Qualified right up to Sergeant, I was."

"Yeah, but what rank were you?"

"Well, I were a *Senior* Aircraftsman. Done two big courses I did. Qualified up to Sergeant."

"Senior Aircraftsman? What's that compared to the Army rank?" asked Ollie, innocently.

Nigel frowned.

"No comparison with the Army. Our ranking system was totally different, *superior* many say," said Nigel, dismissively.

Ollie nodded.

"But there must be some comparison, surely?" said Danny.

"I was responsible for millions of pounds' worth of equipment, *millions*."

Bill Dunne, one of the digger drivers, who stood at the bar waiting for his bacon sandwich, turned to them.

He was a big brute of a man, unshaven with a mop of black and grey curly hair.

"An *SAC* is the equivalent of a bloody *Private* in the Army," he said brusquely.

Nigel looked annoyed.

"I wouldn't say that."

"Don't worry me what *you'd* say. Your mate asked you, and I told him. Fucking Private is the answer. I was a Corporal in the RAF Regiment, so I knows what a stores basher is,

and that's what he was, a fucking storeman. No brains needed, just stack boxes and scribble on paper."
The café went quiet.
People became engrossed in the contents of their drinking mugs.
A little later Nigel spoke quietly.
"I was still *qualified* up to Sergeant though."

TWO

"Presume you's all had the four-course option at our dago spick's no star typhoid restaurant, served by that slimy, thieving, Bulgarian prick," said Bernard Jones, by way of a welcome back for the afternoon's lessons.
Nobody replied.
Jim was going to tell him that Alex was a Romanian, not a Bulgarian, but couldn't be bothered.
"This afternoon I shall introduce you's to the GMB1250 gas monitor."

He held up a blue machine by its strapping. It was about the size of a small shoe box. The front had eight different buttons on it at the bottom, and a glass window on the upper half which they presumed the results appeared on.
"This is it. You's will all get one. Them are calibrimated once a year by GMB Limited, what are specialists."
Hamilton whispered.
"Does he mean calibrated?"
Ollie smiled.
"These machines cost two grand each they do. If you's lose yours, you's buy a new one. If you's damage it, you's pay for the repair," said Jones belligerently.
"Like shit I will," Hamilton whispered.
Jones turned on the overhead projector and played an instructional film, provided by GMB Limited, on the machine that they would be using in the gas fields.
After the film, they were all given their gas monitors and, using a precis for guidance, used them on the dummy gas points in the small room, overseen by Jones.
Oliver doubled up with Hamilton.
Turn on the machine, press a 'Clear' button to get rid of old readings, plug a lead coming from the machine into the gas stand up pipe, press a 'Read' button, and wallah! As if by

magic a series of readings appeared on the screen.
They used the training to good effect but were soon bored by the repetition.
At three pm Jones told them to go for a tea break.
As they walked to the Cafe building Ollie asked Hamilton what he did before joining Thorne's.
"I was a bus driver in London. My ancestors were Jamaican. Met this gal from near Norwich, an' she stole me heart, so here I am."
Oliver looked at the tall, handsome black man with the soft gentle eyes.
"Why Norwich? I mean, why leave London?"
"She's a mummy's girl. Needs to be close."
They got their teas and sat down.
"The old gal ain't too bad. She were a racist to start with, like most Norfolk country people. I find Norwich *city* folk okay, but out in the country they all think I'm going to eat their babies."
Ollie laughed out loud, spraying his mouthful of tea across the table.
He got a cloth from Alex and wiped the table clean.
"What does your lady do?"
"She's a teacher at Swaffham. That's where we live, at her mum's."

"Not always a good idea living with the in-laws, is it?"

Hamilton shrugged.

"Not too bad. We're saving to buy a place nearby. Main problem is me gal makes a lot of noise when we're having it off. So, we often go into the garden shed to do it, or wait for the mum to go shopping, or when she's on the evening shift."

Ollie looked at Hamilton.

"You serious, Hamilton?"

Hamilton nodded.

"Yep. Thursday nights is good cos the old girl goes to bingo, and we does it all evening in front of the fire. Same as when she's working evenings at the supermarket, only then we actually do it in our bed with her volume fully up."

Oliver liked this man. He hoped it was mutual.

"By the way, don't call me Hamilton. Friends call me Ham."

"Okay. I was a teacher too, in Norwich, but just got sick to death of the way the bloody government were screwing education. Not fair on the kids, or teachers."

"Me gal says the same. Lots of her colleagues have left the industry cos they fed up. My Miriam says she thinking of leaving, even though she loves being a teacher. Thing is she works unpaid hours a lot of the time cos there isn't enough staff. She doesn't feel valued by this government. She says they have untrained teaching assistants taking lessons, and all sorts of shit like that."

"I know what she means. Too many exams and pointless league tables too. Puts too much pressure on the kids at too early an age. They don't fund education properly either. Class sizes getting bigger and bigger."

"Are you married?"

"No. I live alone."

"Why ain't a good-looking dude like you married, then? Or, even courtin', at least? You ain't gay, are you?"

"I had a fiancée, but she lost her life in a road accident three years ago. Drunk bastard, head on. He got eight years. He'll be out next year."

Ham scratched his closely cropped hair.

"Don't seem right does it? She's gone forever, and he comes out and gets on wiv his life."

They walked slowly back to the classroom, chatting as they went.

The rest of the afternoon was spent using the machines again, going through fault finding, and abnormal reading procedures. Jones wandered around them giving advice and acting superior.

At five o'clock he looked at his watch and dismissed them.

"Tomorrow we'll spend a little time out in the field. Piss off now. Plug your machines into the chargers by your desks. Switch them on and leave them on your chairs. Back here at eight o'clock sharp in the mornin'. Read your precis sheets tonight cos you'll have a hexam tomorrow."

They walked to the car park.

"Fancy a pint?" Ham asked Oliver.

"Where?"

"Bricklayer's Arms. Almost outside the gates, on the way to Swaffham, just off the A47."

"Okay. Just the one though."

"Of course."

The Bricklayers was an old country pub, long past its sell by date. The landlord, Archie Binns, had long since given up being enthusiastic. After thirty-five years, pleasant enough, but he and his wife Beattie just went through the motions.

Five more years and they were retired.

The gas field had boosted their clientele somewhat, but only during lunchtimes and early evenings during the week. By nine o'clock they often closed up, unless there was a darts match on.

The Cribbage league had long since died a death.
Archie had only little tufts of hair perched on either side of his head. His face was very red, probably due to the large consumption of his own product. He was portly and Beattie ran him a close second, her large bosoms marched a fair way in front of her as she walked.
"Now then gents, what can I get you?"
"Lager shandy for me, what about you, Ham?"
"I'll have a pint of Fosters, please," said Ham.
They were served their pints and took a window seat that overlooked, what was once, a beer garden.
Ollie looked around the bar. It had a tired, worn out look. Dart board, pool table, scarred wooden floor, and yellowed, once cream, coloured walls and ceilings.
After a few minutes as the two men talked Archie came over.
"Working on the gas field are you, boys?"
They both nodded.
"Yes. Started yesterday. Do you get many of the workers in?"
"Yeah. Fair amount, pipe layers mostly, not early on Tuesdays though. Its darts night and they go home to get changed before coming in. Good bunch of lads and lasses. Never any

trouble. One or two miserable buggers, which I assume you'll judge for yourselves in time."

"No locals come in?" asked Ham.

"Oh yeah, quite a few. Friday and Saturday nights mostly, and Sunday lunchtimes of course. We do grub, then. Not like it used to be though. A lot moved away because of the smell and the stigma of having a rubbish dump on their door step. Some that's still living here can't sell their houses now, though. The word has long been out on this little patch."

"Are the locals okay with gas workers then?" asked Ham.

"Mostly yeah, but on the odd occasion, a local resident makes an inappropriate remark and fur flies, but it ain't often. Me, or my missus, nips it in the bud, usually."

The landlord returned to the bar and resumed polishing glasses.

They finished their drinks.

"My round next time," said Ham.

Ollie drove his car through the winding country lanes to Attleborough.

Cotton Avenue.

There were eleven other bungalows in the avenue, all similar to his.

His neighbours on either side were retired. He got on well with them.

He parked in his drive and opened his garage door to let his dog out.

As always, Bess, the golden Labrador ran around him, yelping and jumping to show its joy at his arrival. The dog stopped momentarily for a pee on the grass, then carried on its happiness routine.

Ollie went in and picked up his mail from the front door mat.

Circulars and a BT bill, nothing exciting.

He fed the dog and let her out.

There was a message on his answer phone from his Mum and Dad, who lived in Norwich, asking him how his first day in the new job went. He thought he'd call them later.

'Now. What shall I do for myself?'

He decided on pasta and cooked himself spaghetti, let the dog back in and switched on the television.

"Another riveting evening in Cotton Avenue," he said out loud to Bess as she lay by his feet.

Bess wagged her tail.

He was lonely still.

It was three years since the accident. Three years of sadness, bordering on despair.

His doctor gave him some pills, but after a few days he threw them in the toilet.

His Dad kept telling him to go out more, get a girlfriend, but he couldn't work up any enthusiasm.

He got Bess's lead and took himself and the dog on a round robin walk through St Peter's Meadow.

A few people walked their dogs, and one older couple said, 'good evening' to him as they walked hand in hand leading their old Labrador at a slow pace. Bess wanted to play, but the old Lab just wagged its tail and laid down.

When he got home again he called his parents.

He made the job seem more attractive than it was, so that they wouldn't worry on his behalf.

"Any women working there," his Dad asked, hopefully.

Ollie smiled.

"No, don't think so, but there are a couple of guys that have funny walks, and wear lipstick."

Ham drove his car onto the driveway of his girlfriend's mother's semi-detached house on the Norwich Road in Swaffham.

Miriam's car wasn't there.

She took the swimming lessons for her pupils on Monday afternoon when normal lessons had finished. Another extra duty that was unpaid.

The children's parents had to pay three pounds fifty a week for their children. Two pounds fifty was paid to the Old Thetford Swimming Pool for entrance and a pound went towards the coach that transported them to and from the venue. To some parents three pounds fifty was a lot, and they had to make sacrifices to raise the funds. One little girl called Emily was a single parent child and her mother just couldn't afford to pay. It was an expense too far. Miriam paid for her, quietly, with no fuss, no one was any the wiser.

Mrs Bradstock was ironing when Ham came through the door. The television was on.

"Wotcha gorgeous!" He said.

He pecked her on the cheek.

"How was the job?"

"So, so. Nothing special, but it's a job, A smelly job I think, when I've finished training. It's a rubbish tip."

"Make a cup of tea there's a good lad. But keep your bloody hands off the biscuits. I know how many are there."

He went into the kitchen, put the kettle on, and ate two chocolate biscuits as the water heated up and he waited.

Miriam's mother Milly was a widow. Her husband had died from cancer seven years since. Big smoker from the age of fourteen, the deadly weed had caught up with him.
She worked at the town's Tesco store as a cashier.
He brought the tea in and they sat on the chairs chatting. He told her about his day.
"Think you'll like it?"
"Probably not, but I'll stick it out, 'til something better comes along."
"Our Miriam's late."
"No. She's got the swimmers today, it's Monday."
"Oh yeah, Forgot."
Milly had nearly died of shock when Miriam brought Ham home.
A black man.
She couldn't recall seeing one in Swaffham.
What would the neighbours say?
They'd think she'd started peddling drugs, and what if there was a rape in the area? He'd be first on the list of people the police would interview.
"Miriam look, I'm not a racist, but are you sure? I mean, they're *different* to us. Your babies will be…..well you know, they'll be…."
"*Black* is the word you're looking for Mum."

"Well, yes, but they're different in other ways, don't you see?"

"No. Explain to me how black people are different, Mum."

"Well, they don't think like us, they…"

"Mum for God's sake, how on earth do you know how a black person thinks, and *how* are those thoughts different?"

"I'm not being funny but they don't have good reputations, do they? I mean it's common knowledge that black men are responsible for all the crime in London isn't it dear? And they have the most unemployed, and all the stolen cars and drugs are done by them. They all talk so silly too, and their clothes, well, wouldn't be seen dead walking around with one of them in all that sparkly stuff. We wouldn't have a drug problem in England if it weren't for blackies, everyone knows that. My mother will turn somersaults in her grave if she knows I've let a black man into my house, let alone allow my daughter to….well….you know."

"Who's going to tell her, Mum? I promise not to."

The morning after he moved in she checked his bed sheets. Nothing there.

She didn't know what to expect. Maybe thought his colour would come off and stain the sheets?

She was very surprised at how clean and immaculate he left everything. Not a bit like a black man. She'd checked the cutlery drawer twice, nothing was missing. His table manners were exceptional too.

She thought he'd pick everything up with his fingers, but he didn't.

The first night she heard them 'at it'.

Her daughter was moaning and carrying on loud enough to wake the bloody dead.

She'd heard that black men had enormous unmentionables so maybe that was the reason for all the groaning from her daughter.

She mentioned the noise to Miriam the next morning, but diplomatically said she thought Miriam was having a nightmare.

Miriam was mortified, and after that she and Ham stole down to the shed most nights and used an old 'Z' bed for their liaisons.

Bingo night couldn't come around quickly enough either, nor when Milly had the late shift at work. Luxury, either in front of the fire or in bed, and Miriam could hoot and holler all she liked.

Milly once caught sight of Ham in his underpants. He didn't appear to have a monster 'down there'.
Fact was he was rather a nice chap. Polite, happy, clean, always ready to do odd jobs. He kept the garden lovely.
It was just that she felt embarrassed having a *black* man in her house.
People never *said* anything, but it was the way they *looked*, or so she thought.
He was very popular in the town. Played football for the Swaffham 'B' team and helped out the Lions on their charity days in the Town.
If only he wasn't black, he would be lovely.
She noticed that young women spectators ogled and shouted encouragement when he was playing football, dirty cows, no shame. On heat over a *blackie*.

THREE

"Right. Settle down you lot," said Bernard Jones from the front of the room.
"First thing's first. I hope you's all read your precis through and knows what all the answers is this mornin'."
He handed out a question paper with fifteen questions on it.
Two people had no pens so he handed two pens out with strict instructions on their return.
"Money don't grow on trees, y'know."
Hammond, Ollie, and Nigel finished theirs after a few minutes.
Two others took half an hour and Danny was still incomplete when Jones told the other five they could go outside for a fag. Since none of them smoked they all went to the cafe and passed the answers around that they had given.
They trooped back to the classroom after fifteen minutes, or so, just as Danny came out.

He looked angry.

"I'll swing for that bastard!"

Nigel asked him what was wrong.

"He had to tell me the answers to two or three questions and said I needed to buck up. Cheeky bastard!"

They remained outside the classroom for another ten minutes before Jones called the six back in.

Jones held the question papers in one hand and twirled his scrawny moustache with the other.

"Pretty poor really, considering all the time I've spent going over things with you six. Three of you are okay but the other ninety percent need to sharpen up."

Ham and Ollie smiled at each other.

He went through the questions one by one.

Oliver, Nigel, and Ham realised they had got them all correct.

"I suggest that them's what struggled should read the precis' again. I maybe ask questions on it at any time, and I expect you's to know what the answers is this next time."

Jones brought up a map of the gas field area on the overhead projector.

"Today we am goin' out into the gas field to do some live monitorin'."

He showed them on the map the site where they would be.

They were all given wet weather overalls, bright yellow luminous coats, rubber boats, waterproof gloves and hard hats. Each item had their individual personnel numbers on them.
They all laughed at Danny, his number was 007.
Steve was 003.
"Bollocks! I'm less than half a James friggin' Bond!"
Jones gave each of them a walkie-talkie radio and a gas alarm, that they clipped onto their coats.
He showed them the simple way they worked.
"Again, don't lose your radio. If you's do, you's pay for a new one. Without your radio you's can't function. You's only use it for work calls. I listen to all the calls you's make from the receiver what is in my office, so don't think you's can bugger about with them. If your gas alarm goes off, you's scarper pronto back to the office, don't hang around."
After they had signed for their work clothes, radio and footwear, they got dressed and followed Jones out of the classroom, past the

weighbridge, and out onto the first part of the gas field.

They had to walk uphill for about five hundred metres to get to the first well pipe.

Danny was gasping as they stopped.

Jones smiled at him.

"What's the matter pop star? Too many fags?"

Danny frowned.

Jones turned to Ollie.

"Right Wilson. I want you's to measure this well. Gather round the rest of you's."

Oliver cleared his machine, hooked up, pressed the flow button, and, after two minutes of allowing the flow to activate the machine, he told Jones what the readings were.

Jones nodded.

"Are those readings okay? Or is there somethin' wrong?"

Ollie thought for a moment.

"Pretty much okay, although I think the CO_2 is a little high."

Jones nodded.

"Good. Right, unhook and let's go on to the next one."

Every fifty metres there was another gas well branch outlet to be read.

Jones made each take it in turns to do the reading and, although Steven initially made a mistake in his interpretation of the reading, by

and large the exercises all progressed according to plan.
It really wasn't rocket science.

When they got to the top of the first hill they looked out over the gas field. It was enormous. Stretching for a couple of miles in each direction, they saw the rubbish lorries from the council and private contractors emptying their smelly cargo onto the vast open chasm in the distance.
Clusters of pipe layers were busy installing their black tubing.
Hundreds of sea gulls circled and swooped. Pecking at the rubbish.
Occasionally a mechanically timed bird scaring device boomed, the birds took to flight momentarily, but seconds later they settled back into their scavenging mode.
The smell reached across the valley and offended their senses.
"What a stink," said Danny.
One or two covered their noses and mouths with handkerchiefs.
Jones laughed.
"You think this is bad? Just wait till you's 'as to wade in amongst it to take a prelim readin' on any new pipes. It makes your friggin' teeth go yellow almost, it do. The ones what we is

readin' here is on an old site, and don't 'ardly smell at all, them don't."

"Do we have to do the really smelly sites often?" asked Ollie.

Jones smiled and nodded.

"Yep. Every weekday."

He said it almost joyfully and looked at Hammond.

He thought that it would be a nice job for the *blackie*.

He couldn't see him lasting long, what with the unsocial hours and the shit monitor sessions.

He thought that that hoighty-toighty bugger Wilson would be his second target, too bloody clever by far, and spouting his goody-goody two shoes lefty commie shit.

Be after his job before he knew it.

Mrs Rathbone put Bernard Jones' call through to her boss.

"Mr Jones from Sagittarius End on the line for you, Mr Stewle."

"What is it, Jones?" said Malcolm Stewles, abruptly.

"Oh, nothing really, Mr Stewle. Just thought I'd update you with the new recruit's progress at Sagittarius End, sir."

"Are they all okay?"

"Oh, yes sir, I've trained them up, sir, and they're fine. Just thought you'd…."
"Then why the fuck are you calling me for? I've got better things to do than keep listening to every progress report on all the little nuances in your tiny empire."
He hung up.
Jones looked at the receiver.
'He hung up on me. *Bastard.* Mister *Stewle*, good name that is, cos he is a piece of *shit*'.
He walked out of the office and into the classroom.
Slamming the classroom door behind him as he entered.
"Shut up! Pay attention!"

Malcolm Stewle waited a minute then rang reception.
"Yes, Mr Stewle?"
"Ruth, *please,* don't put that idiot Jones through to me again, unless he's got something *really* important to tell me. He'll be calling me next for a bloody weather report."
Ruth pulled a face.
"Very good, Mr Stewle."
Stewle swung his chair around to face his visitor.
"Now, where were we Reggie?"
Reggie Witter, smiled at his fellow director.

"Why don't you get rid of that old biddy and get some young fruity tart to do your reception?"

"If I did, I'd be like you Reggie, having her across the desk every five minutes instead of working."

"Oh, Malcolm how cruel," said Witter with a twinkle in his eye.

"Yes, but stunningly accurate. Now where were we up to."

"Government rumours that all landfill might be going to Belgium for incineration."

"Is that a *maybe* rumour, a *sure thing* rumour, or just idle gossip from the Secretary of State's office cos she feels lonely and wants some media attention again to boost her bloody already inflated ego."

"Well, Billy Henly, and I, played golf on Sunday, and he was fairly adamant that she's pretty much done the deal with the Belgians. They've got shitloads of incinerator spare capacity, and offered her a deal, apparently."

Stewle scowled.

"Yeah, well, Henly might be a Tory MP but he's still a fucking waster. We gave him forty grand last year for any insider information and all we got was a bloody Christmas card. It had bells on the cover, which he probably thought were appropriate as they were attached to our fucking legs!"

"Mmmm. He seems fairly sure about this one though."

Stewle hauled his nineteen-stone frame out of his chair.

His bejowelled face went red at the effort.

"Come on. Let's go to the boardroom for a drink."

Stewle poured out two large scotches.

They sat in two of the plush red leather armchairs that faced a picture window which gave them a view over the River Wensum.

"You'll need to get Henly to keep us up to speed about the Belgian thing. If it has even a hint of truth, we'll need to formulate a strategy on what we should do. We don't want to be caught with a load of plummeting shares and a company that doesn't *handsomely* pay its way."

"Okay. Will do."

"Right, here's my joke of the week for you."

"Oh God! You and your bloody jokes. Go on then."

"A boss wanted to test a young female accounts clerk applicant looking for a job. He asked her, 'If I were to give you £10,000, minus 14%, how much would you take off?' The applicant hesitated for a few moments then replied, 'Everything but my earrings'."

Bernard Jones drove his 2006 Renault Megane along the A47 to Kings Lynn. He'd had trouble with this heap of junk since he'd bought it.
Brakes, lights, clutch, bloody awful, and he was useless at cars.
None of the new intake could do cars either, useless buggers. Garage costs were going up. Even the two hundred pounds a month salary increase for his promotion didn't help, a newer car was out of reach.
He pulled up outside his house, a two-bedroomed ex council town house. He'd bought it when good old Maggie Thatcher was instructing councils to give them away for pennies, never to be replaced.
One of the front windows was boarded up with some three-ply wood that he'd picked up from work. His five-year-old son Tommy had broken the window when he threw a tennis ball hard against the wall. His aim was not good that day.
'Must get that fixed', he thought to himself for the fiftieth time, as he walked over the small grassy square to his front door.
As he entered, Doreen, his wife shouted out.
"Take them smelly bloody clothes off, before you's come through here."
Same speech, *every* night.

He stood on the inside front door mat and took his jeans, shirt, and boots off and bundled them up under his arm before walking out of the tiny entrance hall, and into the lounge.

Doreen, his podgy wife, sat in her pink dressing gown smoking a rolled-up cigarette and watching television. Her pale skin highlighted the odd red spot pustules on her face. Her bleached hair was letting the dark roots through.

He bent down to kiss her. She turned her head away.

"You bloody stink! And take those smelly clothes out of here."

He sighed and went through the little kitchen and out into an equally small outhouse, He hung his jeans and shirt on a nail that had been driven into a wood baton screwed to the wall.

Dropped his boots on the floor.

Retraced his steps.

Stood in his underpants and socks, looking at the television set.

"Tea will be after this. Go and clean yourself up. You'll stink the bloody house out."

Doreen stubbed out her cigarette on a saucer that lay on a small wooden coffee table in front of her.

"What we havin'?"

"Pie an' chips."

He went to the bathroom and wiped his body over with a wet flannel.

After drying himself and spraying himself with a deodorant, he put on his old tracksuit and went downstairs.

His wife was still watching the Jeremy Kyle show.

He stood behind her for a minute watching the screen where two women were berating some orange haired, spotty, tattooed and multi pierced young man.

"What a load of rubbish. Scum, the three of them."

"It's dead good, he's had them both and neither knew about the other, *and* them is sisters," said Doreen before lighting up another roll up.

"Why you still in your dressin' gown, Dor?"

"Couldn't be bothered to change. Wos the point? No one's comin'. We ain't goin' out."

He looked at her lecherously.

"Oh, thought you might be offering."

She frowned and pulled her dressing gown tight around her body.

"Well, I ain't."

Bernard went through to the kitchen.

He looked in the refrigerator.

"Eureka!"

Four large cans of Mellowes Extra Strong Cider lay there waiting for him. A bottle of cheap sherry lay next to them.

'One for her, four for me'.

He opened a can of cider and sat at the small kitchen table where he opened the post that lay there.

'Bills, bills, and shite. Gas, electric, water. Why do the buggers all come at once?'

He realised he couldn't pay all three this month, not without some other extra income.

'Need to nick something from work and flog it.'

The month before last, he had stolen a lawn mower out of the maintenance shed. It had only been used once when the site first opened. The pipe layers had not locked up again. Handy, that was.

It was a petrol LawnMaster Mk3, which cost nearly three hundred pounds new. A self-employed landscaper who frequented his local pub, The King's Arms, was the happy recipient, he bought it for one hundred quid cash.

No questions asked, no answers given.

There was the usual hullabaloo from the boss in Norwich about the theft.

Jones blamed the Travellers, who had set up site in a field nearby. Everyone knew they would nick *anything.*

He felt he was on safe ground.
He'd reported the foreman in charge's security negligence.
The pipe layer's foreman was sacked, for continuous slack security.
They'd lost a large socket set the previous month, again the suspects were the Travellers. That time Jones had broken the lock to get in.
This one *was* in the hands of a Traveller. Jones sold it to one who ran a lorry business.
Some months before Jones had sold one of the company computers from Beryl Ansteys' office.
She was on holiday. It was almost brand new.
After the latest theft Stewle had sent a security firm to run the rule over the site. Their report had brought about changes.
New, bigger locks everywhere, and a signature sheet for each building to be signed by the last person leaving confirming all windows and doors were locked.
Failure to do so would incur disciplinary penalties.
They had recommended a night security man, but that was an expense too far for Stewle.
Bernard Jones thought he should be on the lookout for some suitable items from tomorrow. Those bills had to be paid.

FOUR

Danny Bentley strummed his guitar and sang a James Taylor song about a lonely young cowboy.
Veronica, his second wife, would be home at six thirty after picking up their daughter from her mother's.
He called her 'Vee', she worked at the local GP's surgery and issued prescriptions. Danny's first marriage had pretty much ended when he caught his wife in bed with his drummer.
He couldn't forgive her this time, he had on the previous occasion when she told him she was drunk and thought it was him instead of a local barman by the name of Max.
He had left immediately, taking just a hold-all, and his guitar.
The slut could keep the rest.
Danny stayed at his brother's house for six weeks.

The break-up of the band was inevitable.

The other guys thought the drummer was more of an asset than he was, so they voted to keep the percussionist at all costs, even if it meant Danny leaving, which is what happened.

Danny and the drummer had traded blows the day he left. Danny sported a black eye for two weeks.

He tried to make it on his own, but the work quickly dried up.

At the end he was just doing the occasional pub and working men's club's gigs. No decent money in that.

Vee was an old girlfriend acquaintance who he bumped into again in their local hostelry. She was out with some girlfriends and Danny was blitzed. She got him into a taxi and took him home.

The morning after, he woke up on a strange couch.

Vee made him coffee and cooked him breakfast, whilst he showered.

That was five years ago. They had lived together in her house, which was owned by her father, from that day on.

Daughter Holly Mary was born on Christmas day, hence the name.

When she got home, Danny read a story to his daughter from a book he had purchased from a charity shop in Sprowston.
Vee made them pasta and Danny could hear her singing in the kitchen.
She was tall, willowy and had long dark hair.
She had an elegance about her, probably from her parents, mother had been a model and father lectured in economics at the UEA in Norwich.
She loved Danny almost from the word go.
He was funny, sometimes vulnerable and always a little sad to begin with.
Over time he changed.
He became surer of himself.
He was gentle with her and adored their daughter.
Danny got a pretty good job as a salesman with BHS and made it up to manager of the men's department in Norwich. Alas, he was one of many that found themselves unemployed when the company folded, and their pension pot had been plundered.
He took the job with Thorne's simply because it was the only one he could get.
Having sent countless job applications out without success, he was belittled and agitated at the treatment he received from the DWP

dole office. They made him feel almost worthless.

In the end he answered an ad in The Eastern Evening News that attracted over ninety applicants.

Thorne's were looking for six men to train as gas monitors, whatever that was.

On his application, he wrote that he'd done it before.

The guy never asked him about it on interview, just told him he would be on minimum wage, forty hours per week, be fully trained, take it or leave it.

Danny still kept his entertainment hand in by playing gigs at small venue clubs such as The Royal British Legion Clubs around Norfolk.

Vee often went to watch him. Noticed women eyeing him up.

"So, what are your workmates like?" said Vee, as she brought the tea in.

The three sat at the dining table.

Danny shrugged.

"Mixed bunch really. Ham is a black man, nice, from London, I like him. Ollie is also a good guy. Intelligent, his wife was killed in a car accident."

"Oh, poor man. What ages are they?"

"Well, we're all about the same I think, around the thirty mark. We all feel the same, that the

job is just a filler until something else comes along that's better."
"And the others?"
"Nigel is a bosses' man, or so it seems to me. Tall and skinny, He's ex RAF."
"Who else?"
"Steve is a shaven headed very big, muscleman. He looks big and tough, but is really rather timid, I think. His last job was as a brickie's labourer. He's married. I think he might fancy the ladies a bit."
"Keep away from him then. Don't want him to give you any idea's."
Danny touched her hand.
"Don't worry, I'm all yours."
"Who else?"
"Jim is a Freddie Mercury lookalike, and he's a gay man. He's an ex-serviceman as well. Was in the Royal Navy. He got thrown out for bopping one of his bosses, an officer, or so Ollie told me."
"Pretty mixed bunch then. What about the boss?"
"Ah, Fagin."
"*Fagin*? Surely not?"
"Nah. We just call him that cos he looks like him. He's a stupid prat. Full of himself and his position. Thick as pig shit. Says he's an Iraq war vet, but Ollie says he's probably a liar. He

made me so angry again today. I felt like punching his lights out again, like I did yesterday."
Vee looked horrified.
"Oh Danny, you didn't? Why didn't you get sacked?"
"No, I mean I felt like punching his lights out yesterday, as well."
Holly sang a song she'd learnt at school that day about how good it is to be nice to people.
Danny thought it was a shame people changed when they became adults.
Later, after Holly had gone to bed. Vee was *very* nice to Danny, and Danny was *very* nice to Vee.

After a week, they were all bored.
Jones spent half a day with them in the classroom going over the same old information, and afternoons were spent in the gas field taking readings and analysing their findings.
Jones took no notice of the readings that they shouted out. He had a standard phrase, 'And what do that tell us', all the time looking at his company ipad.
He stood slightly away from the six. They couldn't see what he was looking at, but all supposed it was online porn.

On the Friday afternoon Ollie shouted out a completely outrageous reading, nothing like the reading on his monitor.

Had it been correct, the field would have exploded. When Jones, still looking down at his ipad, made his standard, 'And what does that tell us'.

Ollie replied, "That we should all be at the pub."

Jones didn't blink.

"Correct. Right, on to the next."

They all trooped off laughing amongst themselves.

In turn, with the exception of Infine, they all gave daft readings.

Jones never batted an eyelid, so engrossed was he on his ipad.

Later that afternoon he told them that they didn't need an extra week training and he would allocate them sections to monitor from next Monday morning after the final exam.

The field was split up into four sections A, B, C and D.

D was the smelliest part of the areas where rubbish laid uncovered, and where lorries constantly tipped the household waste. Two diggers pushed the rubbish into hills and then compacted them.

The seagulls bombed the humans with white splodge shit bombs.

Jones was also responsible for two other nearby sites, at Molbury and Resset Heath, and he said next week he would take two men there and train them to take the readings at the two offsites and show them the 'flare' building where the gas was converted into electricity.

The flare buildings had readings too that needed to be sent each day to Head Office.

These two 'offsites' no longer took rubbish and were covered over and had now taken on the appearance of high rolling meadows.

The gas pipes still protruded out of the surface and gas was still being extracted and would continue until the yield was so low that they weren't viable. The land would then only be suitable for animal grazing. No buildings would ever be allowed to be constructed there.

Jim stood at the counter chatting to Alex.
"How do you like your job, Jim?"
"It's a job. But I dislike the boss."
"Yes, everybody says that they don't like him."
"Do you know the difference between him and a battery?"
Alex looked puzzled.
"No, what is the difference?"

"A battery has a positive side."
Alex didn't understand. Jim explained.
The other five sat at one of the tables watching the television news.
Jeremy Corbyn had just been elected as Labour leader for the second time with an increased share of the vote, and the BBC report indicated that everybody hated him, apart from over half a million Labour members.
"He'll never get in. Where's all the money coming from?" said Nigel, "Is it coming out of fresh air, what a tosser."
"If we scrap Trident, that's two hundred billion. If we scrap HS2, that's close to a hundred billion. If we make companies like Google, Apple, Morrisons, Dyson, Virgin, Boots, Daily Mail, the Telegraph, and all the other rich fat cats who horde money offshore, pay their share of taxation just like we do, *and*, if we increase taxes on the very rich who can afford it. That's where the money would come from," said Ollie.
Nigel sneered.
"Rubbish! If companies don't make profits them won't invest here, everyone knows that."
"The media said that in the late 40's, the 60's, *and* when Blair got in, they *still* invested. Besides, nobody is saying companies can't make profits. Just saying they need to pay

their just taxes. Why should *you* pay taxes out of a meagre seven pounds twenty an hour and billionaires who, if they lived to be a thousand, wouldn't be able to spend one hundredth of their vast fortunes, yet they pay none?"
"Hear, hear, pure bloody greed," said Ham.
"Yeah, well. I thinks they earns it," said Nigel.
"Earn it? It's their workers who actually earn it for them. They breeze around in the most part sitting in high rise offices, or cruise the Med, or the Bahamas, in their multi-million pound yachts."
"I suppose you like this Corbyn idiot?"
"As a matter of fact, I do. He's like a breath of fresh air in British politics. His policies make sense and they're designed to give the huge majority of British people a better life, based on fairness," said Ollie.
"Rubbish! Their figures don't add up."
"And who says that? That they don't add up?"
"Well, all the papers and the telly news. Everyone knows that," said Nigel.
"I see. Who owns the papers and the TV channels?"
"What do it matter?"
"It matters because, one, they provide *no* figures themselves to say Corbyn's calculations are incorrect. Two, the paper owners and television channels all reflect a

jaundiced and in many cases a *lying* slant on things. Three, the media is owned and controlled by the right wing of the British establishment, the same people who profit most from the status quo, and Four, Labour *have* had their figures checked by responsible economic entities, who say they *will* work."

"Maybe so. I'll still vote Conservative. Don't trust this bugger Corbyn," said Nigel.

"Why don't you trust him?"

Nigel shrugged.

"I dunno. Just don't. He looks scruffy. Never wears a tie, and he's not shaved."

"Richard Branson has a beard and never wears a tie. Jesus had long hair, no tie and had a beard. Stephen Crabb, a current Tory minister, has a beard."

"Yeah but them's different. They are all okay."

"Have you ever *listened* to, or read, any of Corbyn's speeches when he's laying out his policies? Have you ever read a Labour Party manifesto?"

"Yeah, course I have."

"So, you know about his policy for the NHS for example?"

"Well, yeah, no. Not interested in listening to *anything* he says."

"The media have done a really good job on you, Nigel. You *hate* somebody, but you don't

know *why*. As a matter of interest, what newspaper do you read?"
"The Sun."

They walked to their cars in the car park.
 Ham said he thought Infine was an idiot.
"Problem is Ham, that there are millions out there that read the main stream papers, or watch the BBC News on television, and they are lied to, to such an extent that the British people blame everyone and everything except those that actually are guilty of causing the problems that we face in the NHS, and in Britain generally."
"Like blaming immigrants, you mean?"
"Yes. Immigrants are a prime scapegoat for Britain's ills."
"You ought to be an MP," said Ham.
"Nah, I'm the sort that I get so angry at people like the Tories and Infine that I want to tear them limb from limb, so I'm no good. You need to be able to keep your cool to be successful."
"Don't you sometimes think that tearing Tories limb from limb would be a great success?"
"No, if you resort to violence, or abuse, you have immediately lost the argument."
They drove to the Bricklayers.

"Evenin' lads," said Archie Binns, his red face beaming at them.
He remembered them from their last visit.
"Usual?"
"Yes please," said Ham.
"Got a good memory."
"Yeah, he has, probably years of practise, it's his bread and butter."
They took their pints to a table by the window.
As they sat down Nigel Infine walked in.
He looked their way and nodded but stayed at the bar when the landlord served him his pint of bitter.
"I think I've made an enemy," said Ollie.
"Maybe. You don't look heartbroken though."
"Yeah. Trouble is, people like him have a vote. It's almost like Rupert Murdoch voting a million times by proxy."
They talked about their job for a while. Ham told him about a Lion's winter cabaret dinner for charity that was coming up in Swaffham, two weeks on Saturday, and would he like to attend along with him and his lady.
"But I don't have a female friend to bring along," said Ollie.
"Doesn't matter. It's just a dinner, and then we get entertained by singers and comedians. Apparently, it's a really good night. Tickets are only twenty-five quid."

Ollie finished drinking his beer.
"Let me think about it. I'll let you know tomorrow, okay?"
"Sure. Don't make it any later. The tickets are selling like hot cakes."
They stood up, waved to Infine, who nodded, and took their leave of mine host.
As Ollie drove home he wondered why he hadn't said yes straight away to Ham's offer of a Lion's Dinner ticket.
His last social outing had been to the local pub with his Dad. That was some weeks ago.
He could get the bus there and a taxi home.
Perhaps he should go.
A few drinks, a nice dinner and a cabaret would make a change from his almost monk like existence.
He still thought of Grace daily.
How they laughed, loved and just existed for each other. Her blue eyes, beautiful face, golden hair, slim frame, and joyful spirit haunted him in the wee dark hours during many a night.
He visited her grave every Sunday and spoke to her, told her about how his week had gone, and how much he loved her, missed her.

Ham did the washing up.
Mother in Law was grateful.

She still couldn't bring herself to giving him a hug, or a peck on the cheek, but she knew he was a lovely man.
Miriam came in to the kitchen.
She put her arms around him and kissed his neck.
"Stop it. Unless you mean it. If you mean it meet me at the shed in ten minutes."
Miriam laughed and kissed him again.
"Dirty bugger. Finish the dishes."
Later, in the lounge, Mrs Bradstock was nodding off in her chair. Ham and Miriam sat watching TV.
 She asked him if he'd invited his new friend Ollie to the Lion's 'do'.
"Yes. He said he'd think about it. It's been awhile since his girl was killed so he should be past the grieving by now surely, although he always looks kind of sad."
"Maybe. Depends on how much he loved her."
"Mmmm. Maybe it's the money," said Ham.
"If it's the money *we* could buy his ticket and tell him it's a freebie."
"Let's see. You're getting very charitable with our money. Thought we were saving up to get married? Or have you gone off the idea?"
She punched his thigh.

A little later Miriam got them two cans of beer from the 'fridge. She handed one to Ham and opened hers before settling down again.
The old lady continued to quietly snooze, even as the cans were opened with a hiss.
"I had thought of asking Annabel along, sort of blind date. What do you think?"
Ham frowned.
"Mmmm, don't know. That sort of thing could be superb, on the other hand it could be a complete mismatched disaster."
"Have you met Annabel?"
"No. Is she good looking?"
"Think I've got a recent group photo from school with her in it."
Miriam went to search for the photo.
"Here it is."
She handed him the photo of the school staff in a group.
Miriam pointed out the woman sitting next to her on the front row.
"That's her."
Annabel was medium height, dark haired, and very pretty, albeit a little on the plump side.
"Nice."
"She's got a great sense of humour, and we laugh a lot."
"Not spoken for then?"

"No. She's had a few boyfriends, but never met Mister Right."
"How old is she?"
"Thirty-one or two, can't remember. I know her birthday is in six weeks though."
"Does she live alone?"
"Yes, in a flat in Hingham."
"Hingham? Where's that?"
"Oh, not far from here. And only about six miles from Attleborough too."
"Well, let's see if he wants to go first. Don't know how to play it about a 'blind date' though. He might get 'shirty'."
"We could say we're picking her up, and would he like a lift too, couldn't we?"
"You are a devious woman, Miriam Bradstock."
Later Ham told her that on Monday afternoon, sometime, he was monitoring on his own, for the first time.
"Take your iphone, play music."
"Good idea. Pity the music won't take the stink away," said Ham
"I dunno, after listening to some of that rapper music of yours, death by stink might be more acceptable."

FIVE

At the beginning of the second week they all congregated in the classroom again and had their last exam before going out to their designated sectors.
Jones pretty much told them the answers to each question under the guise of making sure they all knew and understood the questions.
They all passed.
Jones handed out the ready-made certificates that had their names neatly printed on them.
At lunch in the canteen, there was a lot of relieved banter, except from Nigel Infine who had a bad hangover.
He'd been to the local British Legion the night before and had drunk copious amounts of Abbots ale. He felt he needed it for pre-exam nerves that would keep him awake.
It was cheaper in the Legion than the local pubs. As an ex Royal Marine *and* Royal Air Force man he was entitled to be a member.

His little flat, where he lived alone, was only a stone's throw from the premises. Most nights he'd wobble home.

Nigel had only completed two weeks basic Royal Marine training in Lympstone, Exmoor, before he had asked to be allowed to leave. Not for him this Royal Marine lark, too arduous, all that climbing, jumping, running, and some bastard, or other, always screaming and shouting in his ears.

He felt he wasn't quite cut out for the military. Not *that* military anyway.

The Royal Air Force was much more to his liking, he thought. And so it was. A nice, quiet, cushy job in 'Stores', until he got caught 'nicking'.

He'd never married, he'd lived all his life, apart from his two and a half years in the RAF, with his mother and father who both died within six months of each other from cancer. They left him their three-bedroomed bungalow in their will, as well as over twenty thousand pounds of savings, and their *Toyota Yaris*.

He had sold the house and bought a small one bedroomed flat in the back street almost next to the British Legion, banking the difference of the equity.

Up until now he'd always had a ready excuse when it came to helping out with the Legion's charity events, although he *had* helped out behind the bar a couple of times when they were short of staff. *That* job had its perks, a few freebie pints *and* a couple of quid disappearing from the till into his pockets.

His flat was his castle. He was never overlooked. Just as well. He liked to download porn, especially young girls.

His only visitor had been Naomi Huston.

He'd once nearly got into trouble with Mr and Mrs Huston, his parent's next-door neighbours, over their thirteen-year old daughter, Naomi.

'It were her fault. Stripped off nearly naked, she did.'

He'd invited her round to listen to music whilst his Mum and Dad were at church. She'd been sitting in the garden catching the sun and reading a magazine.

Naomi wore a pair of pink hot pants and a silky white blouse top. She had boobs alright, not too big, just the way he liked them.

She sat in one of the big arm chairs and he sat opposite.

They listened to 'Bad Romance', he liked Lady Gaga,

He had an erection, just watching her did it.

Little titty buds poking through.

All provocative.

If he hadn't started to rub himself she'd never have noticed.
Naomi gaped open mouth at him, then shouted, "Oh my God!"
She got up quickly and ran to the door.
"I'll give you a tenner!" He shouted as the door slammed shut.
His parents went mad.
Even though he proclaimed himself innocent. Naomi's parents thought about the police, Mr Infine Senior talked them out of it.
His mother and father were almost at the end of their tether with their son.
The previous month he had been fined sixty pounds for the theft of a ladies' bag at a bus stop. The lady was partially sighted.

When the six got back after lunch they were given their allocations for the rest of the month.
Nigel was given A site, which was the closest to the site office and Bernard Jones.
Danny had B site, and Ollie got C.
Ham was given the raw open tip site D.
He closed his eyes when Jones announced the allocations. He was rather hoping for Molbury, which was only a couple of miles from Swaffham. Steven got that.
Jim got the Resset Heath site.
"Fuck!" said Ham quietly.

"Never mind mate. It's only for a month, we'll all have to do a periodic stint there," said Ollie.
"Yeah, I know."

Nigel had stayed until the others had left the office.
He thanked Jones for giving him the A site.
"Thank you, Mister Jones, for givin' us the A site. I'll make sure I do me level best for you, sir."
Jones liked this man, he showed proper respect.
"In time, I'll need a deputy to cover as Manager when I'm on me holidays, or away at Head Office. Keep your nose clean and do what I tells you, and you's *could* be that man."
"Oh, thank you, sir. I'll work 'ard for you, Mr Jones, I promise, and if there's anything that you's need to know about the other men, then I'll make *sure* you do know, sir."
Jones smiled at Nigel.
"Very good, now fuck off."
Nigel left the office a happy man.
Jones was pleased too.
So pleasant to have a nark in the enemy camp.

Jim, as usual, was talking to Alex at the canteen counter.

"I'm off to Resset Heath this afternoon with Jones. I have to stay there," said Jim.

"Oh Jim. I *will* be very sad that you are not here. I enjoy talking to you very much. How long will you be away?"

"A month."

Alex smiled.

"Well then, it will not be *too* long before I see you, although even a month seems a long time."

Alex's hands were resting on the counter as he leaned forward talking to Jim.

Jim put his hand on Alex's. They looked into each other's eyes.

There was chemistry there.

"Would you come out with me, Alex?"

"Yes," Alex said quickly, nervously.

"We both live in King's Lynn. We could meet at The Globe Hotel if you like? It's a very nice place, overlooking the river. We could have a drink, *and* a meal, if you want?"

"Yes. That would be nice."

They arranged to meet.

Ham trudged through the smelly bags of rubbish.

Many bags had split, and the raw rubbish had spilled out.

The seagulls dived and pecked at the opened garbage bags picking up food. Their noisy squawks irritated him immediately, and the stench from the rubbish was so bad it stuck in his throat.
A man jumped down from a bulldozer and raised a hand to him as he plugged into the first pipe on his list.
The man was unshaven and had one eye that looked in a different direction from his other one.
He was a bulldozer driver. He seemed to be dressed in rags.
As Ham moved on to his second reading the driver followed him and introduced himself.
Ham found it difficult to know if the man was looking at him or over his right shoulder.
He had a red round face, unshaven, and big stand out ears.
"I'm 'Arry. 'Arry Potter. Afore you say fuck all, that really *is* my name. I drive the dozer. Push all the shit so there's room for more, and then I flattens it down. Bill Dunne drives the other dozer. He's a good man, but as mad as a fuckin' hatter."
Ham nodded.
He wore his scarf over his nose and mouth in an attempt to keep the stink out. It wasn't very effective.

"I'm Ham. The smell here is rotten, isn't it?"

'Arry shrugged.

"Can't say I notice it much. Been 'ere six years. Word of warning, keep a good eye out around 'ere mate. I can't 'ear fuck all when I'm driving what with the clatter of the dozer and the birds screechin'. I've nearly run over a few blokes cos they weren't lookin', including Misery Guts."

"You mean Jones?"

"Yeah. He used to strut around 'ere shouting at the agency workers what was doing your job. I thought one day, Charlie Armstrong were goin' to biff 'im one. He called Charlie a lazy bastard. Charlie squared up to him, but never 'it 'im. I was hopin' he would, but he never. Jones was shittin' himself, I thought he were goin' to cry. The agency never sent Charlie 'ere no more, I reckon Misery Guts had a word."

"Oh, so Jones never did it all himself then?"

'Arry shook his head.

"Nah. He never did fuck all. Just drove the landrover around and shouted his mouth off. He started orf being just like you, takin' the readin's like. Then they had a scare with an underground fire an' the authorities said they 'ad to look at *all* the settin's, so company got more blokes in and he was the only one with any experience like, so he got the charge hand's job. Total wanker he is. He don't never come near me, nor Bill. He knows we might run the bugger over. According to Alex the cafe boy, who comes in every Saturday to give the cafe a good clean, he said he seen Jones doing the readings on weekends so we weren't 'ere. Fuckin' coward he is. Gutless bastard."

For the rest of that day Ham trudged up and down the hills, sloshing through the endless rubbish, and keeping a sharp eye and ear out for the two bulldozers. He never played any music. The stench made him feel physically sick, and his lunchtime sandwiches went uneaten.

Every so often a bird scarer made a loud bang. They startled Ham. He cursed each and every one.

"So glad you've agreed to come, Ollie," said Ham as he brought their beers to the window table.

Ollie gave Ham the twenty-five pounds.

"I can pick you up."

"No, don't do that. It's miles out of your way."

Ham felt embarrassed.

"Well, thing is, man. I have to pick an old friend up from Hingham to take, so picking you up is virtually on my route."

"In that case, great. I'll get a taxi home though, then I can please myself when I leave."

"As you wish," said Ham.

He felt like a thief in the night. Should he tell him now, or spring it as a surprise? He thought that he *would* tell him, but maybe tomorrow.

"You got the shit short straw then."

"Yeah. D Sector. Man, I really stink, I know it. There are two crazy blokes there too who drive the bulldozers moving the rubbish. We met Bill Dunne in the café on the first day. He was the one who put Infine in his place."

"Yes, I remember. Big bloke."

"You've got to keep a good lookout for them, or you'll get run over. Still I'd rather get my shifts over with early in that sewer. It shouldn't come round more than once every six months for us. Miriam made a point last night, she said that they should have showers at the site. She say's she can smell me two blocks away. I'll be even worse now thanks to Sector D."

"I agree. I undress in my garage and just hope no one sees me in my pants running to the house. Hate my neighbours to think I'm a flasher, or something."

"Maybe we should ask Fagin if the company will install showers for the men," said Ham.

"Nice idea, but I can't see it happening somehow."

They saw Nigel Infine pull up in the car park.

"Oh bollocks, here comes Mister Personality Plus," said Ham.

Nigel came in, ordered his drink and came across to their table.

He sat down and smiled at Ham.

"See you got Sector D then. Horrible is it?"

"Yeah," said Ham.

"I got A, best one there is. Not very smelly, or hard walking," said Nigel.

"Yes. But it's the one nearest to the *exit* gate too," said Ham.

Nigel frowned.

"Wadya mean? *Exit gate*?"

Ham smiled. Shook his head.

"Oh nothing. Nothing at all."

Nigel looked from one to the other.

"We only just *started*, they won't be *sacking* anyone *yet*, will they?" said Nigel.

He didn't look too convinced of his ground.

"Yeah, I suppose that *should* be true," said Ham.

"Wadya mean '*should*'. Have you '*eard* somethin'?"

"Nooo. Nothing *really*."

"*Nothin' really*? That means you 'as 'eard somethin'."
"Nope. I never repeat rumours, *never*," said Ham.
Nigel leant forward.
"Go on mate, you's can tell me. I shan't tell no livin' soul, swear on me dead Mother's life."
Ham stroked his chin.
"Well. I shouldn't say anything really, cos it is just a rumour, and probably no truth whatsoever in it."
"What? What's the rumour? Come on man, tell us, I'll not blab, I promise."
Ham shrugged.
"Well, okay then. But promise you'll not tell a soul?"
"I promise, honest I won't," said Nigel, his face now red.
Ham looked at Ollie, then back at Nigel.
"Mmmm, okay then. You know that gypsy bloke that runs the weighbridge?"
"Yeah. Short fat bloke, big scar on 'is cheek, looks like an ex-boxer. Yeah, I knows him."
Ham spoke in a hushed tone.
He leant towards Nigel.
"Well. He said…"
He hesitated,
"Now, you *do* promise not to tell no one."
Nigel looked agitated.

"*No*, course I *won't*, now come on, tell us for *God's* sake!"

"Well, he said that the numbers of the sea gulls over the sites has dropped alarmingly."

There was silence for a moment.

Nigel was perplexed.

"*So*? Who gives a *fuck* about that?"

"Yes, but he said that his families' ancient gypsy folk lore says that when the sea gulls start to leave the sites, the sites are about to close, and close *forever*."

Nigel looked at Ham, mouth open and eyes wide.

He blinked a few times then sat back in his chair.

Ollie could hardly contain himself.

Ham took a swig of his ale.

"What? Are you fuckin' serious? Is that it? An' you believes it? Fuckin 'ell! Gypo's are lying bastards, everyone knows that. Steal your fuckin' teeth they would, an' then tell you the fuckin' Pope done it. Lying tossers them are."

Ham looked furtively around the bar.

"Shush. Watch your mouth. Of *course* I believe it. Don't want to get the Sagittarius End Gypsy curse on me, no thanks," said Ham.

There was silence at their table.

Nigel looked at Ham, then at Ollie, then back to Ham. Their expressions were non-committal.

"That's got to be fuckin' rubbish, ennit?" said Nigel hesitantly.

Ham shook his head, then shrugged.

"Could be, but I'm not going to say nowt else about it. Last bloke who said anything against the Sagittarius End Gypsy's folk lore regretted it, big time."

Nigel's eyes grew big again.

"Why? What happened to 'im?"

"Best I don't tell you."

"Come on man. I shan't let on."

"Are you sure? I don't want no curse on me."

"Cross me 'eart an' hope to die, I won't say nothin' to no one."

"Well, okay then. Apparently, first off, he lost all his hair. It just fell out in clumps. He ran a comb through it and it just came out. Within three days he was completely bald."

"Fuck! Bald you say? Then what?"

Ham took a long swig of his beer.

"A few days later all his teeth fell out one after the other. He was in a cafe, and every time he took a bite out of his bacon sandwich some of his teeth came out with it. Within three days he didn't have one tooth left in his head," said

Ham in a subdued voice, looking around lest anyone was listening.

"Jesus, bloody Christ! But how did them's know it were a gypsy curse?"

Ham shook his head.

"Best you don't know."

"Come on man. Tell us the rest."

"Well. Okay then. But promise you won't let a word of this out."

Nigel shook his head.

"Promise I won't. Shan't tell a soul, honest."

"Right then. According to legend, the sign of the Sagittarius End Gypsy curse is the letter 'C' appearing on the body. A few days later this same bloke was having a pee and he noticed a small sore on his knob. It formed the letter 'C'. As the days went by the 'C' got bigger until…."

Ham shook his head.

"Look. I'd rather not say any more. It might put you off your tea."

Nigel gulped.

"Come on man! Don't fucking stop now! Tell us the rest!"

Ham sighed.

"You sure?"

"Yes, course I'm fuckin' *sure*!"

"On the seventh day, he was having a pee and his knob came off in his hand. Piss everywhere, sprayed all down his trouser legs, and him with his knob in his hand. Apparently, the guy at the next urinal saw it happen and ran out screaming his head off."

"*Fuckin' Christ*! What 'appened to him?"

"Who? The knobless bloke? Or the guy at the next urinal?"

"The bloke with no knob. What 'appened to 'im?"

"Well, so the story goes, he spent the best part of the next six months trying to get a transplant on the NHS. No surgeon would do it. They all knew about the Sagittarius End Gypsy curse, you see," said Ham.

Nigel's face was now *very* red.

"What 'appened to the poor bugger?"

"I heard he got a job as caretaker at a girl's boarding school. The governors of the school thought, with his condition, the girls would be completely safe."

Their table stayed quiet for a few moments. Nigel blinked repeatedly, visibly shaken.

"Well," said Ollie, "I've got to be off. See you."

Ham got up too.

"I'm coming as well."

Nigel sat in silence, a worried and then a puzzled look on his face.

When the pair got outside they both burst out laughing.

"I don't know how you kept a straight face," said Ollie.
"I was laughing inside. He's such a gullible arsehole. Just hope he doesn't ask the weighbridge gypsy about Sagittarius End Gypsy folklore."
"See you later. Take care."
"Yeah. You too."
They both got into their cars and drove away.
Ollie smiled all the way home, and Ham still had a smug expression on his face as he pulled into the drive in Swaffham. Miriam would love the story.

Nigel ordered another pint of beer.
He felt in shock.
'Fuckin' Gypo's, nothing but bloody trouble, those bastards. Fancy your knob fallin' off? How would you pee? He must have had to sit down to do it, like a bloody woman.'
Archie served Nigel his second pint.
"Your mates left you on your own then?"
"Yeah. They're not really mates. We just work at the same place."
"You're a newie too, eh?"
"Yeah. Started with them two, and three others. Our boss has given me the nod on a promotion already," said Nigel.

"Corr. That's quick. You must be some sort of high flyer then, eh?"

"I suppose I am. Our boss is no mug, he can see quality a mile off."

Archie thought Nigel was a big-headed prick.

He remembered that that Jones bloke used to come in here a lot, 'til he got threatened by one of their digger drivers.

"Where'd you live? Nearby?"

"Wymondham."

"I know it. Quite a nice town is Wymondham."

"It is. Tell me somethin'. Has you's ever heard of the Sagittarius End Gypsy curse?"

Archie scratched his head.

"Can't say I have, but there are a lot of gypsy's living around here. Why? What is it?"

Nigel looked around to make sure no one was listening.

"If you get it your hair falls out, your teeth follow, and then your old man down there comes away."

Archie looked non-committal. He felt like laughing but the look on Nigel's face told him not to.

He stroked his chin.

"Result then really, wouldn't you say?"

Nigel looked puzzled.

"*Result*? What d'yer mean, *result*?"

Archie sighed.

"Well. No barber's fees, no painful dentist visits, and, if the old girl has a headache on a Friday night, it don't matter a shit."

SIX

Beryl Anstey sat in her office looking out through the window that faced the weighbridge.
She watched the gasmen trudging out through the light afternoon rain to the gas field to do their daily monitoring.
She'd put streaks in her hair the previous night and felt good about herself.
Okay, so apart from her largish nose her face wasn't wonderful, but not bad either.
She knew she passed muster when she'd done all her bits with make-up.
Her mum told her to look at any man she fancied straight on, then he might not notice her nose.
She needed a man.
She rather liked the look of that one who wore his sunglasses all the time. He had long blond hair and she remembered from reading his

personnel file that he was a musician before he came to this shit hole monitoring job.

'Now what was his name?'

She opened one of the filing cabinets and sifted through the personnel files.

'Ah here it is. Mmmm, *Daniel, Daniel William Bentley*. Wonder if he likes being called Dan? Maybe Danny? 29 years old, nice age that, means he's got all the useless kid's stuff like bloody Playstation and Call of frigging Duty out of his brain. From Norwich. Oh well, can't have everything.'

She turned the page.

'Oh bugger! *Married*! Why are all the best ones bloody *married*? Mind you, married men get divorced all the time. At the moment, I'm after a body not a title, although that would be nice, if he had money. Which he ain't, not workin' at this dump.'

Beryl was a single mum courtesy of a girl's holiday to Ibiza with three other ladies out for a good time and hoping to pull.

Most of the holiday could barely be remembered apart from breakfast around 2pm and being aware occasionally that she was almost totally out of it, sleeping most of the day, and the rest of the time dancing, drinking as much as she could, as quickly as she could and indulging in early morning sex through an alcoholic blur.

On that holiday, it was hardly worth wearing *any* panties. Five different young men or was it six? and a middle-aged club owner.

One night she was pretty sure there were three of them in this guy's bed. Could have been any one of those. She did fail to pull on one occasion, one night, but spent the early hours sitting on the tiled floor of the bathroom hugging her flat's toilet bowl and screaming a Technicolor 'Eureka!' down it every five or ten minutes for over an hour after drinking a bottle of wine, fourteen shots of something, and a pint of lager.

She did remember that the club owner was Spanish, married and about fifty or so. His name was a blank, but he left her a twenty Euro note on her bedside dresser before he legged it at around four am.

The other men were a mix of English, German and she thought one was probably a Swede, but couldn't be sure. She thought the English guy was from Huddersfield or Leeds, or somewhere in the North and was either Robert, or Robbie, or Rob, but again, couldn't be sure, maybe it had been 'Knob'.

Nine months later she'd had a little girl, Mandy.

Her mum Sybil had helped her throughout her pregnancy and after. Her Mum was appropriately experienced, she was a single mum too.

Her man was an American airman from the Lakenheath USAF Air Base.

The day after she phoned him and explained that she was pregnant, he apparently was sent post haste back to the good old US of A. Her first letters to the Base Commander yielded replies of no knowledge of any US airman named Calvin Markswood Junior at the base. Later letters asking for financial support went unanswered.

Mandy was now five years old and attended the Swaffham Infants School.

Beryl's mother put her on the bus each morning at twenty to nine, and met her again after school around four pm. They lived opposite the stop in the village of Necton.

Beryl left home at eight o'clock to start work at eight thirty. She had almost never been on time for the two years that she had worked for Thornes. No one noticed. Jones was always later than her.

After a week-long training and induction period at head office, she was pretty much her own boss in the Sagittarius End office, filling out timesheets, recording readings from the

Monitors which that soppy idiot Bernard Jones brought in every morning, and requesting supplies, all from, and to, the Regional Head Office in Norwich.

She'd been introduced to most of the staff in Norwich during her induction. The boss, Malcolm Stewle had visibly undressed her as she shook his hand. She knew what he wanted. Dirty old git.

Jones always had his tongue hanging out as he loitered around the office for much of the first two weeks of her employment after her training period at Norwich.

He offered her out for a drink in her second week at Sagittarius. She declined.

He looked like an unwashed, ugly, smelly, paedophile, murderer, and what was worse he kept twirling that stupid bloody little tash of his. That wife of his must have been as nutty as him to live in the same house and share the same bed. She imagined him undressed. Puny of limb, foul smelling, with a winkie like a soggy cigarette. *There* was a premature ejaculator, if *ever* she saw one.

Bernard Jones had a good look around Beryl's office when he dropped the engine flare figures and monitor statistics off that morning. There was another computer, but not as good as the previous one he had stolen. The rest of the office stuff had no resaleable value as far as he could see.

In his strolls around the general area surrounding the non-gas site he looked into the secure yard behind the offices. Amongst all the replacement gear for the pipelines that had no quick sale value, he noticed that there was three full reels of industrial size copper wire.

He knew that copper had a high value, maybe as much as a thousand quid a reel.

The storage area was cordoned off with high V fencing, on the top of which were two strands of barbed wire. He had the only site key to the strong padlock that secured the gate entrance, so that was not an option.

He plodded through the day, sick to death of never having enough money.

Jones approached Durrell Nernes, a six foot, heavily tattooed, thickset man, in the King's Arms that night.

Nernes had served two prison sentences for robbery, his family were well known in the area for petty theft and thuggery.

Durrell assured him that he could offload any amount of thick copper wire for him.

Jones pointed out that he would need a couple of very strong assistants to help him get the three large reels into a car trailer.

"Car ain't no good," said Durrell, "Not big 'nough, nor strong 'nough. I'll bring the right vehicle, no worries."

The two arranged to meet at the main gate of the Sagittarius End site on Friday evening.

Nernes would ensure they had two 'strong 'uns' to lend a hand.

Friday night, no moon, cold with drizzle, and four men ready to steal.

Jones carried a sledge hammer, and a Monitor's single glove.

Durrell Nernes and his fourteen-stone son, Wester, carried a swagger, and both smoked rolled-up cigarettes, with a little something in them. They had a third man, Errol, with them. He was a bald giant of a man with black teeth.

Durrell's ancient dark green three-tonner was backed up close to the secured gate.

Two mighty blows from Wester with the sledge-hammer and the gate was open.

The four rolled each of the copper reels. They were very heavy, and they were fifteen minutes into their labours before they were at the lorry with the first reel.

The reels were far too heavy to be lifted by hand. They hauled them onto the lorry using the lorries on board hydraulic lifting gear.

After the copper was safely stowed, secured and covered with a tarpaulin, the three men took their leave of the site manager.
Jones patted his pocket that contained the agreed six hundred pounds and smiled. Before he left the area, he threw the single glove down by the opened gate and hummed a marching song as he walked briskly to his car.

He looked up at the boarded-up window.
'Must get that fixed'.
"Where you been?"
Doreen sat in her dressing gown.
The television was on. 'The Ten O'clock News'.
"Making us some money to pay for the bloody bills. Have you been dressed like that all day?"
She shrugged.
He laid the money on the table in front of her.
Her eyes widened.
"Bloody hell, that's good. As you're up, get us a drink."
Jones went to the 'fridge'.
A bottle of the usual plonk for her, and a few cans of Stella for him. Then maybe a bit of 'physical' if he were lucky. Celebratory.
He handed her the bottle of cheap sherry. As she unscrewed the top he told her of the

night's proceedings. She swigged from the bottle, in between burps.

"You ought to go nicking for a livin'. I'm sure you'd make more money than at that bleedin' rubbish dump, *and* you'd smell a lot better."

"That's all very well but I could get stuck in prison if I got caught. Don't fancy getting' me arse reamed every night for six months by some big black drug dealer."

He did manage a bit of 'physical' later although Doreen spoilt it a little by constantly reminding him to hurry up, as she badly needed the loo.

On Monday morning, just after nine, Beryl phoned Head Office to let them know that there had been a robbery. Mr Stewle came on the line and asked her what had been stolen.

"I don't know really, except I do know there were some big round things with copper stuff in them, and they're gone. The big padlock is smashed. Mr Jones will be in soon. He'll know exactly what the robber got. I don't like to go near the gate cos the coppers will be wanting to do their forensesses things for clues."

Stewle sighed.

"Forensics. Not what you said. It's *forensics*, dear."

"Oh right, sorry."

"Phone the police, and tell Jones to call me the minute he gets in."

The phone went dead.

After she had phoned the police Beryl made herself a cup of coffee and sat watching the latest You Tube trending on her computer.

At nine thirty Jones came into the office with Friday's reports.

Beryl told him about the break in, and what she had done. He looked amazed.

"Bloody hell! Not *again*. What have they taken *this* time?"

"Don't know. Kept away. Just saw the gate open and the padlock on the ground. I know the wooden wheel things with the copper stuff has gone. But don't know what else. Mr Stewle said the cops will be doing the forensets, or whatever it is, so I ain't going near it."

"Very wise. I'll keep well back too but just eyeball what they took."

"Mr Stewle said you was to call him when you knows what the robber nicked."

Jones left, and fifteen minutes later called Stewle and made his report.

"Looks to me like the robbers only nicked the three copper reels, Sir."

"Right. When the coppers have been, ask one of them to give me a call."

"Yes sir. Anything else you'll be…."

The phone went dead.
"Bastard!"

Danny and Steven stood at the bar of The Sportsman, a local pub.
Since working at Sagittarius End they found they lived just two streets away from each other and had arranged this evening out with their wives.
"Amazing that we lived so close and now work at the same dump. In all honesty, I can't ever remember seeing you around."
"Me neither, mind you we've only been here six months, we lived in Yarmouth before that," said Steven.
Their two wives sat at a table, both drank white wine. They seemed to have much in common, got on well from the outset, and had arranged to go shopping together. Danny's wife Vee had a car.
"I just hope he finds another job soon. The stench of his clothing drives me up the wall. He puts fresh on every day and the washer works overtime. Even his bloody car stinks to high heaven now."
Sylvia agreed.
"They should pay them a stink rate to add onto their pay. I haven't felt like cuddling him since his first day there, frightened I might get

something, and pass it on to me Mum. She's past sixty now and the bubonic plague would do for her I reckon, what with her forty a day habit, *and* she likes her whisky. Mind you, her boyfriend Archie hums a bit, I can tell you, an' he don't work at their place."

Danny sipped his beer.

He asked Steven about the site he was monitoring.

"So, what's Molbury like, then?"

"A bloody dump, like Sagittarius, it's a lot smaller and it's not got any open rubbish to monitor, so it don't stink as much, thank God. There's only one bloke there, old boy name of Billy, and he just kind of guard's things. He seems to drink a lot of homemade beer in his little hut, an' sleeps most afternoons. Molbury's a bit like Sagittarius were ten years ago, I suppose, but now it's all covered over and grassed. Best thing about it is you're on your own and you don't have to wear your stupid hard hat, and all the other crap gear. It's not a tenth the size of Sagittarius, either. Worse thing is the frigging rats. Hundreds of the bastards, in the monitoring pits an' in the flare buildings."

"Hate rats, I do. What sort of hours do you work then?"

"Well, they can see from your first monitor what times you're on site so even though you're on your own you can't skive. I get in around eight and leave just after five."
"At least you don't have to contend with that tosser Jones all day."
"That's a fact. How is it at Sagittarius now?"
Danny shrugged.
"Same old shit, different day."
"I know one thing, soon as I can find another job I'm offski, that's for sure," said Steven.
"Me too," said Danny.
The two men re-joined their wives at the table and chatted merrily away for the rest of the evening.

Detective Sergeant Morland knocked on Beryl's door before he opened it.
"Come in!"
The tall silver haired plain clothes policeman entered the office.
"Hello dear. I'm DS Morland from Norfolk Police. You've lost some property I believe?"
Beryl eyeballed the copper.
'Pity he looks like a ninety-year old, bet he was a bit of all-right in his younger days'.
"Yes. They nicked some of them copper reel things from the compound behind here."

The policeman took down her name, address, job title and phone number.

"Is this place manned at the weekends? Where's the compound please, miss."

She indicated the direction of the secure area.

"No. No one here after five on Fridays 'til around half eight on Mondays."

"Can you show me, love, please?"

She took him outside and showed him where the gate padlock had been smashed.

"No one's been here. Me an' Jonesy kept away in case we buggered up any clues."

Morland smiled.

"Well done. Who's Jonesy?"

"Site foreman. His office is in that little building there."

She pointed.

"Righto. Thanks."

Morland walked to the gate and Beryl went back into her office.

The policeman saw clear signs in the dirt that a lorry had been used, he took photographs of the tread marks, boot and shoe imprints and the general area within the compound. He made some measurements, then placed the broken padlock into a plastic bag.

There was a glove laying by one of the gate stanchions. He picked it up, bagged it and picked up another couple of small pieces of residue, that he thought might become useful, and bagged those too.

He walked over to Jones' office.

Jones was reading the Sun when the knock came.

He beckoned the knocker in.

"Detective Sergeant Morland, sir."

"You've come about the robbery."

"I have. You are the site foreman, the young lady in the office yonder tells me."

"I'm the site *Manager*, not the foreman."

"Right. And your full name is?"

"Why do you need *my* name? I never 'ad nothin' to do with it."

"I realise that, *Sir*. I need to make a report, and so I'll need your full name, address, and a contact telephone number."

Jones gave the policeman his details.

After copying down a full description of the items that had been stolen he showed the glove he had picked up to Jones.

"Seen this, or one like it before, Mr Jones?"

Jones face reddened and he coughed.

"Well, yeah. Them's the gloves what my monitor men get issued with. It should 'ave a workers' number on it."

Morland turned the bag over.

"007. Whose number would that be?"

Jones closed his eyes briefly and stroked his chin.

"Erm, that is Danny Bentley if I'm not mistaken. Better just check."

Jones went to his desk and pulled a book out of his top drawer.

He leafed through the book.

"Yep. Danny Bentley, it is. Do you think he done it, officer?"

"I'm not accusing anyone at this stage. Where can I find this Danny Bentley?"

"He's workin' on B site. I can get 'im 'ere if you's want. He 'as a radio."

The policeman nodded.

"Yes please."

Ham waded through all the rubbish to reach one of the monitoring outlets. He'd applied for a security job at a factory yesterday and was hopeful. Better pay, and a hell of a lot better than working in this filth, for pennies.

He had an air pistol in his pocket, which he hadn't fired since he was in London. Pigeons flying off his roof there used to shit all over his car. The pistol got rid of some of them and the noise frightened others away.

He was aware that seagulls were protected, but he just had to get revenge for their bloody

raucous screams and their three-ton shit bombs.
He looked for the two digger drivers. They were busy at the bottom of the site, well away from him.
Ham aimed at one swooping bird but missed. Then he missed a second time. He'd be no good in the forces, he thought.
An hour later, after he'd expended fifteen pellets he decided to change tack and wait until he came across a landed bird. His previous successes with the pigeons was because they just sat still on his roof, or on his shed.
An opportunity arose as a seagull was busy pecking at a rubbish bag. He got to within four metres and was just about to raise the barrel when the bird got skiddish and flew off.
At last one sat nicely for him. He got to within his new five-metre umbrella range, raised the pistol up, targeted the belly of the bird, and then couldn't bring himself to shoot it.
He shouted at it.
"Fuck off!"
The bird flew a couple of metres away and then landed again.
He looked around.
Good job nobody was there to see him acting stupidly.

He chased it.

"Bugger off!"

Seagulls were different to pigeons, he didn't know why, but they were.

His radio came to life. He was wanted back at the office. Pronto.

Danny sat on a pipe in section B. He had his headphones on and listened to Bruno Mars singing 'Magic'.

He thought this guy was just a poor imitation of Michael Jackson. He reckoned he could do better by a mile, given the chance.

He heard something crackle on his company radio.

He pulled his ear plugs out.

"Bentley! Bentley! Are you's there?"

First time he'd had a call. It was that little prick Jones calling him.

He pressed the send button.

"Yeah. I'm here."

"Right, well. You's gotta come to my office straight away."

Danny shrugged.

"Okay. I'm coming."

"Well, hurry up. Police here want to speak with you's."

Danny stowed his ear phones and his Sony in his pocket, picked up his monitor and started

to walk quickly along the trodden pathway that meandered through B Section and onto the dirt road that would bring him to Jones' office.
'Police?'
He racked his brain.
He hadn't done anything illegal for many a moon. Admittedly, his car wasn't insured, but surely the law wouldn't send a copper to his place of work just for that. They'd pounce on him at his house, or in the street.
He smoked a little hash from time to time but never sold any, so it couldn't be that either.
He prayed it wasn't a death in the family.
Just before he turned the corner to Jones' office he put his hard hat on.
A car stood outside Jone's offices.
He entered the building and knocked on Jone's door.
He went in after he heard Jone shout, "Come in."
Jones beckoned him and he closed the door behind him.
"This is him, officer."
So, this man *was* a copper. It *had* to be bad news.
The man stood up and faced Danny.
"Hello, young man, I'm Detective Sergeant Morland, of Norfolk Police."

He held open a wallet that had a warrant card inside.
"Is it me Mum, or Dad?"
The policeman shook his head.
"No. No. Nothing with the family. Let me explain."
Danny looked at Jones.
Jones's eyes were lowered. He was quiet. Listening.
"Over the weekend, sometime between knocking off time on Friday afternoon and first thing Monday morning the storage area had visitors. They smashed the lock and made off with some property belonging to Thorne's. Do you know anything about it? Is there anything you need to tell us?"
Danny frowned and shook his head.
"Me? Why would I know anything about it?"
"Better own up now, Bentley," said Jones.
The policeman scowled at Jones.
"Please. Leave this to me. Keep quiet."
"I know *nothin'* about it," said Danny vehemently.
"Can you give me the details of your movements all over the weekend, please Sir?"
"Yeah. I can, but why me? I had absolutely nowt to do with this shit."
Danny recounted his movements over the weekend and the detective jotted down his

notes, including the details of the people he knew who could vouch for his being where he said he was from Friday night through to Monday morning.

"Have all the other workers here been questioned as well?"

"No, just you," said Jones.

The detective wheeled onto Jones.

"Mr Jones. Please leave this office *now,* so that I can speak to Mr Bentley in private."

Jones pulled a face but left the office.

"The reason I'm questioning you first Mr Bentley is because a work glove was found at the compound where the theft took place."

Danny nodded.

"Yeah. I did lose a glove. Only missed it this mornin'. I could have sworn I stowed it with the rest of my gear on Friday before I knocked off shift. Jones gave me a new pair."

"The work number on the glove is 007. Is that your work number?"

"Yeah it is, but I repeat, I know absolutely *nothin'* about *any* theft."

"I see," said Sergeant Morland.

"Anything else?" said Danny.

"No, you can hop it now. Not going anywhere soon, are you, sir?"

"No. Except for home at five o'clock. Are you goin' to interview my friends and family?"

"Maybe."

Danny left the office. Jones was waiting outside.

"Put your gear away Bentley. You're suspended."

Danny was astounded.

"*Suspended*? But I ain't done nothin'."

"Maybe you's ain't, maybe you's 'as. Better if you's owns up now, it is. I'll give you's a reference if you does."

"Bollocks!"

Danny went to the locker area and stowed all his gear. When he came outside again Jones was nowhere in sight.

Ham came walking up.

"Hiya Danny. How's it going man?"

"Fuckin' arsehole Jones has just suspended me. Apparently, there was some stuff nicked over the weekend an' they found one of my glove's nearby."

"But surely, they don't think you did it, do they?"

"Jones has put the boot in, I reckon."

Danny was near to tears. He got into his car and phoned his wife before driving off.

"Yes, Mr Stewle. I feel sure it were 'im. Left the encribinatin' evidence he did, sir."

"I see. Is the policeman still there?"

"Yes, sir. He went to speak to Beryl again, sir. He said he's wantin' to speak to the weighbridge bloke as well as the two digger drivers on section D he does, an' also the pipe-layers."

"Tell him to call me when he's free, please."

"Yes, sir. I will, sir. Is there…"

The phone went dead as Stewle hung up.

"Bastard."

A knock came on the door and Ham entered.

"Right Veene. Bentley's not workin' here no more, so you's is going to do his monitorin' in section B as well as you's other one in D."

Ham frowned.

"How does that work then? Each section is a full weeks' work."

"You's will do what I tells you's. You's 'as just got to work quicker, instead of buggerin' about."

"It can't be done. I work pretty much flat out just to finish D section by Friday night."

Jones crossed his arms and rested them on his desk.

"Well, that's not good enough. You's will have to stay later, and maybe you's will come in on Saturday as well if you ain't good enough to carry out you's duties to my satisfaction."

"Nope. I'm not working late and I'm certainly not working Saturdays. Neither of those are in my contract."

Jones pushed his chair away from his desk and stood up.

"Right! That's the trouble with you's blackies, you's all lazy. You ain't got no upper class breeding like what us whites 'as. All you's want to do is take drugs and rape white women. Either you's do what I tells you's, or you's is finished here!"

Ham turned on his heels and left the office, slamming the door loudly behind him.

Jones chuckled.

'That's the thing with thems niggers, thems can't not take no constructive criticism, no matter 'ow well intentioned us white people put it to 'em. He'll come crawling back soon though. Where else will a wool-head get a job in Norfolk? Unless, of course, him fancy collectin' the old rubbish bins, or floggin' drugs or pimping.'

SEVEN

Annabel Simpson brushed her shoulder length dark hair.
She looked at herself in the full-length mirror in her hallway.
She felt she wasn't fat, well, maybe just a little. But cuddly, if she only had someone to be cuddly with.
Last applicant had been Archie. He wanted more than just a cuddle, even on their first, and, as it transpired, their only date.
He was a local government official. A graduate and very clever, at council stuff anyway, but incredibly boring.
After a couple of drinks in The London Tavern she gave him a goodnight peck on the cheek at her doorway after their first evening out. He had grabbed her bottom and pulled her to him in a very rough manner.

She slapped his face, and swore he almost cried, before he turned tail, and skedaddled away like a naughty schoolboy.

He called her next day to apologise.

Had he been a little bit subtler, he might have got somewhere, not all the way there, but a little. In any event, she turned down his offer of a cosy meal in Maples, an upmarket restaurant in Norwich.

Her longest serving boyfriend had been Rex, an insurance broker from Hethersett who had a six-year-old son living with him. She thought it was love so she moved into his bungalow. After six months of being a sex and food goddess, mother, washer-lady, cleaner, school dropper-offer, and tantrum reducer, it all got a bit tiresome, especially after a day filled with children demanding all her attention at school.

She moved back in with her Mum and Dad, but that only lasted a few weeks.

She needed her own space, and a nice one bed flat in Hingham made all the right noises.

She would have liked to have been a bit taller than her five feet five, but shoes generally took care of that. Her dark hair was pretty damned good, not too long, not too short, and it was set off by her bright hazel green eyes.

Now Miriam had set her up with a semi blind date for The Lion's Winter Dinner.

She wondered whether she should buy a new dress for the occasion. Maybe black, or possibly red. A bit of cleavage, and possibly some lace to set it off.

Miriam said Ham had told her this guy, Oliver, was really nice. Quite good looking, outspoken about politics, but otherwise a little reserved. Apparently, his girlfriend had been killed by a drunk-driver a few years ago. No girlfriends since.

Alex and Jim chatted over their meal in The Globe.

Jim thought Alex had wonderful eyes and was so handsome, with his wavy dark hair.

Alex thought Jim was a gentle giant.

They found out that they had a lot in common. Music, theatre, country walks. They laughed together at the same things, and when their eyes met there *was* that chemistry.

Later that night they kissed for the first time in the shadows outside the restaurant.

"I have an apartment nearby. We could have a coffee, or more wine," said Jim quietly.

The two men shared more than coffee, or wine, that night, and when Alex left at five am he felt elated, fulfilled, at peace.

They spoke over the next day on their phones and Jim prepared a meal for them both at his apartment, on Sunday evening.
"That was a fine meal, Jim. I enjoyed it."
"Good."
"Have you ever been in love, Jim?"
Jim thought for a moment.
"I think so, yes. I definitely think so."
Alex looked surprised.
"Was there a sad ending to it?"
"I dunno."
"But surely you *must* know?"
"How can I? It's only just happened, being in love, I mean."
They looked into each other's eyes.
"I have a deep feeling for you too, Jim. I don't know if it is love, but I just would like to be with you."
"What will your parents think, or say, when they find out about us?"
A worried look appeared on Alex's face.
"Of course, there are gay people in my country, just as there are here in the UK, but here it is accepted more. In Romania, some people, especially neo Nazi's and other right-wingers, are violent towards men and women like us. My parents are good people, but I don't know if they would be angry at me too, it is not so acceptable there."

"I see."
Alex sighed.
"But you see Jim, it doesn't matter. I am here, with you, and I want to remain with you. If they are angry I will be sad, but I will still be with you, as long as you want me to be."
They held hands across the table. Alex stayed the night again.
Alex told his Mother and Father about his relationship with Jim the next evening. His Father was *very* angry, his mother cried.
"A man? You love a man? You bring shame upon this family. No sodomite will live under my roof. Pack up your belongings and leave. *Now*!"
His mother said nothing.
Alex packed his cases, and phoned Jim. They became a couple that night, living in Jim's apartment.
"Was it awful for you?"
Alex nodded.
"Terrible. My Mother cried. My Father was so angry I thought he would hit me. They said I have disgraced the family."
They sat on the settee. Jim had his arm around Alex's shoulders and as the tears fell he pulled Alex to him and comforted him as best he could.

"Hello Mr Stewle. I just thought I'd tell you that I've suspended that bloke from last Friday."

"Suspended? What *bloke*? Do you mean Bentley? Why?"

"Yeah, that Bentley bloke, what nicked the copper reels, sir. We can't have no nickers in the company, sir. I'm hard on them, I am, sir. Protectin' the company, I does, sir."

Stewle sighed and shook his head.

"Have you got *positive* proof that he stole the copper reels? Has he *confessed*, Jones?"

"Well, yeah. Well, no. Not *confessed* exactly, but the police found his glove in the compound, sir."

"But that's not bloody *proof*, man. I've spoken to Sergeant Morland this morning and he has confirmed to me that Bentley's alibi's all stack up. It wasn't him."

"Must have been 'im, sir. His glove, an' he looks like a thief, with all that long hair, and he wears sunglasses, even indoors."

Stewle shook his head.

"Jones. It is now ten o'clock. By eleven I want you to call me and tell me that you have reinstated Bentley in his job with this company."

"What? Give 'im 'is job back, you mean?"

"Jones. I mean *exactly* that. You had no right to suspend him."

"Right. Yes sir. If you say so, sir."
"I do say so. Furthermore, *before* you suspend, or fire, *anyone* in the future, you are to seek my permission, *first. Do you understand*, Jones?"
"Yyyes, sir. I just thought that as…""
Stewle hung up and swung his chair round.
Reggie Witter sat opposite his fellow Director, whiskey glass in hand.
"Fucking clown, that Jones at Sagittarius End."
Reggie smiled.
"Seems to be, Malcolm. Why keep him?"
Stewle shrugged.
"He's cheap, so provided I get the figures in correctly and promptly, and Sagittarius End produces good annual profits he can stay there. But could you imagine what a hoo-ha there would be if the press picked up on a story where some brain dead dull shit like Jones suspends somebody just because one of his gloves was found near the crime scene, notwithstanding that *all* his alibis for the time within which the copper reels could have been stolen, stand up to scrutiny?"
"Yes. Definitely not good PR for the company, and the man could have brought a civil case against us."
"Yes. I tell you one thing, you may need arse-lickers like Jones in a company, but they try

your bloody patience sometimes with their *total* stupidity."

"I agree. He could, of course, have pinched the copper reels himself and *planted* the glove. Been done before, Malcolm."

Stewle nodded.

"Indeed, but he's far too bloody stupid to think that one up."

"Bastard!"

Jones picked up a biro and threw it across the room. It pinged against a wall.

"Fuck it!"

He picked up his desk book, thumbed through it, then rang Danny's number.

"Hello."

"Is that you, Bentley?"

"Yeah, this is Danny Bentley. Who's this?"

"It's *Mr* Jones at Sagittarius End. Look, I've decided to give you's a second chance. I've decided you's can come back to work."

"Oh, have you? You realise now that it wasn't me what stole anything, do you?"

"Well, er, nothin's proved one way or the other, but I knows you's has a kid an' all so I felt sorry for you's, an' you can come 'ere an' work again, startin' tomorrow at nine."

"Right," said Danny.

He slammed the phone down.

"Shithouse!"
Vee, Danny's wife, was sitting on the settee reading the Evening News.
"What is it?"
"That fucking Pleb Jones has taken me off suspension and says I'm to report back to work tomorrow."
"Oh Danny, that's great. I know the job is terrible, but at least it's there 'til another, better, one comes along. It means they know you never nicked owt, too, doesn't it?"

Jones walked across the yard to Beryl's office. He looked at his watch.
'Eight-thirty. Bentley should be in soon'.
Beryl looked up as he came in.
She'd only just arrived.
"Here's the flare figures for last week. Can you send 'em off to that prick Stewle, please, they're late cos of this thieving' shit!"
Beryl pulled a face.
"You're in a bad one today. I guess they haven't caught the robber?"
Jones laughed.
"I thought they had, but looks like he slipped away."
"Who was it? Some of them Gypo's from Howard's Close?"

"Nah. Them's coppers thought it were Bentley, on account of he left 'is glove by the gate."
Beryl looked shocked.
"Surely, he wouldn't have nicked stuff from his own bosses, would he?"
"God knows. Why not?"
"He seems like a nice guy."
"Look. All them men's is on low wages. They'd nick their mother's last halfpenny, if you's ask me. Anyway's, them coppers changed their mind, some of 'is mates gave 'im an alibi."
Beryl mused for a moment.
"Them copper reel things looked really heavy so there must have been more than one of them anyway, and they'd have needed a lorry to carry them off, so maybe they all done it."
Jones sighed.
"Well, we'll never know now. They 'as scarpered with it, an' the police is useless."
Beryl put the sheets of figures into her 'In' tray.
"What's goin' to happen now, then?"
Jones shrugged.
"Buggered if I know. I binned Bentley, but Stewle told me to reinstate him, so I 'as."
"I see."
"He'll be back in here in a minute to sign a new monthly Health & Safety sheet. Tell 'im to get 'is arse over to B Section, I don't want to see 'im."

Beryl's life brightened.
Jones walked back to his office. His shoulders slumped.
'I'll 'ave to tell the nigger to just do Section D now. Fuck it! He'll think he 'as won."
He kicked a chair.
"Bastard fuggin' beaten me. Me, a white man, an' all'.

Beryl placed the Monthly Health and Safety sheets in the bottom drawer of the filing cabinet.
Danny drove along the A47.
He hated the thought of working at that shithole Sagittarius End, but he needed to pay his way. He knew that if Jones said just one little thing out of line today, he'd *batter* him.
He parked and walked to Beryl's office.
Beryl. Twinkle in her eye.
"Hello, new boy!"
Danny noticed, he smiled at her.
"I've got to sign the monthly H & S sheet."
Beryl had undone two of her blouse buttons.
Danny noticed.
She bent down to extract the Health and Safety sheets from the lowest drawer in the filing cabinet, taking her time.
She knew she had a nice arse.
Danny noticed.

After she placed his sheet on her desk, she indicated where Danny had to sign.
She bent down as if looking at the sheets, her cleavage more apparent.
Danny noticed.
"You're supposed to read it all. All eight pages."
"Bollocks to that. Has there been any new changes?"
"Only that I've dumped my boy-friend and was wonderin' if you wanted to come out for a drink with me Friday night?"
He slowly took his sunglasses off.
She came around the desk and stood very close to him, looking up into his eyes.
He could smell her perfume, and knew she wanted him.
He grabbed her.
They had a long, lingering kiss.
"I can lock the door," she said quietly, into his ear.
"Do that."
The spare desk was very sturdy, and convenient.
At twenty-five past nine Danny hurried to B Section.
He'd had quite an unexpected, but pleasant, start to the day.

He had to pass through part of Section D and saw Ham at the top of one of the slopes.

Ham waved, Danny waved back, and climbed through the rotting bags of rubbish up the hill towards him.

"On Friday, Jones told me you were suspended. He said I had to do your sector as well as my own."

"And what did you tell him?"

"Fuck off."

"Good man!"

"So, what's happened?"

Danny told him, but not about the little episode with Beryl.

"That Jones, he's one big piece of shit, isn't he?"

"No argument there, my friend. Although I think you may be doing a disservice to 'shit' by associating Jones with it. He called me this morning, and told me he felt sorry for me, and that I didn't need to cover your sector. I wasn't going to anyway."

EIGHT

Steve was over from Molbury to pick up a battery and some spares for the site.
He laughed when Danny told him in Alex's café, at coffee break, the saga of his suspension and about Ham's situation.
"What a prize frigging dope that wanker Jones is."
Beryl came in.
She walked straight to the counter and ordered two sausage rolls from Alex. He put them in a bag and, as she turned to leave, she gave Danny the biggest of smiles.
Steve noticed.
Beryl passed their table.
"Hello Danny," she purred rather than spoke.
"Hi Beryl, how are you?"
"Great, thanks. See you later?"

"Yep."

As she left, Steve nudged Danny.

"You're in there, mate."

"I know."

Wide eyed Steve smiled.

"Have you?"

"*What*?"

"*You* know."

"No comment."

"That means you have, you randy git. Hope your missus doesn't find out."

Danny just smiled.

Jones came in.

Blanked both men and went to the counter.

Alex turned from the preparation of sandwiches.

"What can I get you, please?"

"A coffee, an' none of that three-week-old sour milk neither. Don't want to get the shits again," said Jones, in a loud voice.

Alex said nothing and turned to the coffee machine.

A minute later Danny came to the counter. He stood next to Jones.

"I'll have a coffee too please, Alex. Please remember to put plenty of that lovely *fresh* milk in for me. You know, the milk you get in fresh *every* day."

Jones looked sideways at Danny but remained silent.

Alex smiled.

"Certainly sir. I never stock *any* milk except fresh milk bought on the day."

"We all know that Alex. Well, most of us, anyway."

Alex placed Jones' coffee on the counter in front of him.

Jones paid with the right money and left without a word.

After he left the café, Danny went into the office where Beryl waited.

She locked the door and they went into the store room where there was another sturdy table.

This one had two thick blankets doubled over and laid on its top. Sturdy, convenient, *and* comfortable.

Danny noticed.

Ollie felt the outlet again.

Hot. Too hot. But reducing.

He picked up his radio.

"Wilson here in Section C. The outlet on C117 is very hot and the pressure is 76.2."

Jones dipped a biscuit into his coffee and stuck it into his mouth.

"Mmmm."

Ollie waited.

Jones crunched on his biscuit, oblivious to the delay.

Ollie felt the anger rising.

"You still there?"

Jones kept crunching.

Ollie sighed.

"Is that flames I can see?"

Jones spat out the remains of his biscuit.

"Flames? Did you say flames?"

Ollie smiled.

"Oh no. It's a red plastic bag caught on the wind."

"Jesus!"

"Shall I turn the pressure down to, say 50? And monitor it?"

"Yes, turn the bugger down, an' hang around to see if'n it does cool down."
"Okay."
"Wilson? Turn it down to 50."
Ollie looked at his monitor readings and smiled. He'd turned the pressure down to 50 well before he'd called Jones.
The outlet remained hot then warm for half an hour before it settled into 'cool' but Ollie decided not to radio Jones, just yet.
Let him sweat.

Jones walked over to A sector where Nigel Infine was monitoring.
"Everything alright, Infine?"
Nigel turned to face his boss.
"Yes, Mr Jones, all okay here, sir."
Jones smiled.
He liked the respect this man showed him.
Not like the others.
"Wilson on C Sector has a warm fitting, or so he says. Don't know if he's capable of sortin' it, so I wants you's to go up there and see what he's up to. Go up now and come back to me office, an' let me know."

"Righto sir. I'm on me way. I'll report straight back, sir."
Nigel semi saluted Jones and walked off.
'Good man him is.'
Nigel kept a good pace up. He muttered to himself as he strode along.
'Obvious Jones likes me. Recognises leader material, he does.'

Ollie was further along the pipe run. He'd left the heated outlet some time ago as the unit had cooled and pressure had been returned to normal. He thought about tomorrow's Lion's dinner and hoped it would be entertaining.
"Hello Oliver!"
Ollie turned as Nigel approached him.
"What brings you here? Been sacked and saying goodbye?"
Nigel's faced dropped.
"Sacked? Why do you say that? Not heard owt, has you?"
Ollie smiled.
'He's still paranoid'.
"No, Nigel. I haven't heard anything."

"Oh. Good. Jonesy told me to come an' check that your hot, whatever it was, is all okay now."
Ollie was imcensed.
'Of all the bloody cheek'.
"And does he want you to tell him that all is okay now, does he?"
"Yeah, he does."
"Right, tell him that my *Flange Up Change Key* is now 'Off', and all is well. If you can't remember the long title of the part just use the capitals to abbreviate it for him."
Nigel took a piece of paper from his pocket and wrote the information down, as Ollie slowly repeated it. He finished writing, folded the paper and stowed it in his jacket pocket.
"Okay then. Thanks. I'll be off."
"See you."
Ollie smiled to himself.

Nigel reported to Jones.
"Okay. Never 'eard of a part called that, though. 'e's goin' bloody dippy 'e is."
"Yes, Mr Jones. I think the same as what you do. A bit dippy. He don't seem right, an' don't work quick neither, far as I could see."

"Mmm. Right, off you go then lad. Well done."

It was just coming up to one o'clock.
Nigel went to Alex's café.
After being served his coffee and a cheese roll, he sat at one of the tables.
He opened his phone and looked at his portfolio of images.
Ham and Ollie came in together at five past.
"Hi Nigel," said Ham.
Nigel quickly changed pages on his phone.
"Hello."
 "Ah Nigel, my assistant," said Ollie, out loud,
"I ain't your bloody assistant. I 'ad to check you out is all."
"Ah, yes. Nigel is Jones's official checker-outer."
"Just doin' what I was told."
Ham and Ollie stood at the counter.
"Bloody scum-buckets. Him *and* Jones," said Ollie.
"Forget them, Ollie. Looking forward to tomorrow night?"
"Yep. I am. Plenty of ale, and no car to worry about."

"That's the spirit."

Ham pulled into the drive.
Milly's car was not there, which meant Myriam was on her own.
He hurried inside.
Myriam was at the sink scrubbing the stain out of a blouse.
He came up behind her and cupped her breasts.
"Guess who?"
"Three pints please, Lloyd."
"You bloody bitch!"
"Get yourself clean, and *unsmellied,* and I *might* be interested."
Later over dinner they discussed tactics for the Lion's dinner.
"What will Ollie think when he realises our friend is a woman?"
"By then it'll be too late, he'll have to grin and bear it. But Annabel is lovely, you said, and on her photo, she looks nice. He should be pleasantly surprised."

NINE

Ham and Myriam sat quietly as he drove his Toyota Avensis out of Swaffham.
They were both nervous.
Ham hadn't told Ollie that their other passenger would be a woman.
"God. I hope he doesn't get the hump because he thinks we've misled him."
Ham put his hand on her knee.
"He'll be fine with it. She's a friend, he's a friend. No ulterior motive, even though there is."
Myriam frowned.
"Don't know why you didn't tell him?"
"Didn't get around to it. But he's a nice bloke. There'll not be a problem, trust me."
"Don't you think you should phone him, now?"
"No. Don't worry."
The car zoomed along the country roads, as they made their way to Attleborough to collect Ollie.

"Actually, I think he'll be pleasantly surprised."
"I hope so."

Ollie was ready.
He sat in his favourite chair watching television.
He inspected his nails. All in order.
He was looking forward to it.
Few beers, dinner, cabaret.
He wondered what Myriam was like.
Probably a nice black lady, fitting for a nice guy like Ham.
He knew she was a teacher, so they had something in common.
Two beeps told him that Ham and Myriam were outside.
He turned off the television and the house lights, then hurried to their car.
His first surprise of the night was that Myriam was white, and very attractive.
He liked her at once.
Her warm smile was friendly and reassuring.
As they drove through the town the three chatted happily about the Lions and their charity work, and Myriam's job as a teacher.
"You know what teaching is like, you've been there, done that, and come away with the scars, physical and mental."
"I have, and that's a fact."

Ham looked at him via the rear vision mirror.
"We're picking up Myriam's friend Annabel at Hingham, giving her a lift."
"Oh yes. She's lovely, a close friend. I've known her for years, she's a good sort."
Myriam turned around to look at him. To judge his reaction.
He was surprised. Not upset, but surprised.
He thought that maybe this was a Ham inspired blind date. What harm could it do? He was intrigued.
He thought though, that they were sneaky buggers, but smiled.
"Is she meeting someone there, then?"
Myriam looked across at Ham, seeking inspiration.
"Well um, no. She's on her own and I thought it might, you know, cheer her up. You don't mind her being at our table, do you? She's nice."
"No. I don't mind at all," said Ollie.

They soon came to the small pleasant village of Hingham. It's main claim to fame was that an ancestor of Abraham Lincoln emigrated from Hingham to the USA in the 1600's.
Annabel's flat was above a furniture shop.
Ham parked beside it and Myriam rang the bell on the wall to the apartment.

Her voice resounded from the white speaker grill.

"Coming!"

Myriam regained the car, and shortly after, Annabel appeared.

Ollie opened the back-seat door for her and held it open.

She floated past him and gracefully slid onto the seat.

She wore a long gabardine raincoat.

Myriam was right, she *was* nice, and her perfume was beautiful.

As he got in his side he smiled at her and offered his hand.

She had a firm grip for a woman.

"Oliver."

"Annabel. Nice to meet you Oliver."

Myriam turned to them and started small talk.

Ollie sat quietly.

He couldn't see her figure, but her face was nice, with long dark brown hair teased into ringlets.

He briefly glanced sideways at her, being careful to be discreet, but Myriam noticed.

She had browny hazel eyes. They seemed to change colour from green to brown, and back again.

Nice teeth.

'Stop it', he said to himself, 'You're behaving like a bloody horse trader.'
She *was* impressive though.

They arrived at the Civic Hall in Swaffham.
Ham parked in the adjoining car park and displayed his parking ticket that had arrived with his pack some weeks before.
Myriam and Annabel walked ahead, arm in arm, chatting and laughing.
Ham gave Ollie a sideways glance.
"What do you think? Not mad at me, are you?"
"For what?"
"For bringing Annabel, and not telling you earlier."
"She's very nice, and I've never been set up on a blind date before."
Ham bit his lip.
"No, no. It's not *really* a blind date. She's just a friend of Myriam's. I've never met her before either. She was on her own, so were you, and I thought that maybe, you'd like to, you know, share the evening….."
"On a blind date."
"Oh, *bugger*."
"Ham, don't worry. She's okay, and I'm quite happy, so relax."
"Really?"
"Yes."

"Do you like him," asked Myriam, in a whisper.
"Think so. Don't really know. Bit early."
"He was a teacher."
"You've told me that, three times."
"Sorry. I'm nervous."
"I know."
"Will you see him again, do you think?"
"Myriam. I haven't even seen him *once* yet. Now for goodness sake, *chill*."

The hall had been bedecked with all the Lions' banners.
After the ladies had placed their coats in the cloakroom, Ham directed them to their allotted table. This was a four-seater, as were many others, some were arranged to take six, and eight.
The stage had musical instruments and chairs ready for the musicians.

Myriam and Annabel told Ham what they wanted to drink. The two men went to the bar.
"What would you like?"
Ham looked along the line of beer taps.
"Fosters, I think, please."
Ollie made the order.
"Nice figure," said Ham.
Ollie looked back in the direction of their table.

"I have eyes you know."
"Just saying."
They carried the drinks back to their table.
As they sipped their drinks the musicians appeared and the people in the rapidly filling hall applauded.
The band played a medley of Elton John hits. Nobody got up to dance.
"So, you teach at Myriam's school, too?" said Ollie.
"I do. You used to teach, as well."
"Yes. In my former life."
"Will you go back to it, do you think?"
"Doubt it. Certainly not whilst the Conservatives are in power, anyway."
"You live in Attleborough, don't you?"
"Yep. I'm thinking about moving to Norwich, though."
"You don't like Attleborough?"
"It's okay, but I'm job hunting, and I think Norwich would suit me better."
"More night life?"
Ollie shrugged.
"Not really bothered by that."
"What about your girlfriend?"
"Don't have one. What about you?"
"Yes, I've got one. Her names Brenda."
"Oh. So, you're, um, er, gay, are you?"
"Yes. Here's my vibrator."

Annabel produced her lipstick.
She removed the top and turned the end. The red lipstick appeared.
Ollie looked at the lipstick, then up at her.
She had a wry grin on her face.
"I don't have many orgasm's, but the colour's very becoming, don't you think?"
Ollie looked bemused.
"Annabel! You're bloody incorrigible! Take no notice of her Ollie, she's not a lesbian," said Myriam.
Ollie smiled. A relieved smile. She *was* embarrassing.
"More drinks?" He asked.
He needed the sanctity of the bar.
He took the order and went to the counter. Ham followed.
Myriam looked angrily at her friend.
"Annabel, that was *terrible.* You hardly know him, and you come out with something like that. He looked so embarrassed."
Annabel grimaced.
"Just a joke."
"A poor one."
The two women sat in silence and watched the musicians.
Ollie ordered.
"Can't believe she said that," said Ham.
Ollie smiled.

"No harm done. Bit of a surprise, that's all. Her way of lightening the atmosphere."
Ham laughed.
"I don't know about lightening, but she certainly changed it."
Ham paid.
"I thought it was okay. Unexpected, but okay," said Ollie.

Ollie put the drinks on the table.
Annabel leaned over to him.
"Sorry. Did I offend you?"
Ollie smiled.
"You certainly did."
There was an embarrassing silence for a moment.
"Fancy telling me you were a teacher."
Annabel smiled back at him. Grateful.
Ham and Myriam got up to dance.
"Would you like to?" asked Ollie.
"Not right now, a bit later."
They chatted about teaching, and then broadened the conversation to life in general and politics.
Ollie was surprised and delighted that she knew a fair bit about the UK political arena.
They agreed on many things.
Myriam and Ham came back to the table.
"Not dancing?" said Myriam.

"Annabel was too afraid to leave the table unattended in case some of your friends hoovered up our drinks."
Annabel stood up.
"Come on then, Mr Hardy, show Stanley here, how it's done."
He took her hand.
Myriam and Ham watched them go.
"See? They'll be fine now," said Myriam.
"Probably. As long as he doesn't ask her where she gets the batteries…….for her vibrator."

Ollie loved her perfume.
Slow romantic ballad. It suited his mood.
They danced close together, but not too close.
Ollie tried to think of something witty to say.
Annabel enjoyed being in the arms of a man again, especially this man.
Conversation wasn't needed.
She felt good in his arms.
He wanted to kiss her.
Ham and Myriam looked on from their table.
"They look a good couple, suited to each other, I'd say," said Myriam, almost triumphantly.
Ham smiled.

"Early days yet, but yeah, they look good together. Hope she's not a Tory, or that will be the end of that."

"Don't know what she is, but I doubt she's Conservative. She's seen too much shit from the cuts at school, I think."

The music came to an end and they waited for the next.

"Okay for another?" said Ollie.

"I'm game, if your broken toes can stand me stamping on them, again."

"It's okay, I think this next dance is called 'The Limp'."

The evening progressed.

They danced, drank, had a very nice dinner, laughed along with Ham and Myriam, and both slowly got very 'merry'.

As the evening drew to a close, Ham phoned and confirmed the ordered taxi for Ollie.

"I'll drop you off in Hingham, if that's okay?" said Ollie.

"That's just fine, just don't drop me off a cliff."

"I won't."

They walked, hand in hand to the entrance, at one o'clock.

Myriam and Ham had bid them a 'good night' at the table.

They watched them go.

"Well. That was a really, great result. They hit it off, didn't they?"
Ham had to agree.
"Yup. I was worried to start, but it all turned out super."

He put his arm around her shoulders in the taxi.
She snuggled up against him.
He desperately wanted to kiss her.

TEN

"Can't you's nick somefing from work again?" Jones frowned.
"I can't keep nicking stuff every time we needs to pay a fuggin' bill."
Doreen sat smoking. Enjoying her favourite afternoon tv show.
The programme was about a young man who was caught by his wife having sex with her mother. Jeremy Kyle was calling on stage friends and relatives who knew all about the affair. There was a lot of shouting.
"Well, you have to do somefing, or else we'll be up in the court."
Jones went into the kitchen.
The fridge was full of beer and wine.
He took out a can of Rabstags, eight percent. Nice and strong, just what he needed right now.
He drained the can as he stood staring out of the kitchen window.

"Fucking council. Bastards never leaves me alone."

He couldn't see why he had to pay up, they never did bugger all for him.

He'd tried different banks for a loan but got turned down. Poor credit history.

He binned the empty can, took out another.

When he returned to the lounge Doreen was leaning forward, peering at the television and rolling a cigarette.

She wore green shorts and a tight-fitting pale blue tee shirt that showed her rolls of belly fat.

"Well. I'll…"

"Shush. This is dead good, this is."

Jones looked at the television.

The husband and wife were nose to nose shouting at each other. Two stage managers were keeping them apart. The randy mother in law sat with her hand over her mouth, watching.

Jones swigged his beer and went through, in his mind, all the different parts of the gas field where he felt that there might be something worth stealing to sell on.

He decided to go to the site tomorrow, Sunday, when there would be no one around, and he could evaluate one or two prospective sources of revenue items.

The television show came to an end to rapturous applause and cheering from an audience that clearly appreciated the unbelievable crassness they had just witnessed. Doreen loved the show. Never missed.
She scratched her head.
"Dead good that were."
She lit her rolled cigarette.
"Well? Fink of anyfing?"
Jones shrugged.
"Maybe. I'll need to have a look tomorrow, when no one's around."
"I is sure you'll find somefing worth 'avin',. you's always 'as."
Jones nodded.
"Sure, I will."
Doreen smiled, got up, and sat on his lap.
He took her cigarette out of her hand and took a long drag of it.
She took it back.
He slid his hand up inside her tee shirt.
She ran her tongue around his ear, blowing smoke.
He coughed.
Foreplay.
"Best we go upstairs, in case the kid comes in," said Doreen.

The next morning, Jones drove to the site.
It was quiet.
He went to his office and took a bundle of keys from his desk.
It started to rain as he walked across to the Admin Office.
Nothing new.
Computer, not a top brand and hardly worth a light. Filing cabinets, printer. Printers are as cheap as chips these days, it's the frigging cartridges that cost the money.
He needed three hundred quid and he needed it *now*, not later, if he were to stay out of court.
Poxy Council.
The Admin Office yielded nothing, nor did the stores yard. He knew his office had bugger all, and the Café was useless. There was a replacement tool kit in the generator complex. He'd stolen the old one last year and flogged it to 'Middy', a self-employed plumber who frequented the pub. They only raise fifty quid at most. Not worth it.
He scratched his head.
The weighbridge office also yielded nothing.
He looked at the safety notices on the notice board.
One notice warned of heavy machinery operating.
"Eureka!"

Jones hurried to his office and secured it.
He drove like the wind to the Kings Arms.
The people he sought weren't there.
He waited.
He knew they *always* visited the pub at lunchtimes.
He hoped the paddy scum wouldn't let him down today.
As he finished his third pint of Adnams, his quarry came in.
Tall thin Penny and rotund Ronan Brady strode up to the bar.
She with dyed red hair, prominent front teeth and long legs. He with no hair and the girth of Big Ben.
Tattoo's abounded, on both of them.
They were tanned. They owned a villa on the Costa del Sol.
Big John, the landlord was already pouring their orders.
They both drank pints of cider.
Jones left them for a couple of minutes whilst they consumed some of their drink.
He sidled over slowly.
"What oh Pen, hiya Ronan. How's things?"
They both nodded to him.
Penny thought he was a gobshite.
"Wonder if I could interest you's in a bit of business, like?"

"What sort of business?" said Penny.
Broad Northern Irish accent.
Jones ushered them away to a quiet corner table where the three sat down.

Doreen was shocked.
"Fookin' 'ell, Bernie!"
Jones smiled.
"A grand for us, and a kick up the arse for that bastard Stewle."
Doreen laughed out loud, cigarette smoke pulsing out of her mouth.
"Jesus! Bugger me! I's can 'ave me hair dyed."
"Piece of cake. They supply the transporter, I supply the keys, and open the gate for 'em. That's it."
"But Stewle will smell a rat, won't he?"
"Nah. Fookin' brain dead is that tosser. I'll make it look like an outside job, again."
Doreen went to the kitchen and returned with two cans of strong ale.
"'Ere. Get this down yer gut. You 'as earned it, you 'as, I reckons. What do thems Paddy's do for a livin' then?
"Plant hire mostly, but they do a fair bit of buy an' sell, too."
"When will you's get the money?"
"We's doin' the job on Wednesday night, after everyone's buggered off. They'll pay me when

the stuff is safely on the transporter, and away."

"An' what's it called? This thing you're nicking?"

"It's a caterpillar digger and compactor."

"Caterpillar? Don't thems turn into butterflies, or moffs, or somethin'?"

"This little, or should I say, big, bastard, can move mountains, an' they cost about sixty to eighty grand, new."

"Jesus! But you're only getting' a grand. Don't seem right, somehow."

"Yeah, but, them's the ones what are taking the risk. I just break in the Plant Office, get the keys, go to the main gate and cut the chain with bolt cutters. Then I 'ands the keys over, and buggers off, with a thousand quid in me pocket."

"What will your swanky boss say when he finds out?"

"I don't give a toss. He, nor the stupid coppers, can prove owt. I pay the council blood suckers, an' still got dosh left over. Nice evenin's work, that is."

"What do thems Irish do with it?"

"Dunno. Don't care. Probably lease it out to builders, I s'pose."

On Wednesday, an hour before midnight, Jones kicked in the Plant Office door.
It took three hefty lunges before the lock sprung and the door flew open.
He wore gloves.
He shone his torch on the board attached to the far wall.
Different keys hung on hooks.
He picked up one bunch of keys and left the building.
Ten minutes later, he stood in the shadows by the back entrance to the site, keys in one hand and bolt cutters in the other.
Waiting. Nervous.
He heard the roar of the transporter before he saw the headlights.
A car followed it.
Jones walked over to the main gate.
The large transporter pulled up.
Hissing air brakes.
He applied the bolt cutters to the large chain and cut through.
"Where's the digger?" said Ronan.
"Around the back of this office," said Jones, indicating the Plant Office.
They both walked around the office.
There were two diggers parked side by side.
"Which is the newest of the two?"

Jones had no idea which one was the newest, he had just taken the first bunch of keys with 'Digger 1' marked above it on the board.
He nodded towards the digger on the right.
Ronan never questioned him.
The digger started at the second attempt, and Ronan drove it around to where the transporter driver had reversed in.
After fifteen minutes, the digger was on the large vehicle and secured.
The transporter drove off.
Ronan started to walk to his car.
"What about the money?"
"Oh yeah. How much did we say?"
"A grand."
Ronan smiled and handed Jones an envelope.
"Count it."
Jones looked inside.
"No need. I trust you."

"God! You're a clever boy, you is," said Doreen.
She had waited up for him.
Jones put the envelope on the coffee table and went to the kitchen to get a drink.
Doreen shouted out to him.
"Bring me one!"
He returned with two cans of Rabstags.

Doreen had the money strewn across the table.

They counted it.

Spot on.

One thousand pounds, all in twenties and fifties.

They sat, side by side, drinking their strong beer, and enjoying the scene.

"You is clever Bernie, that's for sure. Top boss at your job you is, an' you keep bringin' the bacon in when we needs it, you does."

Jones preened himself.

"I'm always a step ahead of the underthings in this world. Specially the brain-dead fuckers in the company. No one outsmarts me, they don't."

They finished their beers and had a few more to celebrate.

"Course, I'll get questioned by the coppers, but who gives a shite. Them's not clever, either."

Doreen patted his knee.

"No one's more cleverer than you is, Bernie."

"Does I get me reward?"

Doreen stood up.

"You does, but no trying on what you did the other night. Don't want it like no bloody queer bloke."

ELEVEN

Alex and Jim sat side by side at the Theatre Royal in Norwich.
'Funny Girl'.
Musical triumph, the revues said.
They weren't wrong.
As they stood up giving the players applause, they both smiled at each other.
"With your voice Alex, you could be doing that for a living," said Jim.
"I *wish*," said Alex.
They walked slowly up the aisle to exit the auditorium.
Jim leaned over and said quietly, "I love you."
Alex beamed, and looked into Jim's eyes.
"Me too."
He briefly held Jim's hand and squeezed it.
No one noticed, or if they did, they didn't mind, or care.
"Have you asked your Mum and Dad, if they'll come to our wedding, yet?"

Alex looked troubled.

"No. I am afraid to even visit them, still."

Jim nodded sympathetically.

"I know it is hard for you. But maybe they have sort of mellowed towards you being gay, by now."

"Maybe, but I doubt this is true. I wish it was, a thousand times a day, I wish it was."

They walked through the inner city and just before they reached The Castle Hotel, Jim pulled Alex into a shop doorway and kissed him.

They held the kiss for a while but were interrupted.

"Dirty fuckin' queers!"

A harsh voice shouted.

Six youths stood looking at the two.

They had been drinking in 'The Murderers' pub.

Jim and Alex started to walk past them.

One youth, his head shaved, and pony tail dyed bright green, kicked Alex hard on the backside.

"Hope it don't spoil your fuckin' pleasure tonight, bum boy!"

Jim swiveled around and punched the youth in the face.

He fell backwards, eyes watering and blood seeping from his nose.

The other youths ran at the two of them aiming kicks and blows.

"Filthy poofs!"

Alex fell down under different blows from three of the gang, and they started to kick him.

Jim punched another youth and sprang to protect Alex.

He was tripped.

The boots came thudding in.

"Did you get spoken to by the rossers today, Danny?"

"Of course. If that twat Jones mislaid his biro, they'd interview me first."

Steve swigged his beer.

The two wives stood at the opposite end of the bar talking to Vera, the landlords' wife.

"I told them they could check my freezer if they wanted to," said Steve.

"Yeah. It's gotta be professionals what pinch somethink as big as a bloody digger. I told them I left it, as I couldn't get it in the boot of my car. They weren't amused at me treatin' it like a joke."

"They've had a load of stuff nicked off the site. Don't know why they don't employ a night watchman. Their insurance must be sky bloody high by now."

"What's a digger cost. Anyway?" said Danny.

"Ollie told me he looked it up on his ipad. Second hand, around thirty to forty-grand."
"Bloody hell!"
"Apparently, 'cause it's a compactor as well, that's why it's expensive. They're over seventy-grand, new," said Steve.

The taxi pulled up outside Annabel's flat.
"Come in, for a coffee?"
"No. Better not, it's getting late."
"Oh. Have you got to get up early tomorrow for church, then?"
"No, no. I don't do church."
"Well, come on then, you big Jessy."
Ollie paid the driver the full fare, as if going to Attleborough.
The driver smirked.
"Have a nice night, sir."
Cheeky bugger. But Ollie smiled.
Annabel's apartment was a one bed.
Compact, but well laid out in pastels. Pleasant on the eye.
He thought she had good taste. Must have, if she invites me in at 1.30am, on a Sunday morning, for a coffee.
They sat drinking coffee and she told him about her early life being brought up by Aunt Edna and Uncle Ted, after her parents died in

a boating fire on the Norfolk Broads when she was seven.
Sadly, Aunt and Uncle both passed away within weeks of each other when she was in her late teens.
They moved on to talking politics.
She snuggled up.
They kissed.
Caressed.
She took him to her bed.

Jim could see light somewhere. Bright, white light.
He tried to open his mouth.
Later, he saw the bright white light again.
Someone was there. Dressed in a light blue or white dress.
He couldn't be sure.
She spoke softly, but he couldn't really hear.
"Can you hear me, Mr Mortimer?"
The voice drifted away.
It must have been later, because it was a man this time.
He wore a white coat.
A bright light came into his eye, first the right eye, then the left.
"Can you hear me, Mr Mortimer?"
Jim opened his mouth.
Nothing.

Later, he heard the man again.
"He's awake, for now, anyway."
Warm, peaceful.
He heard some soft beeping, a long way away.
"Good morning, Mr Mortimer. How are we, today?"
He could see the outline of the white figure.
Different. A brown, or grey, face.
He couldn't move. Didn't want to.
Warm, quiet.
Later, he could make out some white coated people around his bed.
They looked down at him.
He knew they were speaking, but it was just low murmuring.

Jones hummed to himself in his office on Monday morning.
Life was good.
Council all paid off, and money in his pocket.
Even his missus was happy. She was having her hair done and getting herself a new dress from Marks. Posh.
His phone rang.
"Jones, it's Mister Stewle here. Just been informed that Mortimer was attacked on Saturday night, and is seriously ill in the Norfolk and Norwich. Unlikely to be back for months. Get a replacement. Same pay and

conditions as the others. Let me know when it's done. You'll have to get a new tea man too, the Romanian lad also got attacked. He died on Sunday morning."

"Bloody hell!"

"The new night watchmen start on Wednesday night. They're *not* yours. They'll report directly to me, in Norwich. Show them around. They'll use your office, so get them a desk, some high viz stuff, and a site walkie-talkie. Names are Hunter and Bayfield. They'll take it in turns to work on a roster that Human Resources make up. Give them the spare set of keys."

"Yes. Very well, Mr Stewle. Anything from the Police, about the digger, sir?"

"No."

The phone went dead.

"Twat! Never nice to me. Treats me like a friggin' skivvy, he do. I beat him this time though. Where's you digger gone, Mr Stewle?" Jones smiled to himself.

'Not all gloom and doom. The Romanian little turd died, eh? Need a new café person? Wonder if Doreen wants to do it? Bit of money for us. We could jack up the prices an' make a decent killin'. Need *someone*, quick.'

Nigel Infine sat in the British Legion lounge bar.

He was going to leave half an hour ago, but a couple came in with their two children. Girl and a boy. Teenagers, just.
He kept smiling at the girl. She looked away.
Shy, but she wants me.
He could imagine having her in his flat. Stripping her, securing her to his bed. Raping her. Turning her over and violating her. She'd enjoy it.
She spoke to her father. He looked at Nigel.
The father walked over to Nigel's table.
"Don't like the way you're leering at my daughter, mate."
"Don't know what you mean."
"Just stop it. Next time I come over to see you, it will be to give you a bloody good clout. Got it?"
Nigel shrugged.
"I ain't done nothing."
The man stared down at Nigel, then returned to his family at the bar.
The young girl turned her back.
'Bitch!'
Nigel finished his drink.
He took a taxi to Rose Lane in Norwich.
The usual suspects were out patrolling the area, looking for punters.
Nigel selected Rosie. It wasn't her real name.

Rosie was a druggie. Bleached blond hair. Nineteen, but looked younger.
Short skirt, T shirt. No bra, small boobs.
"How much?"
"Twenty."
"Where?"
"Just around the corner. My place."
They walked through a dark lane to a row of old townhouses.
Very small bed-sit. All yellow decoration, with dark brown settee. Scruffy.
"Where's the bed?"
Rosie pointed at the settee.
"Tha's it. Want me to pull it out?"
"Yeah."
She pulled out the bed and laid on it.
No panties.
He was ready.
Got between her legs. Tried to kiss her.
"No. Not that."
She averted his lips.
He sat up on his haunches.
"Come on. Won't 'urt you."
"No. Just fuck me, that's all."
"Pull your top up, wanna see your tits."
She sighed and pulled her T shirt up.
Fifteen minutes later Nigel walked back towards the taxi rank.
He was twenty pounds worse off but felt better.

She wouldn't let him take her from behind.
Unadventurous cow.
Maybe next time.
He would drive his car there. Park it outside her little room on the street.

On Monday Ollie phoned the ICU at the Norfolk and Norwich hospital, on his mobile, to get an update on Jim's condition.
"Serious. As well as can be expected. No visitors yet. Maybe next week."
He passed on the news to the other gasmen and employees in the café at lunchtime.
The atmosphere was very subdued.
Alex and Jim were well liked.
"Who did it?" said Ham.
"Police say they don't know, yet," said Ollie.
"But if it happened in the City centre, they *must* have CCTV coverage of it, *surely*?"
"Probably. Dunno."
"I'll put a notice up when I know about the funeral. I daresay some guys will want to attend.
Jones came in.
He smiled at Doreen, serving behind the counter.
"Any news, Jonesy?" said Steve.
"*Don't* call me Jonesy. It's *Mister Jones* to you."

"Any news, *Mister* Jonesy?"
"About what?"
The gasmen looked at each other.
Angry. Glaring.
"*Jim.*"
Jones shrugged his shoulders.
"He's alive. The spic is dead. That's all I knows. New bloke startin' Thursday, to replace 'im. My missus is running the café."
"What injuries has he got?" asked Ham.
"How the fuck would I know's? I ain't his mother."
"But you're his boss. Would have thought you'd take an interest," said Ollie.
Jones shrugged.
"All I know's is, he won't be back soon. Maybe never."
"Poor Alex," said Ham.
"Nobody deserves what happened to him," said Ollie.
"Maybe he gave some English bloke a bit of spic foreign lip," said Jones.
"And you think that that merits a beating?"
"Well, if some foreign shite head started slaggin' me off in mine own country, I thinks I'd biff 'im one."
Ollie looked at Ham and Steve.
They looked angry but remained silent.

"Everythin' a'right wiv the new café lady, boys?"

Ham turned away from Jones.
"Get home okay, Saturday night?" said Ham.
Ollie smiled.
Wonder if Annabel told Myriam, who in turn told Ham.
"Yep. And thanks for a very nice evening. Really enjoyed it."
"We did too. Think Annabel had a good time. Did she say?"
Fishing. He knows nothing.
Ollie smiled
Ham noticed.
"She never said anything, but I think she did."
"What time did you get her home? Can't remember what time you left."
Myriam obviously wants a report.
"Oh, about twenty minutes after we left. You got the taxi for us at one, wasn't it?"
"Yeah. One."
"So, I got her home around twenty past then," said Ollie.
"Ah, right. *So*, you got to your home around half past, then?"
Ollie wanted to burst out laughing, but held it in.

"D'you know, I never looked at my watch. Just went straight to bed."
"Mmm. I see. Straight to bed, eh?"
"Yeah, Straight to bed."
"Ah, right."
Ollie stood up.
"Well, better get back to earning a fortune."
"Fancy a pint, after?" said Ham.
"Okay."

TWELVE

Ollie sat in the visitors seating area. Staring into space.
"Mr Wilson?"
A nurse stood before him.
"Yes."
"You can see Mr Gillespie, but please don't stay longer than five minutes or so."
Ollie got up and followed the nurse into the ICU.
Gentle beeping.
Patients with wires attached to monitors. Some had masks on their faces.
Nurses checking machines. Blue and green lights pulsing above each bed.
The nurse stopped at a bed.
She stooped down and spoke softly to the patient.
"Mr Gillespie. I've got a friend here to see you."
Jim's eyes flickered, then opened.
"Hi Jim."

Jim opened his mouth and croaked.
"Hi."
Ollie sat down in a chair by the bed.
"Everyone at work sends their best wishes."
Jim spoke softly.
"Thanks."
"The police say they've got good CCTV of the cowards that attacked you. They're hopeful of arrests."
Jim sighed. His eyes sad. Dull.
"Alex is dead. Brain injuries."
Ollie nodded, his eyes also sad.
"I know. Such a lovely young man."
"We were getting married soon."
"I know. I'm so sorry, Jim."
"Not your fault. I never had a chance to say 'goodbye'."
Silence. Sad silence.
"Is there anything I can do for you?"
"No….. Yes. See if Alex's parents….. are okay."
"I'll do that."
"Don't know what's going to happen about the funeral."
"Don't worry. I'll take care of it."
Jim sighed. Drained.
The nurse came.
"I think that's enough for one day, Mr Gillespie."

"Yes. Okay," said Ollie.
Jim's eyes were closed.
Ollie turned to the nurse.
"Can you tell him I'll come again, soon, please?"
"Of course."

Ollie knocked on the door of Alex's parents.
The door opened a little.
"Mr Emil."
Bloodshot eyes looked back at him.
The man said something that Ollie didn't understand.
"I was a friend at work of your son, Alex."
"Alex? Are you homosexman?"
"No. I came to see if I could do anything, for you."
"Come in."
The door opened wider.
Ollie was beckoned through a sparsely furnished room to a dining/kitchen area.
A lady sat in an upright chair.
She looked up at him. Pain in her eyes. A little surprised.
The man said something to the lady in Romanian.
"You knew my son?"
"Yes. I worked at Sagittarius End."
"Some English kill him."

Ollie sighed.
"I know. Bad men, evil men."
The lady nodded.
"Your son was a good man."
"He was homo, but we loved him."
"Yes. There are many homosexuals in Britain, and the majority are good people, men and women."
The man said something. Harsh, angry.
The woman replied.
He threw up his hands and went out the door.
"He wanted marry his friend."
"Yes. His friend is called Jim. He is a nice man, like Alex. He asked me to come to see you, to make sure you were alright."
She looked surprised.
"He did? Why? We never meet him, never."
Ollie looked at the sorrow in her face.
"He loved your son. Just as you did."
Tears rolled down her cheeks.
"Yes."
The man came back in.
The woman spoke to him in Romanian.
The man looked at him.
"You want drink? Have beer, coffee, vodka."
"No, thank you. I can't stay very long. Do you need me to do anything?"
The man spoke.
His voice had a tremor to it.

"When put my son in earth?"
"I don't know. There must be a post mortem first. I can find out, and let you know."
The man shook his head.
His eyes full of tears.
"No understand."
The old lady's shoulders shuddered.
The old man put his arms around her and drew her close.
She said something to her husband.
"I will come back. To tell you," said Ollie.
"When?" said the old man.
"Tomorrow. In the evening, around seven o'clock. Is that okay?"
"Yes. We have no money to bury him."
"Please. Don't worry."

Beryl Anstey hit the 'send' button.
The previous day's figures zoomed across the waves to the Norwich office.
Eleven o'clock.
Another two hours before Danny came.
God! She couldn't get enough of him.
She thought of him at night in her bed.
Wanted him beside her, all the time, he was so lovely, handsome, funny, and bloody sexy to boot.
She hated his wife, never met her, but hated her.

The new digger/extractor would be delivered today, and a man from the Head Office branch would arrive to check it over before signing for it. He'd just better not come whilst Danny was there. The office would be locked anyway, and she certainly wasn't going to unlock it and spoil their love-making. Screw them.

Jones came in to pick up the typed-up weeklies.

"New digger arrives today," he said.

"What time?"

"Anytime now. Give me a call when it comes."

"Right. The new bloke and the night-watchmen start on Thursday."

"Yeah. The watchmen ain't got nothin' to do with me. Them's coming in later for me to show 'em around. The new man, Bishop, is under me, though. Don't forget now, shout me when the digger comes."

She thought he was an idiot.

As if he wouldn't hear the roar of a bloody great transporter, that carried ultra-large loads like diggers, when it pulled up outside his office.

She hated him. Hook-nosed, smelly, arrogant, lazy, arse-licker.

Oliver Wilson had dropped a note in to her telling her that Alex would be buried on the twenty-fifth.

Such a shame. Lovely young man.
She didn't mind if he was a poof.
Hairdressers and top dancers are all poofs. And waiters.
The café was rubbish now that Jones' wife Doreen had taken over. She had stopped using it. Didn't want to catch anything because of that freaky, dirty cow. She knew that most of the site workers, and the factory workers from the processed food plant opposite, had stopped using the café.
"Going to the funeral?"
Jones looked puzzled.
"What funeral?"
"Alex, of course. The café boy who was murdered."
"When is it?"
"Twenty-fifth."
Jones looked at the calendar pinned to the office wall.
"That's a Saturday. Shan't be goin', not on a Saturday. Tha's me pub day."
Jones sauntered off.
'Tosser!'

Ollie went to the ICU.
No nurse on the desk, so he walked to Jim's bed.
Empty.

He stood, slightly shocked at where Jim had lain.

"Can I help you?"

An Asian nurse, very petite and smiling.

"Oh yes. Sorry. I was looking for Mr Gillespie. He was in that bed."

"He has been transferred to Carrow Ward."

Ollie breathed a sigh of relief.

"Is he okay? Why's he been moved. Is he getting better?

"Yes. He's out of danger now. They'll update you in the ward."

The nurse gave Ollie instructions on how to get there.

Jim gave him a wry smile as he approached the bed.

"How you doing, mate?"

"Not so bad," said Jim, sadly.

"Everyone at work sends their regards. Is there anything you need?"

"No. I'm good, thanks."

"Any news on the scum that did it?"

"Yes. The police liaison officer said the six blokes were all picked up this morning, after I formerly identified the CCTV pictures, and are now in custody. They've all been charged with murder, and attempted murder, plus a couple of other things, I can't remember."

Jim looked pale, worn out.

"Good. How long before you're out of here?"
"They hope to get me out for Alex's funeral, whenever that will be. Probably be a wheelchair job, though."
"Okay. I'm going to see Alex's parents now. Giving them the news. Anything you want me to add?"
He drove to the house.
Mr Emil answered the door.
He nodded and beckoned Ollie in.
Mrs Emil stood up when he came in.
She indicated a chair for him to sit.
He told her about the charges.
She knew.
The police liaison officer had already called.
"Thank you for telling us. You good man."
The old man sat down.
"Is his fren okay?"
Ollie was surprised at the question.
"He's slowly getting better. He can't remember many things from the past, and he is blind in one eye now. His fractures are mending, and he will need dental work."
Ollie indicated with gestures as he explained.
"We will go in the burying," said Mrs Emil.
Ollie's face lit up.
"Oh good. It's at Gayton. Three o'clock."
They both nodded.
"I can come and collect you."

The old woman said something.
The man replied.
"No. Is okay. My brother take us, he give money for burying."
"Please don't worry about that. It's all been paid for."
"But who……who paying?"

Ollie picked up Annabel from her apartment.
They walked hand in hand to the White Hart.
Quiet in the restaurant part, just two other tables with people at them.
He told her about the hospital visit, and about calling on Mr and Mrs Emil.
"So sad for them. Jim too."
"Yes, but it shows you the spirit of good men, too. All the money for the funeral has been raised by the guys at work."
"Oh, that's a lovely gesture."
She put her hand on his.
She *really* liked him. He was such a caring, intelligent, nice bloke. He was *her* caring, intelligent, nice bloke.
They drank wine, chatted, and she told him a couple of risqué jokes.
He told her one back that was nearer the 'knuckle'.
Her laughter made the other guests look her way.

She didn't care, she was happy.
Later that night as they lay in each other's arms, he told her about the fatal car accident, and how it had affected him.
He felt calmer afterwards.
She kissed him, cradled him.
Made it better.

THIRTEEN

"How come the takin's keeps gettin' lesser and lesserer?" said Jones.
"Buggered if I knows. I reckon your blokes as got it in for us."
"Maybe we should put the prices back down to what them were."
Doreen sat on a tall stool eating from a packet of crisps. Her once white pinny, over her jeans, and blue tee shirt was stained.
"Not worth doin', if you's do that."
"I see you've stopped doin' pasties, *an'* pies."
Doreen shrugged.
"Wha's the sense? I have to go all the way to Smith's the baker in West Winch, pay 'im, then come all the way back. It's a lot of buggerin' around, twenty minutes, and these shites what come in just ain't worth it."
"I used to like them pies. So did the lads."

"Well. They don't come in no more, so what's the sense? Not worth traipsin' all that way just for you's."

"They might come back if you started doin' them same grub as what the spic used to do."

"Fuck that. I ain't runnin' around early mornin' for those arse-soles. They're always moaning, coffee's not hot, cheese rolls is stale. That black sod even complained about the tea last week. I told him he ought to come in earlier when it's first made, stead of at half twelve when it 'as stood for over 'alf an 'our."

Jones lit up a cigarette.

"Don't matter about no bloody darkie anyway. They'll eat an' drink shit all day, them will. Used to it, in the jungle, they is."

"Yeah. That advert on the telly to give 'em clean water, why? If them's die from drinkin' shit, its nature's way of keepin' their pop'lations down, ennit?"

"It is, you is right there girl, an' no mistake."

"Does he get the same wages as what the white English blokes get?"

"Yep. Got to, it's the law."

"Disgustin'. Coons should go back to that Bongo fuckin' Bongo land, an' leave us good English people alone."

Detective Sergeant Morland sat in his Superintendent's office discussing the thefts from the Sagittarius End site.

"We've had as many spotters as we could get, which isn't many, out all over the UK looking for the Digger. Lists and photo's gone to every UK station, and the Customs boys, too. Nothing."

"Mmm. Gotta show up sometime. Probably in a barn somewhere, and they're waiting for the heat to dissipate."

"Yeah. We've been on to all the likely suspects looking for the copper reels, too. They're probably in the same bloody barn as the digger."

"Taking a lot of manpower is this case. Manpower we no longer have, to be honest, what with the cuts and everything. What else?"

Morland shifted in his chair.

Bum ache. Getting old.

"I've got two undercover boys from Monday, for four days. I'm going to get them into the local pubs. I'd have liked to keep them for longer but powers that be say, no can do."

The Super shook his head.

"Good idea about the local pubs. Still think there's an insider at 'it'?"

"For sure. I suspect the mark is an old timer at the company. The thefts started well before the six new boys arrived."

"Glove a plant, then?"

"Yes. Could be Jones. He had access to the glove lockers."

The Super pursed his lips. Thought for a moment.

"Bit too obvious, don't you think?"

"Maybe."

"Have you checked the bank accounts? The digger must have yielded a few bob."

"Not yet. You happy to sign up the Proceeds of Crime forms?"

"More than happy."

They moved on to the two other cases that Morland was working on.

Steve and Danny both tasted the wine.

"Well?" said Steve.

Danny licked his lips.

"Bloody good. Nice taste, I can feel it's powerful, too."

"Yeah. I put extra sugar in it, to pep it up."

The two sat in Steve's lounge, sampling Steve's home-made wine.

Both wives were out, late-night shopping.

Steve refilled the glasses.

"I can really feel it now. Strong."

"Yeah. Only costs about sixty pence a bottle to make. I get thirty-three bottles out of a kit."
"Good is that. How long from start to drinkin'?"
"Three weeks."
"Brilliant."
"I'm sendin' off for another pack tonight. Only eighteen quid. They deliver in three days."
Danny held his glass up to the light, then drained it.
"If I get one too, will you show me how to make it?"
"Sure."
When Vee and Sylvia got back with the shopping, both men were very happy.
The two wives tried the wine too, more than once that evening.
Later, Danny and Vee walked home.
Each carried a bottle of Steve's wine.
The forgotten shopping lay in the boot of their car and that remained outside Steve's house until next morning.
They were not particularly steady on their feet.
Neither brushed their teeth, nor did Danny manage to undress.
Vee managed her dress zip.
She woke with the garment loose around her waist.
Rubber lips. Dry.
Danny lay on the floor snoring.

"Get up Dan. It's nearly eight, you'll be late."
Five minutes later Danny drove to work.
No cop cars, which was fortuitous. He would have definitely turned the blow job green.
His mouth felt like the Sahara, but at least he got there for eight-thirty.
Jones was not around. Safe.
He put a bottle of the red wine in his locker and walked over to B site. The wine was for Ollie.
He didn't notice his locker door slowly open behind him.

Jones came back to his office.
He saw Bentley's locker door was open.
He closed it. Noticed the wine.
"If I catch 'im boozin' at work, I don't give a shite about Stewle, I'll sack him," he said to the four walls.
He lifted up the wine.
Pondered a moment.
Too risky.
Replaced it.
After he had completed yesterday's output figures and was just about to take them across to the office, Doreen walked in, red faced. Angry.
"What's up?"
"What's up? I'll tell you's what's friggin' up!"

She glared at him.
"Well? Come on then, what?"
"Friggin' Pizza's. That's what is friggin' up!"
"Pizza's? What d'ya mean, *pizza's*?"
"Them buggers eatin' them that's what!"
"Who? What? Wadya mean?"
She pointed out of the window.
"The bloody Pizza prat came and delivered pizza's to that fugger wos-'is-name."
"Who?"
"The posh bastard, wot you say loves Corblyn."
"Wilson?"
"I dunno."
"Do you mean, the pizza delivery man came *on site* to deliver pizza's?"
"Well, no. Not *past* the gates. But that bugger came down, picked them up he did."
"I can't stop 'im from doin' that."
"What? You can't do *nothin*'?"
She wagged her finger at him.
"Takin' away our business, that prick is. No wonder our trade is shite. Pizza's are nickin' it. 'im and that black bastard is sittin' in 'is car, and eatin' the friggin' grub right this minute, now, and them's don't come in the café at all, not even for a cuppa tea, they don't, *never*. Well, 'ceptin' for Nigel."
Jones sighed.

"I'll 'ave a word."
Doreen turn and left, muttering.
She walked to the café.
A pipe-laying worker stood at the counter. Waiting.
"Wadya want? Ain't got no pies."
He looked taken aback.

"How's things with Annabel?"
Ollie wiped his mouth with his handkerchief.
"Great. We get on fine. We're going out for a meal with my Mum and Dad on Friday."
Ham smiled, inwardly delighted.
Myriam will be out buying bloody hats on the weekend.
"Where?"
"The Mulberry Tree in Attleborough."
"Oh yeah. Is it any good?"
"Yeah, excellent. Top quality, never varies."
"Getting serious, is it?"
"Don't start. No wedding bells, *please*. We're just *friends*. Good friends yes, but only friends."
"Okay. I get it."
Quiet.
They ate their pizza's and drank coffee from their flasks.
Couple of minutes passed.
"Can I be your best-man?"

Ollie laughed.

"Bugger off!"

When their forty-five minutes was nearly up they both started along the muddy track back to their sites.

They met Danny on the way.

He didn't look too good.

"Hi Dan."

Danny gave them a brief smile.

Eyes dull and red still.

"Hungover. Steve's home-made wine."

"Fire-water?" said Ollie.

"Yes, but good, and cheap to make."

"Run your car on it?" asked Ham.

"Would blow the bugger up," said Danny.

"See you."

After Danny had gone about twenty yards he turned and shouted to Ollie.

"I've a bottle for you in me locker. Give it you tomorrow, at lunch. Ham, one for you when I've made it."

"Okay, thanks," said Ollie.

"You wouldn't drink it, would you?" said Ham.

"Probably not but it might be okay as a drain-clearer."

"It's important, *very* important," said Jim.

The Trauma specialist looked worried.

"Mr Gillespie. You need another two weeks in here before you are fit to leave."
Jim sighed.
"My soul-mate is getting buried on Saturday. I just *have* to be there."
"Look. You had a fractured skull, five broken ribs, a punctured lung and lots of internal bleeding. Your condition is such that it would be courting disaster if I allowed you to go to this funeral on Saturday. You *must* see that."
"I do. I only want to be away for two hours at the most. There and back."
Tears glistened in Jim's eyes, then cascaded down his cheeks.
Doctor Ranjid placed his hand on Jim's.

Ollie was getting ready to pick Annabel up.
The phone rang.
"Hello."
"Ollie, it's Jim."
"Hi Jim. Great to hear your voice."
"Thanks. Look. I need your help."
"Right. You have it."
"Thing is, my doctor doesn't want me to attend the funeral on Saturday. He says I'm at least two weeks away from being well enough to leave the hospital."
"Oh dear. Well, he's the specialist, Jim."
"I'm going, Ollie. Even if I have to crawl."

"Mmm. You say you need my help. How?"
"I need to have two able bodied men to push me in my wheelchair from this hospital to a suitable vehicle. Take me to the funeral, then return me to the hospital, afterwards."
"When you say, 'suitable vehicle', what do you mean?
Jim explained what the doctor had said.
He gave Ollie some details of people to contact.

The meal at The Mulberry Tree was a success.
Ollie's Mum and Dad loved Annabel. They were so relieved that their son was at last awakening from his sad bereavement journey.
The meal was good, the talking never stopped, and Ollie's Mum cried when they departed at eleven o'clock.
"I'm so glad he's found you, Annabel."
The young couple walked to Ollie's car as his parents departed in theirs.
"That was lovely," said Annabel.
"Yup. Enjoyed it. Didn't bore you, did they?"
"No. Not at all. Your folks are adorable. Invited me for Sunday lunch weekend after next, too."
"Don't remember that. When did that happen?"
"When you were in the loo, pointing Percy."
"Never invited or told me about it."

"No. They said specifically they thought you should stay away, you might put me off my roast beef."

He swung her round and kissed her.

A taxi driver sat waiting in his cab for a fare.

"Get a room, mate. Much more comfortable."

Annabel laughed.

"He's too tight. Any car park, or alley, will do for him."

The cabbie smiled.

They drove off.

"Want to see my hovel? We can have coffee."

"Okay," said Annabel.

Bess was delighted to see her master.

Annabel made a fuss of her.

When Ollie came back from the kitchen with their coffees, the dog lay by Annabel's armchair, head resting on her foot.

Ollie looked down.

Smiled

"Looks like you've made a friend," said Ollie.

"She's great. I always wanted a dog. But I've had to settle for you, just now."

After coffee, he gave her a tour of his bungalow.

The tour ended at his bedroom.

Annabel stayed the night.

Ollie was up early the next morning.

He left a note and some taxi money for Annabel.
He looked down at her as she slept.
Peaceful. Everything about her was peaceful.
She was lovely. Kind, funny, considerate. He loved her eyes and her laughter.
He wished he could clamber in beside her again, but duty called.
At seven-forty-five Ham pulled up in front of the bungalow.
Ollie was ready.
They drove to King's Street in Norwich.
Not a lot was said. They knew what had to be done.
The depot was closed, it being Saturday, but an ambulance stood parked.
By the side of the vehicle was a St John's Brigade staff member.
Barbara Vincent was a trained nurse, but now worked as an administrator for the Brigade.
Her blond hair, tied into a bun, was in stark contrast to the black ambulance. She wore a black uniform with St John Ambulance 'flashes' on each shoulder.
She smiled at Ham and Ollie as they pulled up.
"Right on time," said Barbara.
"Thanks for doing this," said Ollie.
"How could I refuse? Sajeer Ranjid is an old friend, and the cause is right up my street."

"Were your bosses okay with it?" said Ham.
"What bosses?" said Barbara.
She had an impish smile.
Ollie locked his car and the three got into the front of the ambulance.
Fifteen minutes later they arrived at the Norfolk and Norwich University Hospital.
They parked at the ramp by the A and E entrance as directed and waited.
They didn't have to wait too long.

FOURTEEN

"Where's Ham?"
Myriam turned from the sink.
Her mother was making up a shopping list at the kitchen table.
"Gone somewhere with Ollie."
"Doin' what?"
"God, you're a Nosey-Parker this morning, Ma."
"Just wonderin', is all."
Wry smile.
"Miss him, do you?" said Myriam.
Milly Bradstock frowned.
Pointed the biro at her daughter.
"Watch it, you."
Myriam smiled.
She knew her mother had become fond of Ham.
He did so much for her, odd jobs, gardening, even shopping.

"They've gone to the funeral of that young lad who was murdered by those yobby pigs in Norwich. He worked with them."
"Oh, I see."
Milly added an item to her list.
"Bit early though, eh?"
"Yeah. I thought that."
"Maybe he's getting' some flowers, or something."
Myriam wiped her hands on a towel and sat opposite her mother.
"Ollie's getting on well with Annabel, apparently."
"Oh good. I like Annabel. What's this Ollie bloke like?"
"He's the one who works with Ham. Nice chap, he was a teacher but gave it up. His girlfriend died in a car crash. Not her fault, the other driver got eight years in prison."
"How blummin' awful."
"Yeah. Ham said he'd be back at about one. He'll pick up your list, and then take me to Sainsburys."

The large package arrived.
Steve signed for it.
He phoned Danny.
"When you pick me up at ten, you can put the home-brew pack in your motor."

"Great. When shall we make it?"
"Well, we should get back from the funeral around one or two. We can make a start on it then. Did you get all the kit stuff from the Mall?"
Danny looked at the large plastic container and other wine making paraphernalia sitting in a corner of his kitchen.
"Yep. Got it all here. Twenty-two quid for the lot. Got some extra sugar too. Want to make it strong, like yours."
"Okay. Good shop that 'Happy-Brewer'."
"Sure is. See you later."
The two male nurses gently helped Jim onto the wheelchair.
Jim was in pain, but never uttered a sound.
They pushed him through the ward to the lifts.
At the bottom Ollie, Ham and Barbara were waiting.
One of the male nurses handed Barbara a large package.
"You've been briefed, I believe."
"Yes," said Barbara.
The four men lifted Jim and his chair into the back of the ambulance.
Barbara looked anxiously at her charge.
"You okay, Jim?"
"Yes. Don't worry."

When everything was secure, the ambulance drove off. Ham and Ollie sat with Jim.
No one spoke.
Ollie and Ham watched over Jim nervously.

Blue sky, cold. Winter's day.
At Gayton Cemetery Steve and Danny were positioned by the open grave, ready to help Ollie and Ham steady the chair as the lift lowered Jim in his chair to the ground.
Beryl waved to Danny. A little wave.
He nodded back.
Steve noticed. Smiled to himself.
Thirty people surrounded the grave, the weighbridge man, the two digger drivers, Beryl and all the pipe layers. Even Wally, the new man was there. A representative, Bill Owen the Chief Clerk, from the Norwich office was also there. Notably absent was Jones and Infine.
Bill Dunne, the digger driver, stood with Danny and Steve.
"Did they get the arse-holes then?"
Steve nodded.
"Yeah. Apparently. CCTV."
"Hope they get's life. Not *fourteen* years, *life*, but *proper* life."
Mr and Mrs Emil stood to one side with Mr Emil's brother.

The ambulance arrived.
Jim was lifted down. He was ashen. His eyes bright with withheld tears.
As his wheelchair touched the ground, his workmates applauded him.
He managed a smile and raised his hand in acknowledgement.

Nigel Infine selected Rosie again.
He'd thought about her most of the night.
He followed her into her bed sit.
He'd parked outside her place, then walked back through the alley to where he knew she worked. No other girls around. Too early.
She saw him and walked towards him.
"You free?"
She held out her hand for the money.
"I'll give you a tenner more if you'll act like my girl-friend."
"What do you mean?"
"You know, kissing and that."
"No. Not that. Fuck me, but no kissing. I told you last time, not that."
"Twenty-five then."
"No."
"Thirty."
She thought for a moment.
Thirty would allow her to score for the rest of the day.

"Okay."

Ollie made a nice speech about Alex.
Jim had given him some pointers, so he could talk about the young man's childhood in Romania, as well as his little café that was so well thought of.
He was aware of the Emil family hugging each other and crying.
The Priest blessed the coffin, and it was lowered into the ground.
Alex's father lifted some soil and dropped it onto the casket in the grave. His tears followed it.
Jim's head was in his hands. His body shook as he sobbed.
Ollie and Ham each put a hand on his shoulders.
Nothing to be said. Shock. The sudden impact of grief. Love gone forever.
Three figures appeared in front of the wheelchair.
The three Emil's gently touched his head.
He looked up. His face full of misery as tears coursed down his cheeks.
Mrs Emil bent down.
Kissed him on the forehead.
Jim put his arms around her, and they held the embrace.

The two Emil men watched, their eyes also etched with the pain of loss.

"You come our house when you okay," said Mr Emil. Voice trembling.

Jim nodded.

"Thank you."

The mourners came up to Jim. Sad faces.

They touched his shoulder, shook his hand then drifted away.

The four men lifted Jim back into the ambulance.

He was exhausted.

The nurse briefly checked him over.

Barbara closed the back door on the three men and drove back to the hospital in silence.

Dr Ranjid was waiting anxiously at the A and E ramp when they returned.

Barbara and he shook hands, he kissed her cheek. Old friends.

The Doctor and the two male nurses, accompanied Jim in his wheelchair back to the ward.

The St John's ambulance returned to King Street with Ham and Ollie on board.

"That was bloody sad," said Ollie.

"Good turnout for Alex though. Nice to see the Emil's being so conciliatory towards Jim."

They said their sincere, 'thank you's' to the nurse.

They both hugged her. A job well done, with much relief at the end.

The two men drove to Ollie's bungalow.

"Fancy a pint. Got some Stella in the fridge."

They drank the beer in silence. Reflecting.

"I just don't get it."

"What?"

"Why are people so filled with hate that they have to hurt or kill someone, just because that someone is different?" said Ham.

"In my opinion, it's born out of a lack of education. Hate isn't a *natural* phenomenon, it is taught, sometimes by parents, sometimes by newspapers, television, books, or by other people who have a vested interest in dividing humanity to make it easier to rule over them," said Ollie.

Ham thought about this for a moment.

"Yes. Never thought of it like that. I've been abused by people who don't know me, because of my colour, yet if those same people were blind, they would have nothing to abuse me for."

"Indeed, but if you pit black against white, or Muslim against Christians, you make those sections of people weaker. When people come together, unite, they are stronger, when divided their strength is dissipated. Generally, those people that are homophobic,

Islamophobic, anti-semitics, or racists, don't even realise that they are being manipulated to serve the needs of others. Those *others* are normally political parties, or capitalists, who are almost always very rich, and need division and confusion among the masses to maintain their system. Hatred for a group distracts them from identifying the *real* problem areas in our society."
"What's the answer then?"
"Getting the truth to the masses. Showing that hope and compassion, not hate, is the way forward. Corbyn does that."

When Ham left, Ollie phoned Annabel.
"Was it awful?"
"It was sad, but in some respects, it had a good outcome. The Emil's made their peace with Jim."
"Oh good. How was he?"
"Weak, exhausted, not well, as you would expect. Not well enough to get out of his hospital bed, anyway. That's what love does for you, I guess, it gives you superhuman strength."
"Yes. Thanks for leaving the money. I actually charge more than what you left for an all-night session."
Ollie laughed.

"I was expecting change."
He hung up and supped more beer.
Sad, happy, melancholic, wishing he could change the world.

Danny and Steve drove home in silence.
When they arrived, Steve came into Danny's house.
He'd promised to help Danny, as this was the first attempt at wine-making that Danny had made.
Danny got them two beers out of his fridge.
They sat drinking.
"Poor Alex. Poof or no poof, no one deserves that."
"No, they don't. It's funny, isn't it? When I think of two men kissing or that, I feel a bit sick. But when I think about two women kissing, it makes me horny."
Steve nodded.
"Yeah. I feel like that as well. I think it must have been our parents making us think that poofs are awful, when I don't really think they are."
"Me neither, they're just slightly different to us. That's all."
They made Danny's batch of wine.

His wife, Vee, came in as they put the large plastic container in the airing cupboard on the top landing.
"Thought you two were going to that funeral?"
"We have. Got back and made the wine. Be careful how you put stuff in the airing cupboard. It's stored in there to ferment."
"Okay. You want tea?"
"No thanks. Just having beer."
"Was there many there?"
"Yeah. Quite a few, all the lads from work. That tosser Jones wasn't there though."
"Jim Gillespie came. In an ambulance. Ollie and Ham fetched him. He didn't look good at all," said Steve.
"Was he the other gay boy?"
"Yeah. He looked terrible, so sad, as well as ill," said Danny.
"Terribly sad, is that," said Vee.

Nigel Infine took his battery off the charger in the crew room.
Jones was smoking.
"Anything to tell me?"
Nigel shook his head.
"The others are *always* moaning."
"What about?"

"Oh, you know. No showers, wages aren't enough. Things like that. They say the café is shite now, and slag your missus off."
"Bastards. Lucky to 'ave a job."
"I tell them that."
"You married?"
"No."
"Got a girlfriend, or is you's queer?"
"No, not queer, Sort of, got a girlfriend."
"Whadya mean, 'sort of'? Either you 'as, or you ain't."
"Well."
"*Well* what?
"Truth is I shags a woman in Norwich. Pays her a little, an' gets it when I want."
Jones was immediately interested.
He licked his lips.
"So, she's a prossie, then?"
Infine looked perplexed.
"If you's pay 'er, she's a prossie."
"In a way I s'pose she is, then. Yeah, she *is* a prossie, but I kiss her and that."
"Does she let you do what you want with 'er?"
Infine smiled.
"Oh yeah. *Anything.*"
"Sucks you off?"
"Whenever I tell 'er to."
Jones took a long drag of his cigarette.

"Bet she don't let you fuck 'er up the arse, though."
"Course she does. Told you, *anything* I want."
"How much do she charge?"
"A tenner."
"Is she a looker or what?"
Infine then described Rosie, and where he met her.
Jones stubbed his cigarette out.
"Best you get to your site."
"Right. Thanks."
After he'd gone, Jones sat staring out of the window.
"Bet he's a lying bastard."
He thought that he'd try in on with Doreen tonight.
He started as his office phone rang.
"Sagittarius End. Can I help you?"
Stewle answered.
"Why weren't you at Alex Emil's funeral?"
Jones gulped. Speechless.
"As his boss, you should have attended."
Brief silence. Jones panicking.
"I um *was* there, Mr Stewle, sir."
"I sent Owen there to represent the Head Office, and he said you definitely *weren't* there."
"I...er...me wife was taken suddenly very poorly. Faint and sick and all. We's...er...we

got there early and er...me wife was taken very ill, had to take 'er home, had to leave, afore any of the others got there, sir."
The phone went dead.
"Bastard!" said Jones, looking at the phone.
"None of 'is friggin' business what I does on me day's off."
He slammed the phone down.
He took Friday's figures across to the office.
It was locked.
He banged on the door.
Nothing.
He looked in the windows but couldn't see Beryl.
"Bitch. Where the fuck could *she* be? 'er car's in the car park. Probably reading a book on the shitter. Lazy bitch."
He went to the café.
Doreen sat reading 'The Sun', cigarette dangling from her mouth.
"You ain't s'posed to smoke inside, 'specially in a café."
"Whose to tell? 'Ardly get anyone in, specially this early.
"Just got a bollicking' for not goin' to that queer's funeral."
"Who orf?"
"That bastard Stewle."
"Fuck 'im. Up to you if you's goes, or not."

"Tha's what I told 'im. Twat."
"Can't expect you's to go to no queer boy's funeral. Better off dead them is, if you's ask me."
He walked back to his office and lit a cigarette.
On his desk was a 'flyer'.
The author was one of the pipe-layers.
'Christmas *Party*?'
He took a closer look.
'Works Christmas Party? I never said there was goin' to be no friggin' *party*. Better not be expectin' me to put no money in.'
He read the flyer.
'Baston Inn, Swaffham? Never 'eard on it.
Never been to a works party before.
Two bottles of free wine to each table.
He supposed that, as the boss, he ought to go. Otherwise that bastard Stewle would be on his case.

In the store room, Danny and Beryl heard the front office door being knocked.
Beryl was naked and Danny wore only a tee-shirt and socks.
Danny looked at Beryl.
They giggled.
"It'll be that tosser Jones, with Friday's figures."
Danny pushed her back down on to the table.

"Shall I go and take them off him?"
Beryl giggled.
"Yeah. You go as you are."
He looked down, and laughed.
Beryl held out her arms.
"Take me, instead."

FIFTEEN

Bill Dunne finished his first of two flasks of coffee, popped the stopper on and screwed the cup on the top.
'Better than the shit that Jones' old bag serves up.'
He thought of Alex and the funeral. It had stayed with him all weekend.
'Poor little bugger. Never done no 'arm to no one, he didn't.'
He'd read in the EDP that the six thugs were up in court that morning, all charged with murder, amongst other things.
'Hope the twats *do* get life.'
The other digger driver was already on the move in his digger and was pushing garbage up the slope on Section 20 of D Site.
Bill saw Ham working on the adjacent hill. They waved to each other.
Pipe layers were also close by, inserting new gas pipes into the ground.

Bill started up his digger. It burst into life on the second push.
Nearly new this one. Replaced the other one that was stolen.
He lowered the digger blade and started to push the waste up the hill.
After an hour, he noticed an old manikin in the rubbish, it was uncovered as the wave of bags and other rubbish rolled to one side.
'God. The shite some people throw away.'
He reversed, stopped, and then ploughed forward again.
The manikin rolled over with the garbage.
The shop had left the blouse on.
'That's floppy for a manikin, that is. Still got hair on it's 'ead, too. Thought they put wigs on shop models.'
Something was not quite right.

The Police car pulled up beside Bill and Ham.
Both were still in shock.
Jones came running over. His eyes wide and sweat on his brow,
He hadn't driven over. His car was uninsured. Left it in the car park, unobserved by coppers.
"Show me. You two stay here," said the grim-faced constable.
The digger driver took the policeman to the body.

It was a young woman.
Her face was dirty and badly bruised. One eye swollen and closed. Her tongue was half out of her mouth, it looked swollen, and almost cut in half.
One of her arms lay at a strange angle. Broken.
The policeman told Bill to take Jones and Ham, and go to the bottom of the incline and wait there.
Twenty minutes later sirens and flashing blue lights heralded the arrival of more police and crime scene personnel.
"I reckons she's been gang-banged, prob'ly by gyppo's, or blacks," Jones blurted out.
Ham clenched his teeth but said nothing.
Bill looked sideways at Jones and shook his head.
He and Ham walked over to the digger parking spaces.
He lit up a cigarette.
"What a tosser that idiot is," said Ham.
Bill nodded.
"He's a prick, *and* I noticed a bit of make up on his face this mornin'. Fuckin' ponce."

Jones dialed up on his mobile phone.
His hands shook.
His wife answered.

"What d'ya want?"
"Doreen. It's me."
"I *know* it's friggin' you. You's come up on the friggin' screen. What d'ya want?"
"The digger driver just found a girl on D site, she's been shagged by some blokes, and murdered. They 'as dumped her. Digger driver found 'er. Dead she was. All beat up. I reckon it's gyppo's or some blacks. Coppers is all over the site."
"Jesus! An' she's dead, you say?"
"Dead as a friggin' door-nail. Only 'ad a little top on, nothin' on the bottom bit. Face all beat up. White she was."
"Could be that nigger what done it."
Jones thought for a moment. A smile appeared.
"Maybe. I said that. She probably asked for it, showing off 'er tits like that," he said brightly.
"Them are always murderin' some young white girls an' women."
"She *was* on *'is* site. Could *well* be 'im. Maybe I should tell the coppers?""
"You say coppers all over? Thems might see our motor. No insurance."
"Nay. Parked it at the back of the car park, out of the way. I ain't daft."
He thought he might tell the police that it was Ham, the blackie, what most likely did it.

Malcolm Stewle's Bentley was stopped at the main gate by a policeman.
"I'm the MD of this site. This is Tony Baxter, our company lawyer."
He was instructed to pull into, and park, in the site car park.
Jones was waiting. Nervous. Twitching almost.
"Mornin' sir. Terrible what 'as 'appened, sir."
"This is the company solicitor. Show us where she is."
Jones took them to D site.
They walked quickly.
Jones talking all the way. Gibbering.
Stewle silent.
Police kept them away from the slope.
A detective came over.
"I'm Malcolm Stewle, MD of the company."
He handed his card to the policeman.
"Detective Sergeant John Baker."
"Dead woman, I hear," said Stewle.
"Yes. No ID. Young woman, around seventeen to eighteen. White. Slim. Five feet two, approximately. Fair hair. Any of your staff fit that description?"
Stewle looked at Jones.
"No. Only 'as two women. Beryl, the office girl, and me missus in the cafe. Them don't look like that."

"Anything we can do?" said Stewle.

"Not really. Just help us to keep everyone away from the area for a couple of days, until we tell you it's okay."

"Right. Will you keep me informed?"

"Yes."

"Jones. Make sure you do that. Brief the men. *All* the men."

"Yes sir. Does you's think it might be a blackie what done it, sir?"

Stewle looked at him. Disgust on his face.

"Why did you say that"? said Baker.

Jones shrugged.

"Well, they is always rapin' white girls ain't they? An' it's Veene's site. He's black. Shifty an'...."

"Oh do shut up!" said Stewle.

Baker shook his head.

Stewle looked at Jones, contempt on his face.

"Just do as you're told man, for *God's* sake."

"Right you are, sir."

The detective handed out his card to Stewle and Jones.

Danny and Beryl kept peeping out of the window.

They watched the police cars, and the general toing and froing.

"Best I leg it up to my site, before I'm missed."

Beryl pulled him to her.
"When can we spend the night together?"
He pulled himself away.
"Dunno. Soon, maybe."
He unlocked the door and left.
'Definitely getting a bit clingy. Best I stop it soon, *very* soon.'
He would never leave Vee.
She had given him so much, and she was such a lovely person, not to mention his fantastic little girl.
Beryl was for convenience, like chocolate bars. His reverie was broken when his radio crackled.
"Bentley! Bentley! Where are you?"
'Bugger!'
Danny had to think quickly.
"At your office. I came for another battery for my monitor. Other one's packed in."
"Well, I ain't there."
"Yes. I know."
"Stay there. I'm comin' back. Wait there."
Danny took the battery out of his monitor and waited for Jones to arrive.
He saw Malcolm Stewle and the lawyer stride past.
Stewle barely gave him a look.

Two minutes later the Bentley shot out of the car park, past Danny and out through the front gate.

Jones came huffing and puffing. His large nose was dripping.

Ham was just behind him.

He unlocked the office.

Behind his back Ham winked and gave Jones the 'finger'.

Danny smiled.

"Mornin' Ham."

"Hi Danny."

Jones shouted out.

"Never mind friggin' gossiping. Get yourselves in 'ere."

He exchanged Danny's battery, and handed Ham a security jacket.

"Get that on, an' make sure no bastard gets on to D site, 'ceptin' coppers. You's can still monitor some of the pipes just on the edge of the site. Don't want you skivin' any more than what you does normally."

Danny and Ham walked away from the office.

Beryl stood at the door of her office.

She waved. Danny didn't.

"Pleasant sort of chap, that Jones, don't you think?"

"Yeah. In a sewer rat, kind of way."

SIXTEEN

Steve and his wife Sylvia were drinking the wine he had made three weeks ago.
She sat in an armchair, he lay on the couch.
The television was on.
BBC Look East said a woman's body had been found at the Sagittarius End landfill site.
"Heard it on Radio Norfolk this mornin'. Thought at first it were gonna be that RAF chap what disappeared. They think *he's* in a landfill somewhere, in Norfolk," said Sylvia.
"No. It's definitely a woman at our place. We're warned off part of the site. Not that it bothers me. Me being at Molbury, an' all."
"Don't you's finish there this week?"
"S'posed to 'ave done, but Jonesy says, cos of the murder, we 'as to do a double month on our sites. Good for me, but shite for poor old Ham. He's got the crappiest shite hole to monitor."
"Someone must have dumped 'er there."

"Yep. Must have moved the barriers somehow."

"Maybe it's one of your blokes what done it."

"S'pose it could be."

"Don't you 'ave any CCTV there?"

"Nope. Too bloody tight."

Steve topped up Sylvia's wine.

BBC Look East News was on the television.

"'Ere, ain't thems the blokes what kicked that poof in who worked at your place?"

Steve turned to the television.

The news report said all six stood in the dock charged with murder. The trial was likely to last for six to eight weeks, but wouldn't start for three weeks, by which time Jim would be well enough to attend as a witness for the prosecution.

"Bastards!"

"How's his boyfriend?"

"Jim? Should be out of hospital in three to four weeks. He'll not be able to work for a few months, or so Ollie says."

Sylvia sipped her wine.

"I don't think I'll 'ave any more after this glass, Steve. I feel right squiffy."

Steve laughed.

"Good for you gal. Danny said Vee got very amenable after just one glass on Monday night."

"What d'ya mean, 'amenable'?"
Steve reached over and gently squeezed one of her breasts.
"Oh, I see."

Jim lay quietly.
He thought of Alex, now laying in the soil. Of the good times they should have had, but never would.
His love gone. Stolen.
The doctors had told him that one eye was damaged beyond repair.
He'd made his statements to the police.
He was still in pain but had asked the staff to reduce the painkillers.
Bad enough being half-blind without sowing the seeds to becoming a junkie.
Ollie had visited him today.
Cheered him up.
Such a good guy. He told him about work, and what was happening in the world outside.
Ollie made a lot of sense when it came to what's wrong in Britain. Never thought about it before. Never even knew it was the Socialists who started the NHS and the British welfare state.
On the visit before last he'd brought Ham, the black man who looked like Harry Belafonte. He made him laugh telling stories about the racial

discrimination he had experienced in Norfolk, and his mimicry of Jones.
Jim didn't think he'd go back to working on the gas field again.
The doctors said he'd need a sedentary job for a year or so.
Nice that Alex's folks were kind to him at the funeral. He knew their pain. Felt it himself. Wouldn't go away. Body broken. Heart too.

Ollie had showered and was dressing.
He was picking Annabel up at twelve.
He smiled at the thought of her.
How lovely she was. A bright light in his dull, mediocre life.
He'd planned the day.
Driving to Norwich. Walking the dog on Mousehold, then the two of them having lunch with his parents at their house on Vincent Road. After that, who knows?
He still felt guilty, as if he was committing adultery.
His sad face looked back at him from the mirror.
He shouldn't feel like this.
Guilty, but so looking forward to being with Annabel.
He loved looking at her hazel eyes. Her face set off by her dark hair. Their kisses seemed to

get more intense, not in a sexual way so much but in a recognition that he was hers, and she was his.

She never mentioned Grace, even though she looked back at them from her photographs as they had walked into the lounge together for the first time.

Later, when he was on his own, he collected the frames and put them in a side cabinet. An hour later he put them back out again. Ashamed.

After putting Bess into the back of his car, he drove to Hingham.

Annabel came to the door.

Happy, smiling.

She had been waiting all day to kiss him, hold him.

They embraced.

A long kiss that promised more.

He looked into her beautiful eyes.

She was so lovely.

"Bess is in the car."

He said it almost as an apology.

She looked over his shoulder.

"Best we get moving then."

She made a fuss of the happy dog.

They drove to Norwich. Talking, joking, laughing.

After parking opposite the café overlooking the city they walked hand in hand along to the Valley Drive.

The large trees formed a canopy over them, and Bess loved to run in the large open spaces beneath.

Ollie threw a tennis ball and the dog gleefully chased after it and brought it back, dropping it at his feet.

"It's your birthday soon. Before I buy you a tool kit that I can play with, any ideas for me on what you might want?"

She smiled at him.

"How did you know it was my birthday? Did Myriam tell you?"

He threw the ball for Bess.

"No. I read it up in the Doomsday book."

They drank small beers outside in the café and looked out across St James' Hill to the fine city of Norwich. The Cathedral pointing to the heavens.

"They have a big bonfire on St James' on Guy Fawkes night, loads of fireworks, hot dogs coffee, mulled wine, and stuff like that. Families love it."

"Sounds a fun evening, especially the mulled wine."

"Maybe we could come this year," said Ollie.

The waitress brought a dish of water for the dog.
"My birthday. A book would be nice, I think."
"What? 'Famous Five', or 'The Woodentops'?"
She made as if to punch him.
He feigned terror.
"*No*, something more intellectual, the 1979 Beano Christmas Annual, now *that* might fit the bill."
They finished their drinks and walked to the car.
Lunch was arranged for two o'clock.
Bess was ready for another lay down, and five minutes after being welcomed by Ollies' parents she lay on the rug in front of the coal fire.
Ollie and his Dad talked football as they sat in the comfortable armchairs.
Mrs Wilson and Annabel disappeared into the kitchen, each carried a glass of sherry.

"How's things?"
"Fine. Hate my job at the moment, but fine."
Mrs Wilson checked the oven.
"No, I meant with you and that son of mine."
"Oh, Yes. Lovely. We enjoy each other's company. He's a nice person."
Edith Wilson smiled. Her wrinkles standing out around her eyes.

"And so are you, Annabel. He's a lot happier since he met you. I can see the old sparkle returning. He's been grieving for far too long."
"He must have loved Grace a lot."
Edith sipped her sherry, put the glass down, then placed her arm around Annabel's shoulder and looked into her eyes.
"He did, but now he's got you. You make him happy, I can see that. Does he make you happy?"
"Yes."
"Do you love him?"
"Yes," said Annabel quietly.
She surprised herself how easily it came out.
She blushed.
"Yes, I do."
"Good."

SEVENTEEN

"It's a bloody nightmare, that site," said Stewle.
"Yes, well. If it were easy, everyone would be making millions like us," said Reggie Witter.
"I know, but it never stops. Constant thefts of anything not battened down, and now murder."
"*Another* murder."
Stewle looked perplexed.
"No. Only the one. The girl."
"Don't forget the chap who ran the café."
Stewle shrugged.
"Yes, well, he doesn't count really. Off the premises, not British either, so who cares? Certainly not me."
"Still haven't even identified the girl yet, I hear."
"No."
Reggies sipped his Scotch.
 "I see you got rid of the old biddy receptionist."
"Yup. Saved myself five grand a year."
"How so?"

"Got a school leaver. Nice tits and only need to pay her the minimum wage."
"Sound judgement, I'd say. Have you…..you know?"
Stewle shook his head.
"Not yet."
"Be careful. We can't afford Conservative party donors being blitzed for touchy feely, as well as our servants in the government."
"I know. But I might take her with me on a business trip in the new year."
"You old dog, you."
"Well, *you* suggested I change my receptionist."
"That's it, blame me."
Both laughed. The whisky flowed.
"Anything on the stolen digger yet?"
Stewle shook his head.
"The police tell me all the ports are on the lookout for it. They reckon these things are normally sent abroad to third world countries. They're doing their best, but just don't have the manpower these days."

They were behind the café counter.
Doreen bent down to pick up a bag of tea bags.
Jones grabbed her breasts from behind.
"Get off!"

She pushed him away from her with her bottom and stood upright.
"Stop *doin'* that!"
"Aw, come on, Dor. We's only 'ad it once in the last four weeks."
The café door opened.
Nigel came in.
Doreen smiled.
"'Ello, Nigella."
Jones came around the counter and walked back past the newly arrived Nigel Infine.
"Hello Mr Jones."
"Why aren't you's on your site, Infine?"
Infine looked hurt.
"It's me lunch break."
Jones looked at his watch.
"Just make sure you're back there at a quarter to."
Infine smiled.
"Oh yes. I never overstay, Mr Jones, never. Fact is, I always get back five or ten minutes early."
As Jones got to the café entrance Infine called out to him.
"'as they caught the bloke what did that girl in, yet. Mr Jones?"
Jones turned abruptly to face him.
"Why ask me? I don't know nothin' about it. What 'as you 'eard?"

Infine shook his head.

"Nothin'. Not 'eard nothin'."

"Well, if you does, you come straight an' tell me."

"Yes, Mr Jones. I'll do that, I will, sir."

Infine went to the counter.

Doreen looked at him. Blank. No expression.

"Yes?"

"Tea an' a bag of crisps please, Doreen."

"What flavor? Not a mind reader you know."

"Oh, sorry. Cheese an' onion please."

"Ain't got no Cheese an' Onion. Got plain."

"'ave you got Chicken flavor, or bacon flavor?"

Doreen frowned.

"No. Just *told* you, only got *Plain*."

"Right. Plain, please."

He took his tea and crisps and sat at one of the long tables.

He picked up an old copy of the Sun.

Inside was a picture of a young female model on a bicycle.

Reminded him of Rosie.

He thought he might pay her a visit later. Worth the extra for a bit of kissing as well as sex. He wondered how much she *would* charge for anal. Jones had mentioned it and it excited him.

At five o'clock he drove to Rose Lane.

Rosie wasn't around.

He walked to her little bedsit.
No response when he banged on her door.
A woman walking by, whom he recognized as a prostitute, told him nobody had seen her for days.
She said *she* was available.
Big and blousy, he wanted young and slim.
He drove back to Wymondham. Fed up.
Maybe she's got a fella or stopped doing it.
That evening at the Legion he sat by a window and read the Eastern Evening News as he drank his beer.
The bar manager gave him a surprised look.
"You okay?" asked Ernie, making his rounds to collect empty glasses.
Infine looked up.
"You look as if you've seen a ghost, Nigel."
Infine's face was ashen and his hand shook as he held the paper.
"No. I'm alright."
He didn't sound convincing.
On the front page was an artist's impression of a young woman.
The young woman looked remarkably like Rosie.
Under the picture was the heading, 'Do you recognize this woman?'
She had been found murdered, her body left at a landfill site.

He finished his beer and left.
'Was it Rosie? Certainly looked like her. She wasn't home.
It were *my* landfill site. *Shit* and *double shit*.
Contacting the coppers was a definite no-no.
They'd do him for using her.
They might even think *he* killed her, if it *was* her that was dead.
His fingerprints might be in her bedsit. *Shit* and *treble shit*!'
He had no friends, no one to seek advice from.
He spent a restless night in his flat.
At work the next day he fretted and found it difficult to concentrate.
He decided to talk it over with Mr Jones at lunch time. He'd understand.
Mr Jones would know what to do.

"Did you's do 'er in, then?"
Infine's eyes widened.
"No! I never would."
"You fucked her though."
"Yeah. I did that, paid 'er as well, but I never done 'er in, never do that."
"Police will think you did."
Infine, almost in tears.
"What will I do?"
"Maybe you's ought to confess. They'll only bang you's up for about ten years then, if *that*.

She *were* a prossie, so she don't count as important."

"But I never did it, Mr Jones. I ain't no murderer, honest. I just fucked 'er and kissed 'er."

Jones looked angry.

"She let you *kiss* 'er?"

"Yeah. I 'ad to pay 'er extra for that."

"What else did you do to 'er? You's told me she took it up 'er arse."

Infine sighed.

"I knows I said that, but I didn't. Just shagged 'er, and kissed her a couple of times."

"So, you lied to me."

"Well, only a little. I just said it cos you asked about it."

"Right. Well. Either you go to the coppers and confess, or, you's keep your gob shut, and 'ope no one finds out."

"But I never did *nothin'*, honest."

Jones lit up a cigarette.

"Seems to me you probably did it, an' if it seems like that to me, it'll seem like that to the law."

Infine's face was very red.

His eyes glistened with tears.

"Weren't me."

"Best you come clean, an' tell the truth. You'll be back out of prison in no time."

"But I never done it. I *swear*."

"They'll definitely take it easy on you's if you admit it. If you don't, an' keep sayin' you didn't do nothin', they might keep you's in for life. You'll die in prison."

Infine sighed. Forlorn.

"Anyway. You get yourself back to your site, an' think about it some more."

Infine almost stumbled out of Jone's office.

He cried as he walked to A site.

Jones sat back in his chair.

He took a deep drag of his cigarette, closed his eyes and smiled.

EIGHTEEN

Danny and Steve sat in Danny's lounge.
Vee was picking up Holly from her mother's.
"If you leave the wine for three weeks after it's bottled it tastes fantastic," said Steve, holding his glass up to the light.
"Yeah. Pity we can't flog it on at a profit," said Danny.
"Mmmm. We could do the next best thing, though. We could sell the kits."
"How so? The packs all have the manufacturers' details on 'em. Sell 'em once an' then they goes direct."
Steve nodded.
"Yep, but only got the makers details on the *outside* packaging. The inner bits don't have any writing on them at all, just plain cardboard little boxes with the numbers to coincide with the guide. If we made a copy of our own guide on plain paper, and a cardboard little case to

put the four contents inserts in, we could sell it at say five quid more than we buy 'em in for."

"Okay, but we'd have to advertise, an' that ain't cheap."

"True. But we could get a ready market from the guys at work. They like it an' they'll tell their families and friends."

Danny perked up.

"*Yes*. We could put some of our bottles on the tables at the Christmas 'do' for free, tell the lads it's all from our own kits and woosh, we're off an' running. We tell 'em we has the outlet to ourselves. An' we supply 'em."

Steve, animated.

"Shit yeah! When they taste it, an' find out how cheap it is, they'll rip our 'ands off!"

"I'll talk to Scott."

"Baston Inn? Is that the pub on the old A47 just outside of town, with the big car park behind it?"

Ham was sitting at the dining table making posters up for the Sagittarius End Christmas party on his laptop.

"Yeah. Never been inside, but Scott, one of the pipe-layers, reckons it's a really nice pub."

Myriam came up behind him and looked over his shoulder.

"Why are *you* doing the posters? *You're* not organizing it, are you?"

Ham turned and pulled her on to his lap.

"No, but I don't think Scott is much of an IT man. He asked me to do the posters. Only need half a dozen."

Myriam put her arm around his neck and kissed his forehead.

"How many will be going?"

Ham shrugged.

"Dunno. Depends on the numbers invited. Maximum the pub can cope with is fifty, according to Scott."

"Are we going?"

"Yes. If you want to. Ollie said he was going to ask Annabel if she wanted to go."

"Yes. That would be nice. What date is it?"

"Friday the twenty second."

"Right. I'll put that in my diary. Do you think Mum might come?"

"Ask her after I've checked on spaces with Scott. Where is she, anyway?"

"Working. She should be home any minute."

"Apparently there's going to be quite a lot of free wine."

"That's good. We can walk there *and* back. Be sober when we get home, what with you carrying Ma and all."

Ham laughed and then kissed her.

"Taxi there an' back. I'll book it up later."
"Combination taxi? Ollie and Annabel?"
"Maybe. If they go."
Myriam squirmed around on his lap to see what the poster looked like on the laptop.
"Mmm. That felt nice. No chance of any 'how's yer father' then?"
"Maniac. Ma will be home soon."
"Rather have you, any day."

Detective Sergeant Baker hung his jacket on the back of his chair.
A few minutes later his 'team' came in for the morning briefing.
The Chief Constable stood at the back of the room. An observer.
"Right, gentlemen. I have received the coroner's report this morning, along with forensics findings. The young woman's cause of death was strangulation. She had had intercourse, and there had also been anal penetration. Her tongue had teeth marks where the perp had bitten her with such violence that her tongue was almost severed. She had also severe bruising on her face and body, indicating she had been punched or kicked before death. We have recovered what we believe to be the perp's DNA from the body. There was blood and skin under the

nails of her right hand. Her left arm, wrist and three fingers were broken."

Baker looked up from his notes.

"Parsons. Any joy with the padlock, or the gate?"

"No. Sarge. All clean. Wiped, I reckon."

"Okay. We're starting at the site. B team, under Jim Chapman, will go there today and interview all the workers. The forensic team will be with them taking DNA's. They know the script. Any questions?"

Silence.

"Good. On you go."

The policemen and women made a noisy exit from the room.

Chief Constable Myrus Greenberg, tall, handsome, and a stickler for discipline, came over to Baker.

He waited until the last officer had left.

"What do you reckon?"

"Could be a worker. Someone who either had a key, or, it could be a dodgy geezer who can pick locks."

"Scratches, plus DNA should point the finger."

"Yes sir. I expect an early arrest."

"Good. Keep me up to speed. That bloody landfill site has been a pain in the arse for ages."

"Yes sir."

Ollie had time. He opened the only letter that morning.

Norwich Intermediary School asked him to attend for interview on Friday the 29th.

at ten thirty.

He'd applied for three posts only last Tuesday. This lot must be stuck for teachers. He'd have to lie to Jones. Maybe a hospital appointment might suit.

He phoned Annabel.

She was pleased.

"Not a bad school. Kevin Humphreys is the head. He was with me at uni. Nice guy, bit of a drip, but okay with it. Genuine. You'll get on with him."

"What? Because he's a drip?"

"Idiot! Drips attract. You'll be fine."

"Gee, thanks."

"You're welcome. Gotta go. I'm saying prayers this morning, can't keep my fans waiting."

He nearly said, 'Love you'. It had almost rolled off his tongue.

He drove to Sagittarius End.

Nigel Infine was standing at the car park.

"You're to stay in the office building. Coppers want to speak to us."

He looked ill. His eyes red, face pale.

"You okay?"

Nigel gulped.
"Yeah. Why shouldn't I be? I never touched her. Weren't me!"
It came out in a rush.
"Never said it was, Nigel. *Whatever* you're talking about."
"The rest of 'em are in the office, 'cept Steve. He's comin'."
Ollie walked to the office.
Jones came out as he neared the door.
Cigarette in hand. He lit it.
He looked anxious too.
"Get in Wilson. Back in a minute."
Ollie entered.
The whole of the site workforce was there.

"Right Nigel. Need you's to run an errand for me."
"Yes Mr Jones. But ain't the coppers here to see us all?"
Jones shook his head and put his hand on Infine's shoulder.
"Don't worry about that. It's only a little chat, nothing' serious."
Infine looked relieved.
"Oh, right."
"Want you's to go into Norwich for me. Go to the airport and get some leaflets on planes to Spain."

Infine looked confused.

"But, er but....You can get all that on the internet."

Jones frowned at him.

"No. I want the brochures from the airport, and you's can get flight details for tomorrow to Spain from the booking agent."

"Is it *really* urgent, Mr Jones, cos I..."

Jones pointed at him.

"Either you's want to do this for me, or not. What is it? Yes or no?"

"But...."

"Come on! Either you does it *now*! Or else I'll get someone else who wants *promotion* to do it for me. An' don't forget, I knows that you's fucked Rosie, an' that. Course, if you's do this little errand for me, I shan't tell no one about *that*."

At the mention of Rosie, Infine's face paled.

"Oh, okay. I'll go *straight* away. Only be an hour or so, there an' back."

"Yeah, well that's the thing. As a thank you for doing it, you's can 'ave the rest of the day off. Bring it all in tomorrow."

"But you's said you wanted to know about flights today to Spain?"

"Yeah. I do so I can cross reference them. You don't 'as to worry about that, just get the friggin' info!

"Right. Okay."
Infine didn't sound too convinced but he went to his car.

Ronnie Askwith and Alice Munday arranged the small clear containers in a line. Each had the name of an employee on them, as supplied by the Norwich head office.
Ronnie addressed the 34 men and Beryl, who stood next to Danny.
"Right. Thanks for coming everyone. I'm Ronnie and this is Alice. We're from the Norfolk Police Forensics department. A woman's body was found on this site, and this is just to eliminate you from the investigation, that's all. As I call your names out, please come forward and we'll get your DNA off you. Only takes a minute. Small swab inside your mouth's and that's it. We shan't retain them after we've cross referred them in the lab. They'll be destroyed."
Jones sat by the desk on which the small containers lay.
The employees lined up. Each told Ronnie their name in turn. Ronnie took a swab, placed it in the small plastic container with the person's name on, supplied by Alice, and she screwed on the top and placed it on the table.

Jones went in third then sat back in his seat by the table.

The line progressed but was interrupted by Doreen bringing in a tray of teas and biscuits.

She set them down on a table in the middle of the room.

She beckoned the two DNA collectors across and, after getting their requirements, handed them their teas.

"Would you like biscuits?"

Ronnie took one. Alice declined

"I'll just go back and get another tray for you's all," she said to those that had no cups.

The two forensic scientists looked put out but said nothing.

Doreen hurried away to get more cups.

Infine picked up the brochures and spoke to the female in the Booking Information Office.

There were no flights that day to Spain.

He had to pay three pounds to the car park which didn't please him. He hoped Jones would reimburse him for that.

This whole episode seemed very strange to him. Why didn't Jones do the bloody job himself? Still, it kept him away from the smelly sites for an hour or so. That was a plus.

He was still in shock over that EDP newspaper picture of Rosie.

Might not have been her but looked the spitting image. He'd have to find another young woman now, if she were dead. This time he'd demand kissing, right from the start.
He kept thinking that his fingerprints *must* be in her bedsit.
The police would interview him for sure.
He wondered what the fine was for using a prossie.

Two women came forward and identified Rosie. Both were prostitutes.
It emerged her real name was Elizabeth Patricia Holmes. She had come to Norwich from Northumberland, two years previously.
Baker and his crew went immediately to her bedsit in Rose Lane.
After the locksmith opened the door, Baker entered, and beckoned the white suited Forensic staff to enter.
Blood on her bed, up one wall, and across the carpet where she must have been dragged.
Lots of fingerprints, taken by the specialists, along with swabs of the blood, and human debris on the bed sheet.
Two police photographers took photographs.
Baker stood outside smoking when the scientist heading up the team came out to him.
"How goes it?"

"Plenty of everything. We'll get it all analysed and I'll have it to you asap."
"Thanks."

NINETEEN

Danny and Steve laughed as they put the extra sugar into the two wine mixtures.

"This'll send the bastards into orbit," said Danny.

"Anything on that woman found in the rubbish?"

"Nope, news just said some were giving DNA to eliminate them," said Steve.

"Amazed that the wicked witch brought tea and biscuits for everyone."

"Yeah. Not like her to be benevolent to her husband's serfs."

"Probably both the tea and the biscuits were three years past their 'eat and drink by' date," said Steve.

Danny nodded.

"Prob'ly."

They finished off the wine and stored it in the cupboard next to Steve's boiler. They had removed the wooden partition, so the warmth got to the containers.

"Better get my skates on. Got to meet Scott at eight."

Scott and Danny went into the Baston Inn.
Old pub but recently refurbished. Bright, new fittings. Real ale.
The landlord, John Spence, was a young, slim man with blond, permed hair and a goatee beard, also dyed.
Apart from the goatee, Danny and he could have been twins.
They sat at a side table with the landlord to firm up their requirements for the Christmas party.
He wasn't too pleased about the free wine but brightened after Scott agreed on a fifty pence per bottle 'corkage' payment.
The final tally of people was 64.
The two men chatted by their cars for a few minutes. Scott said that £64 corkage for the wine was very acceptable, and Danny agreed.
From his perspective, it was good business.
Steve agreed when Danny told him.
"Bound to lose a bit as we start the business."
The two budding entrepreneurs took 100 empty used bottles out of the local restaurant's bottle bank skip.

They agreed they'd need more.

After all the labels were taken off and the bottles cleansed, they were ready to start bottling when the wine was ready.

The first cog in their business empire was in place.

"Daniel Robin Bentley. I am arresting you on suspicion of the murder of Elizabeth Patricia Holmes on or about the 15th of December 2017. You do not have to say anything. But, it may harm your defence, if you do not mention, when questioned, something which you later rely on in court. Anything you do say may be given in evidence. Do you understand?"

Danny stood, his wrists manacled. Forlorn, lost, unbelieving.

He nodded.

"This is a joke, isn't it? I never did nothing to this woman. I don't even know her. Who the fuck is she?"

"We have your DNA, Danny. You might as well come clean right now. Save yourself a lot of anguish lad," said Detective Sergeant John Baker.

"It's not me. You've made a mistake."

Danny was led out of Jone's office by two constables to a waiting police van and placed

inside. It drove away with its blue lights flashing.
The Detective turned to Jones.
"Thank you for the use of your office, Mr Jones."
Jones beamed.
"It were a pleasure. Glad you 'as got the bugger. Knew 'e was a wrong 'un I did."
The policeman and his colleague glanced at each other, a slight smile on both faces.
The policemen left.
Jones hurried across to the café.
He burst through the door.
"They 'as got 'im! It were that fucker Danny Bentley. it were!"
Doreen's eyes were wide.
"Bloody 'ell!"
He hugged his wife.
She hadn't seen him this happy since he'd received the money for the digger 'sale'.
She thought he was going to start dancing.
"Got to tell Anstey!"
He hurried to the Admin Office.

Beryl went cold and burst into tears when Jones brought her the news.
"He couldn't!" she sobbed.
Her hands covered her face.
"Not him. Can't be."

Tears fell.

Jones was surprised at her reaction. He expected her to be shocked but not to behave like this.

"'E's only a Monitor. Soon get another in his place, don't worry."

She sat down at her desk, head in hands.

Jones left.

"Stupid cow!"

As soon as he reached his office he made a general broadcast over the radios.

"Bentley 'as been arrested for killing that girl!"

He sat back in his office chair and lit up a cigarette.

He thought everything had turned out just fine. Didn't need Infine after all.

The Wymondham Custody Sergeant booked Danny in.

The police allowed him a phone call. He couldn't get hold of his wife, so he phoned Ollie on his mobile number.

"There *must* be some mistake, Danny?" said a shocked Ollie.

"I've told them that, but they say they have my DNA. How could they? I don't even know the fuckin' woman. As far as I know I've never met her in my life."

"Okay. What do you want me to do?"

"Well. I need a lawyer, and my wife will need to be informed if you don't mind, mate?"

"Of course. I'll attend to it straight away. Can I bring you something in? Anything you need?"

"Can't think, but I'll get Vee to let you know if there is. Her phone must have been out of signal. Couldn't get her."

Ollie knew by the sound of his voice that Danny was close to breaking down.

"Don't fret yourself mate. I'm sure this is all a terrible mistake, and we'll laugh about it over a pint soon. I'll get you a brief right now, and then I'll tell your missus. Try to relax. I know it will be hard to."

"Thanks Ollie."

They took Danny to one of the cells.

He sat on the bunk head in hands.

Ollie and Annabel stood hand in hand on top of Saint James' Hill.

The view of Norwich was getting hazy.

Ollie occasionally threw the tennis ball down the slope and Bess ran to fetch it. Sometimes her speedy hind legs overtook her body and she tumbled and cartwheeled down the hill.

After getting the ball, she laboured back up and dropped it at Ollies feet. Panting. Tail wagging.

Annabel made a fuss of her, and Bess was thankful for the respite, but none the less always ready to go again if Ollie threw the luminous green sphere for her.

After a while they walked back to the car.

Ollie put a metal dish down and filled it with bottled water for the dog to drink. It slurped gratefully.

When Bess was sated, Ollie helped her into the boot. The two back passenger seats were down, and a large grey rug served as her bed.

Annabel and Ollie walked across the road to the Britannia Café.

They took two seats that gave them a view of his car, the distant Norwich and the hills of Mousehold.

"What happens now?" said Annabel.

Ollie sipped his coffee, then shook his head.

"Don't know. I'm still in shock."

"His wife must be devastated," said Annabel sadly.

"She was. It just doesn't add up. Why on earth would a happily married man go to a prostitute, and then murder her afterwards?"

Annabel stirred her drink.

"I presume he'll have an alibi?"

Ollie nodded.

"Yep. He has. It's the DNA that is the puzzler. Just hope the cops do a proper investigation

and not a flimsy, we got our man, don't bother with anything else, sort of thing."
"Who did you get as a lawyer?"
"Roland Maynard from Prince of Wales Road. He's actually a barrister, good at these type of cases, apparently."
Annabel looked surprised.
"God. I bet *he* didn't come cheap?"
Ollie shrugged.
"He's got a good reputation."
He didn't tell her that he had stood surety, initially for five thousand pounds.
It was now getting dark. They finished their coffees and drove to Hingham.

Steve couldn't believe it either after he received Jones' call.
Danny was a bit of a rogue, sure. But never 'murder'. He had a lovely missus, and besides he was having it off with Beryl on the side. Why would he kill some girl? Nope he wasn't capable, and he was going to make sure the coppers at the Wymondham nick knew it.
He phoned Vee, no contact, so he phoned Sylvia.
"What's up love?" said Sylvia.
She was walking across Sainsbury's car park. Bag of shopping in one hand. Phone to ear.

"God! I don't *believe* it! He wouldn't, he *couldn't*. He's not that sort of bloke, is he? How do they *know* it's him? Oh my God! I better had get 'round to Vee's and give 'er some support. She must be in bits."

Tears glistened in her eyes as she stowed the shopping bags in the boot of her car.

Steve continued up the wind-swept hill to his next monitor point.

"As soon as I knock off I'm going to the 'nick' to see what's goin' on."

Steve completed the next monitor then rang Ollie. Engaged.

Nigel raised his fists up to the heavens and shouted out.

"*Yes. Yes. Yes!*"

Two of the pipe layers working on the next hill looked his way.

Nigel laughed and laughed. His laughter was almost hysterical.

The pipe layers looked at each other.

"'e must a won the Lottery."

"Or 'e's stark ravin' friggin' bonkers!"

Nigel walked gleefully on to his next monitor point, laughing all the way.

"I knew it weren't me. Fuggin' Danny done it!'

Ollie told Ham on his mobile phone what had happened.

"Don't believe a word of it, man," said Ham, scratching his short-cropped head.

Ollie agreed.

"I'm going to Wymondham this evening after work to see if there's any news, anything I can do for him."

Ham watched the Forensic team and the lone policeman carting their equipment to the two police cars at the base of Ham's section.

"The coppers look as if they're finished here now, puttin' their gear away. Will you let me know what transpires tonight?"

"Will do."

The two police cars drove away. The site was deserted.

Ham called Jones up on his radio.

"The police have left. Do you want me to do some monitoring now on D site?"

Jones sighed.

"No. Wait a minute. I'll pass you's my orders in a minute. Stay there."

"Okay," said Ham.

Ham opened up his ipad and played a music Youtube take.

Jones wandered off to the toilet and relieved himself. He strolled over to the Admin office.

Beryl sat, red eyed, at her desk.

Jones was surprised.
"What's up with you, then?"
She looked up at him.
"Why do you bloody think? Danny's arrested, of course.""
Jones smiled.
"Is that all? 'e should get strung up."
Beryl burst out crying and ran to the toilet.
Jones put his head back and laughed.
'That'll learn that bastard to wear sunglasses all the time!'
He whistled as he walked back to his office.
The world was now a much better place.

Ham sat on his plastic hard hat.
He wondered if that shite-house Jones had forgotten him.
Suddenly his radio burst into life.
"Veene! You there?"
Ham turned off his ipad and confirmed he was.
"Don't bother with no more monitorin' on the site. You's can come to my office an' clean it up."
Ham looked at his watch.
3.30pm.
'Soon be dark.'
Ham stowed his gear in his shoulder bag and began to walk slowly down the hill to Jone's office.

He had meant to ask Ollie if he and Annabel were going to the Christmas party on Friday.

Baker sat in front of his boss, Chief Inspector Morley Roberts.
The file on Rosie's murder lay open in front of him on his desk.
It was a neat office. Painted grey.
A picture of Queen Elizabeth the Second was the only wall adornment.
No piles of papers, nor wall charts, everything was orderly and in its place.
One desk, computer at one end, telephone at the other.
Four wooden chairs forming a semi-circle faced the desk.
Two filing cabinets stood against one wall.
His office window looked out across the street to the Waitrose car park.
"So that's the only evidence you have John, the DNA?"
"Yessir. But that's fairly conclusive, don't you think?
Roberts squirmed in his seat. He winced.
"Trouble is, his alibi is rock solid for time of death, etc. None of his clothes has any blood on them, and also, his car is clean as a whistle. How did he get the girl to the site? No evidence at all that he was in her bedsit, no

fingerprints, plus he has never displayed scratch marks, or cuts, and we know the girl put up a struggle. There's no getting away with it, this case is an accident waiting to happen for us. The CPS are not happy. You'll have to get something to strengthen the case against him."
Baker pursed his lips, looked down at his hands in his lap. Didn't know what to say. He thought the DNA was ample.
"I'll get my men to go over everything again, sir."
"Yes. I think you should. Bentley is meeting his lawyer in half an hour. It's Maynard. As you know there's no buggering about with him."
Baker looked surprised.
"How could a bloody gasman afford a brief like Maynard for God's sake?"
Roberts shrugged.
"Beats me. But he did, so you had better firm up the case, and be quick about it."

In the visiting/interview room.
Roland Maynard shook Danny's hand, and smiled. Good, strong teeth and a dash of gold amongst them on one side.
Maynard was very slim, six feet tall and had long grey curly hair. He wore pince-nez rimless glasses that perched on his nose. He had a

facial resemblance to the Duke of Edinburgh but walked with a slight limp. His dark blue suit looked expensive as did his bright red silk tie.
The room had no windows. Grey wall. One desk. Three chairs. The door had a one-foot square reinforced glass window. A camera and audio stick protruded high up from one wall.
Maynard pointed to the wall.
"The police will be recording in sound and vision via those things."
Danny nodded.
"They can't use it as evidence though."
Maynard sat down opposite Danny.
"Before we start. I've not got a lot of money saved up. How much will your fee be, please?"
Maynard looked surprised.
"Oh, that's all taken care of, Mr Bentley. So don't worry."
It was Danny's turn to look surprised.
"Taken care of? Who by?"
"Oh, I thought you might have known. A Mr Wilson, Oliver Wilson. He said he was a friend of yours."
Danny's mouth fell open. Ollie.
"Oh. Yes. Yes he is."
"Now. I've had a chance to review the police case, so just enlighten me on your take of all the circumstances, as you see them."
Danny cleared his throat.

"I just didn't do it. I never met the woman, and I can verify I weren't nowhere near Sagittarius End, nor that girl's house in Norwich. I just don't know how they got my DNA to match up. It, it *can't* be me, it just *can't* be. I'm innocent."
"Well, DNA is normally conclusive. Did the police take your DNA here?"
Danny shook his head.
"No. It were at Jone's office, we all stood in the room an' had it done, one after the other."
"Really? Who is Jones?"
Maynard leant forward.
"He's the foreman of the site. His missus even brought in tea and biscuits for everyone halfway through."
"Did she now. I see. Can you describe to me exactly how it all took place that day? The DNA taking, I mean."

Twenty minutes later Maynard left the interview room and asked the Custody Sergeant for directions to Baker's office.
A young PCW was directed to accompany him to the office.
It was empty.
"Can I help you Roland?" said Detective Sergeant Wood, who shared the next office with Detective Sergeant Maybanks.
Maynard turned to the voice.

"Oh, hello Sam. Any idea where John Baker is?"

They shook hands. Acquaintances from way back on various criminal cases.

"He's away to see a Mister Stewle, boss of Thorne's site Sagittarius End at the Norwich branch office, I think. Can I help?"

"Are you on the Sagittarius End murder case?"

"No. That's John and Aubrey's baby."

"In that case, no. Thanks anyway. I'll maybe catch him later. If you see him ask him to get back to me, would you? I'll send him a text in the meantime. It *is* important."

"Righto. Will do."

Maynard retraced his steps, along with the PCW.

DC Wood watched them go.

'Wonder why the daft bugger doesn't call him? Bloody lawyers.'

Maynard knocked on Morley Roberts half opened door.

The Chief Inspector beckoned him in.

"Okay, Middlechurch, you can resume your duties.

The young policewoman left.

The lawyer closed the door behind him.

After shaking hands, Roberts pointed to a chair and Maynard sat down.

"How can I help you, Roland?"
Maynard stroke his chin.
"Well Morley, it's like this. I am loath to drop any of your forensic people in it, but their performance was far too slap dash on this occasion. I'm talking about the Sagittarius End murder case and Danny Bentley in particular."
Roberts leant forward, his elbows rested on his desk and his hands under his chin.
"Right. What's worrying you?

Stewle offered DS John Baker whiskey or wine.
"No thanks. On duty."
Stewle nodded.
"Of course. Coffee then, or tea, perhaps?"
"Coffee would be fine, please."
Stewle made the coffee order to his Receptionist.
Baker cleared his throat.
"As you know, we have arrested a certain Danny Bentley, on suspicion of the murder of Elizabeth Holmes. Her body was found in one of your landfill sites, Sagittarius End."
"Yes. And?"
"I need his employment details, and, more impotantly, any observations you might have regarding him."

"Okay. I don't think I know anything about him, except he was once suspected of being a party to a theft from the site of some copper wire, but he had witnesses to prove he was elsewhere at the time of the theft. I'll get Jones, the site foreman, to get that to you. He knows him far better than me. Do you need it immediately?"
"Thing is, I'd rather not get it from your man Jones. He obviously has an intense dislike of Bentley and I need something of a more impartial nature to help build up the case."
"I see. Mmm in that case……"
Baker's mobile phone rang.
"Sorry."
He answered it and listened.
His face lost its colour.
"Right. Yes sir. Straight away."
Baker swallowed hard as he put his phone back into his raincoat pocket.
He looked up at Stewle's inquisitive face.
"Something's come up concerning the case. I need to get back to Wymondham."
Baker stood up, extended his hand.
They shook hands.
Baker hurriedly departed.

TWENTY

Milly was sitting in her favourite armchair knitting a scarf for Ham.

Myriam had just lit a fire and was watching it take.

"Do you want to come, or not? I need to know now, really. Ham has to pay for the tickets today, or tomorrow at the latest."

Myriam looked cross.

Milly Bradstock closed her eyes.

"It's just that you'll all be youngsters and I'm not."

"It's a party Mum, not an age thing."

Milly sighed, then shook her head.

"No, Myriam. Thanks for askin' me, but I'm happy here, watchin' telly."

"Okay."
The front door opened and closed.
Ham came in. Happy. smiling.
"Evenin' all."
He looked at Milly then at Myriam.
Frowned.
"What's up?"
"Mum doesn't want to come to that works party of yours."
"Oh, that's alright."
Relieved if truth be known.
"Not your thing eh, Mrs B?"
Milly smiled. Grateful.
"Exactly."
"Well, I've got some good news," said Ham.
"What?" said Myriam.
"They're making all the people at work take another DNA test. Danny's been freed."
Myriam wide eyed.
"How lovely is that? You said he couldn't have done it from the word go."
Milly stood up.
"I'm going to make a cuppa. Don't tell us any more 'til I get back."
Ham nodded, smiled.
"Okay, don't forget biscuits."

Tears spilled down Sylvia Skipmore's cheeks.

Vee Bentley sat beside her. Stunned. Her eyes dark and dull from lack of sleep and worry.
"Knew it couldn't be 'im. Never," said Sylvia haltingly.
She had her arm around Vee's shoulders.
Steve looked from Vee to his wife.
"As soon as Ollie told me, I came straight home. Jones wasn't around, and his car had gone, so I won't be missed. Don't give a shit if I am. This is more important than bloody work," said Steve.
"It was Ollie who told me," said Vee quietly. She sighed.
"Danny must have given him my number. I never thanked him. Just never thought of it. Been a nightmare, just want him home."
Holly sat on a side chair looking fearfully at her mother. She knew something bad had happened but knew nothing of the details except that her Daddy was in a prison.
"I reckon he'll be here soon. Ollie said he had an immediate release, and that were an hour ago." said Steve.
As he spoke the front door opened.
Holly ran from the lounge shouting.
"Daddy! Daddy!"
They all stood up.
Danny came in, Holly in his arms.
Vee almost fell against him.

He clasped his two women to his body.
Tears, lots of them.

Steve refilled the wine glasses.
They all looked at Danny.
He sat by Vee and Holly, holding their hands.
"Ollie did it all. Hired Maynard the lawyer. And paid him. Don't know how much, but he's a top geezer and I reckon he were expensive. Ollie picked me up from Wymondham and dropped me 'ere. Wouldn't take no money. Wouldn't come in. Said he 'ad to meet 'is girlfriend."
"So, what happened then?"
Danny was silent for a moment, collecting his thoughts.
"Well, after I'd seen Maynard. The coppers came and took me into a room. Maynard was there, so were some bloke in a suit. He said he wanted another DNA swab."
Danny leant forward and picked up his wine glass. Sipped it. Licked his lips.
"He took a swab off me. Then they took me back to the cell. About two hours later a copper came, unlocked the cell, an' told me I were free to go, the charge was dropped."
Steve shook his head.
"Bloody 'ell! Must 'ave been a friggin' nightmare 'til then."
Danny agreed.

"It were. You get to the state where you think everyone and everything's against you an' that you 'ave no friends. You imagine all sorts of shit to be honest. The second DNA swab proved it weren't me. Maynard offered to drive me home, but Ollie was there too, so I came home with 'im."

"Why didn't you bring 'im in?" said Vee.

"As I said, he had to meet 'is girlfriend, somewhere."

Vee looked up at Danny. Kissed the back of his hand.

"Did they say what happened? You know, to get it all so wrong."

The copper's apologised. Maynard explained that the DNA must have got mixed up or somethin'. The swabs weren't taken in a proper *manner,* whatever that is, apparently."

"Useless. Could've ruined your bloody life, man," said Steve.

He raised his wine glass.

"Anyway. Here's to getting there in the end."

"Hear, hear. Works party on Friday. We get our little business started then," said Danny.

They all raised their glasses again. Holly raised her lemonade.

Ollie sat on a wooden chair in Reception at the Police Station in Wymondham. Roland Maynard sat on another.

Maynard shuffled his bottom on the chair and grimaced.

"They've had these blasted chairs since the year dot."

Ollie smiled.

"Thanks for doing this," said Ollie.

Maynard held his hands up.

"No need to thank me. Just doing my job. The boss here tells me the DNA's for the others will have to be taken again. This time, in a police, properly controlled, environment."

Ollie nodded.

"Yes. I must admit the DNA taking last time was a bit shambolic, in Jone's office."

Maynard smiled.

"Yes. I know."

"Will you send me your bill?"

Maynard shrugged.

"Yep. It won't be much. Hardly anything for me to do. Police method was so sloppy, made my job easy. You and Danny gave me the ammunition, I just fired the bullets. At least we know it definitely wasn't young Danny who murdered the girl."

Just as he said this the corridor door was unlocked, then opened. Danny came out. A relieved sad smile on his face.

Doreen Jones sat watching the television. A rolled up cigarette dangled from her lips. She sucked on it. Nothing. 'Bloody roll ups. Go out every bleeding two seconds. When I'm rich I'm only goin' to smoke ready mades in a packet.'
She wondered what the hell could be wrong with *him*.
He'd come home early. Cursing and swearing. Straight into the kitchen. Drank her whole bottle of sherry, nearly.
She'd gone into the kitchen. He was sitting drinking from the bottle.
"Wha's the matter? Did you's get the sack or summit?"
He looked up at her. His eyes wild, angry, frowning, frightened. His face was usually pale but today it was flushed at the cheeks.
"They let that bastard Bentley off."
"Bentley, who's Bentley?"
"Danny friggin' Bentley. The one they 'ad for that tart what them's found."
Doreen relit her cigarette with the gas lighter for the stove.
"I thought 'e murdered 'er?"

Jones drained the bottle. Slammed the bottle down on the table.

"He did. Now they'll blame me. Twats!"

Doreen blew out the smoke.

"Why would them blame you? You never done it, did you?"

He shouted at her, his eyes blazing, spittle flying from his lips.

"Fuggers! Course friggin' not. But they've got to pin it on someone."

He opened the refrigerator and took out a can of strong cider.

"They 'as it in for me. You wait and see. Bastards!"

"You never *done* anything, so you's ain't got nothin' to worry about, 'as you?"

He sat down and took a long draught of the cider.

His eyes were red. He had a haunted look.

She looked down at him. *Her* eyes widened.

"Bernie. You's didn't do nothing to that prossie, did you's?"

He took another swig from the can.

"Don't matter. They'll say I did. All of 'em, got it fuggin' in for me. I know them 'as."

Doreen licked her lips. Worried.

Something was dawning on her.

"When you's came 'ome the other night you's had scratches on yer face. You's said it were cos you fell in a bush, tripped over you's said."
Jones said nothing. His eyes were downcast.
"It weren't no bush was it?"
She looked at him. Her eyes narrowed.
"It were *'er* what scratched you, weren't it?"
He looked up at her.
Pleading.
"No. Listen Look. She was breakin' into the stores, that's what it were. Breakin' in she was. I tried to stop 'er running. She scratched me an' I belted her. She fell over and banged 'er 'ead on the table. Tha's what must 'ave killed 'er. Weren't me, it were the friggin' table. I...."
Doreen slapped his head. Hard.
"You fuggin' shit! You is a fuggin' *liar* you is. You *killed* 'er. It said she were raped an' *you* done that as well. Stuck it in 'er arse you did too. I knows it were you what did that to 'er now, you's always lately asking me to let you do that. Paper's say she were 'abused' but I know's what that means! You fuggin' pervert!"
She hit him again.
"Bastard!"
He started to cry.
She slapped his head.
"No use you fuggin' cryin'. You 'as *ruined* us, you 'as. Me an' the kid, *ruined* we is."

TWENTY-ONE

Ollie, Steve, and Ham were helping the landlord of The Baston Inn to set up for the party that evening. Nobody had seen Jones yesterday, or that day, so the three skived off early.

"I never saw 'im yesterday neither, nor the day before, with a bit of luck he's too ill to come to work for six months, by that time we'll all have different, better, jobs," said Steve.

Ham laughed.

"No, you wouldn't have seen him. Not at Molbury. Jammy git."

"Gets a bit lonely there, though, not all a bunch of roses, mate," said Steve, feigning sorrow.

Ham pulled a face.

"Oh, you poor, poor soul. Tell you what I'll do. I'll swap you Molbury for my pleasant-smelling shit hole section, how's that? You can start on Monday."

Steve looked at the ceiling as if mulling over the suggestion.

"Thanks anyway. Don't think I'll bother. Don't want your missus to have a go at me. She must love the smell of your work clothes by now."

Ollie butted in.

"His dinner is *always* ready and, on the table, when he gets home on account she can smell him before he hits Swaffham."

They bantered away until they had finished off the tables.

Decorative Christmassy tablecloths, red candles encased in small glass containers, cutlery, wine and water glasses plus Steve and Danny's wine. They had decided on three bottles per table. Two red, one white. Their own labels on the bottles. Crackers finished the tables off.

"Thanks for the assist boys. Let me get you a pint for all your help," said Landlord John Spence.

After John had pulled the pints they sat in one of the alcoves.

"Well done, again. For helpin' Danny, Ollie," said Steve.

Ollie shrugged.

"Didn't do much. Maynard did his job quickly. I think we all knew Danny couldn't have done such a thing," said Ollie.
"Wonder who *did* do it?" said Ham.
"She were dumped by someone who didn't work there I reckons. No person with all 'is marbles would get rid of her on his works premises, surely?" said Steve.
"Poor woman," said Ollie.
Ham and Steve nodded.

An hour later Ollie arrived home.
Annabel had let herself in and, after letting Bess into the back garden, made a couple of small sandwiches.
They embraced, kissed and one thing was leading to another when Annabel pushed him away.
"Down boy. Time to eat. It's only a tiny snack as we're off out in an hour or so, but I bet you haven't eaten for hours."
Ollie smiled at her.
"Right you are. I need to shower, too."
"I brought my party frock, it's in the car."
After he had showered Ollie looked through his mail.
A bill from Maynard. £150. He was very pleased with that.
Later they sat watching the news on television.

On Look East, the presenter merely said that the man held on suspicion of murder with regards Elizabeth Holmes had been released without charge.

Ollie told her how Maynard had wasted no time in destroying the police case. He didn't mention that he was footing the bill from Maynard. He *had* savings, he felt sure Danny didn't.

Ollie got up from the table and kissed Annabel on the forehead.

"Two things to do before we set off. First is to make sure Bess has a piddle."

He opened the back door and Bess hurried out.

"I'm pretty much ready, whenever you are," said Annabel.

He sat down and faced her.

She thought how handsome he looked. Lovely hair, lovely eyes, lovely man.

He took her hand in his.

"Annabel. I know we've only known each other for a short time, but I think we've got to know each other…sort of…um…fairly well. I've become fond of you, well not just fond, but….um…well, *really* fond is what I mean and I, well….."

He got down off the chair and onto one knee. His face was scarlet. It matched hers.

"Thing is…well…".
He fumbled in his jacket.
Annabel's eyes were brimming.
Ollie took a small box from his pocket and opened it. The ring had a large diamond in the middle and three smaller diamonds leading off either side.
"I was wondering if…well…would you…um…will you…er…marry me? I know I haven't got a good job at the mo…."
She shot off her chair and pushed him backwards to the floor.
"I thought you'd never ask!" she blurted out.
She kissed him where he lay as the tears of joy rolled down her cheeks.

"I *told* you it was debatable, and now the CPS think we are bloody clowns!" said Chief Inspector Roberts.
"Well sir, I can explain, you see….," said Detective Sergeant Baker.
"No, you *can't* explain. That's the bloody problem. How did your coppers and the forensic people, under *your* control, allow such a circus to take place? The CPS will pick us up on every trivial little thing from now on."
"I believe it became a bit of a muddle when the tea lady brought in drinks and……"

"Ye Gods and little cod fishes! Your bloody excuses get more and more bloody lame! Blaming it on a bloody tea lady! I have now had to authorise a forensic team from *Suffolk* to go to Sagittarius End to conduct the DNA collection next Tuesday, as I can't trust your lot to do it right and I need to show that we're clear, clean and above board with our investigations. Now get out of my sight and type up a bloody report as to where you are with your investigation of this woman's murder."

"Yes sir."

Baker left.

Tail between his legs. Angry. Worried. Humiliated.

Truth be known, his investigation was going absolutely *nowhere*. After Bentley's DNA showed he was not the killer, he had nothing.

He spoke to the Suffolk Forensic department chief and got his instructions on how the room should be set up for the DNA sample taking on Tuesday.

After the call he drove to Sagittarius End.

Needed to detail with that prick Jones how he wanted the room to be arranged for next Tuesday. Couldn't get the bastard on the phone and that silly woman in their admin office said she hadn't seen him for a couple of

days. There must be no hiccups this time. How the hell they got it wrong last time was beyond him. Although it was a bit of a circus when that old fart had brought in the teas and biscuits.
Beryl Anstey gave him the keys to Jones' office.
He spent the next two hours positioning everything so that it was as per the Suffolk Forensic boss' instructions.
He went over the lay out three times to make sure everything was as it should be.
He returned the keys and told Beryl that nobody should alter the lay out of the rooms. Beryl told him she was so glad Danny was cleared.
"Well, he ain't exactly cleared yet," said Baker gruffly.
"Well, it said on the radio this morning he was."
"Yes. Well. We'll see."
Beryl watched him drive off.
'Tosser'.
Nigel Infine came down one of the inclines.
She watched him approach.
'Wonder what this wretch wants?'
"Hello Beryl."
He smiled at her.
She stood. Stonefaced.
He went past her towards Jone's office.
Stuck up bitch.

"You's can't go in there. Jones ain't 'ere, anyway."

He turned.

"Who says? I need another battery. This one's fucked."

"The copper's say. All set up for Tuesday."

Infine frowned.

"Coppers? Tuesday? Wa's 'appenin' Tuesday?"

His face had paled.

"I thought *everyone* knew. We're all gettin' our DNA doing again. Was screwed up last time. Made a mistake. Thought it were Danny. It weren't 'im," said Beryl.

"But it *were* Danny. Him was arrested an' everythin'."

"No. Not Danny. Someone else."

He almost burst into tears. His bottom lip quivered.

Beryl shrugged.

"Anyways, you can't go in Jones' office. Copper says."

"Where *is* Mr Jones? I got to 'ave a battery, I 'as. Can't do me job otherwise."

"Dunno. Don't care. He's a prick. Ain't been here for two days. Maybe him's sick."

Infine spat on the ground.

"Give us the key, Beryl. I got to get me another battery. Won't touch nothing, I promise."

Beryl thought for a moment, then turned.
"I'll get the key, but I'm coming with you's."
"Righto," said Infine.
'Maybe she wants me to bang 'er on Jone's desk. She looks as if she is dyin' for it.'
A couple of minutes later Beryl reappeared. Keys in hand.
"I'll let you's in, but don't touch nothin'," said Beryl as she walked past him towards Jone's office.
She unlocked the door and walked inside.
"Don't touch nothing. Just get another battery and bugger off. Shouldn't be in 'ere really. Coppers said."
The chairs were all laid out in two rows, with their backs to the front. Two large stands stood behind them, screening off the front of the room.
Infine looked at the set up.
"What time 'as we got to be 'ere for the DAN thing?"
Beryl gave him a withering look.
"*DNA*. DNA not *DAN*. Ten o'clock sharp, the copper said."
He placed his battery in a charging point and picked up another from one of the charged portals.
"I never 'ad mine done last time."
Beryl looked surprised.

"Why not?"
"Jones sent me to do a job in Norwich."
"Well, you're getting' it done this time. Everyone is, includin' me."
He walked back up the incline.
'If they made a mistake last time, they could make a mistake this time. Make it out to be me. I 'spect them 'as me fingerprints from 'er place. *Fuck!* Ain't fair. I knows I didn't kill 'er. I shagged 'er yes, but never killed 'er. Wouldn't do that, *never*."
He checked a few of his site points. Some were heating up quite a bit. They'd been doing that a lot lately. He turned them down. Jones wasn't there. He was his own boss today.
Infine sat down after a while and pondered Tuesday.
Dreaded it.
They just better not make no friggin' mistakes.
He thought his best plan was to tell the head copper that he knew Rosie. She was a prossie, and he had used her a few times, but he never hurt her. No. He would never have done that. He liked her, she was young. Young like a school girl is. He had never done nothing to any school girls. Wanted to, but never had. Course, he wouldn't tell no coppers that. They just better not get his DAN wrong. They could

take as much blood as they liked, as long as they got it right.

"Annabel *Wilson*. Has a certain ring to it, don't you think?" said Annabel.
Ollie smiled as he drove his car out of Attleborough.
"I wasn't *serious* you know. Got that ring out of a cracker last Christmas, been keeping it for a special occasion, for a laugh."
She elbowed him.
"You bugger!"
Annabel slipped the ring off her finger, wound down the window and made as if to throw something out.
"Whoa!"
He braked.
"Only joking."
She laughed and held up the ring.
"Fooled ya!"
They both smiled.
"We have a fair bit to discuss, don't we?"
He looked briefly across at her.
"Planning? You mean?"
"Yup. Where? When? How many guests? Who to invite? Honeymoon? Just to mention a few."
He nodded.
"I was thinking a ferry crossing to Zerbrugge and getting the head steward in the bar to do

it. Give him a tenner and drink a pint of duty free each. Come back the same day."
She put her hand on his thigh. Squeezed.
"Have you got Scottish blood?"
They pulled into Myriam's drive.
Their plan was to get a taxi home after the party and pick the car up on Sunday.
Myriam met them at the front door. Ham was behind her.
After all the greetings were completed Myriam guided them into the lounge. Milly gave Annabel a big hug and shook hands with Ollie.
"He's better lookin' than you said, Myriam," said Milly.
"Mother! You're embarrassing the poor man."
Ollie laughed.
"No, I love it," said Ollie.
Annabel pointed a finger at Milly.
"I can see I'll have to watch him with you around, Madam."
They all sat down in the comfortable lounge.
"You did well to get Danny off, Ollie," said Myriam.
"Wasn't me. It was his lawyer," said Ollie.
Annabel kept adjusting the high collar of her dress. Always with her left hand.
Myriam shouted.
"Annabel!"
"What?" said Annabel sweetly.

Ollie was aware. He smiled. Broadly.
"What is it? Am I missing something here?" said Ham.
"The ring! Is that what I think it is?" said Myriam.
Annabel grinned.
"I found it in the playground this morning. It's only paste and plastic."
Myriam came across and took Annabel's hand. Peered closely at the ring.
"How beautiful. Lovely. Are you two engaged or what?"
Ollie shrugged.
"S'pose so. She said she'd beat me if I said 'no'."
Congratulations all round.
Hugs, kisses, shaking hands.
Milly kissed Ollie.
"Goody, goody. I can have a new hat now."
Ham shook his hand.
"I've never been a best man, just in case you're short."
Ollie smiled.
"No experience then. Mmm……maybe I'll ask Jonesy."

"You's can't just sit there all friggin' day. You got to go to work, see what's 'appenin'. You

don't go to work they'll think its suspicious like."
Jones. Hungover.
Looked up morosely at his wife.
She pointed at his mobile phone which was laying on the table.
"Your phone's been goin' off all mornin'. I looked at it a couple of times. Your boss Strewn-whatever-it is fuggin' called once an' that silly tart Anstet, whatever 'er name is, called twice. Another call twice came up as DS Bakery, whoever him is."
"Fuck! Him's a copper," said Jones.
He bit his lip.
She shook her head and went into the lounge.
Her fingers trembled a little as she rolled a cigarette.
'We is in shit street now an' no mistake. Him'll go to prison all 'is life, me an' the boy will be poor as them poor people what I seen on the telly. Livin' in a friggin' shop doorway. Can't pay the mortgage. No money, no 'ouse, no bugger all.'
She lit her cigarette.
She heard him talking to someone and listened at the door.
"Yes Mr Stewle. I've been proper poorly. Flu', but I'm going in lunchtime."
Stewle drank some of his coffee.

"I should think so too. I *shall* be at your Christmas shin dig in The Baston Inn. Shan't stay more than ten minutes, just showing my face. I have to be in Birmingham for a meeting for the next day, early."
"Righto Mr Stewle Sir, Look for…."
The phone clicked. Purring noise.
"Fuggin' bastard. He *always* does that! How the 'ell do he know about the Christmas piss up. I never told 'im.'
Doreen came in.
"Who were that on the phone?"
"Stewle."
"What did him want?"
"Just to tell me 'e's comin' to the Christmas thing in Swaffham."
She sucked in a lung full of smoke.
"Did 'e say anythin' about that tart?"
Jones shook his head.
"Nah. Nothin'."
She almost smiled. Her eyes brightened.
"Well, that's *good,* ennit? It means that the coppers ain't said nothin', so maybe you'll get away with it."
He finished off the can of strong cider.
"Got to give DNA on Tuesday."
"Wha's that mean? What is it?"
"The rossers put a stick thing in your gob."
"So?"

"Them can tell if you's is the one, or not. Them's match it with somethin' else. S'all something scientific. It ain't *never* wrong."
"Bugger."
She went to the fridge. Took one of his cans of strong cider.
It hissed as she pulled the ring on the top.
"If I'd known this lot were goin' to 'appen. I'd 'ave let you's stick it up me jacksie."
She swigged from the can.
He looked up at her.
"We could do it now if you's want?"
She pulled a face. Disgust. Pathetic.
"Don't be a numpty. Too late now you bloody moron. We is in big trouble now. Or rather *you* is. I reckon they put you's in nick for life, for what you 'as done."
"I told you, she were *thievin'*. It were an accident. Anyway, Infine told me you could do anythin' to her, anythin'," said Jones morosely.
"How would he know?" said Doreen.
"He's done 'er every way. He likes a woman takin' it in 'er arse, he told me. Paid 'er he did, a lot of times."
Doreen shook her head.
"Fuggin' idiot! Fuggin' liar! If you's want to get off this, you's need to act normal. Go to work, an' we'll need to go to that Christmas party

shite at Swaffham all 'appy as if we 'asn't got no cares in the fuggin' world."
Jones looked at his watch.
"Bit late now."
She slapped his head.
"Don't keep *doin'* that!"
She stood over him. Threatening.
"I will keep doin' it if you don't get off your bleeding arse, an' go to work!"

TWENTY-TWO

Danny needed his monitor.
It was in Jones office complex.
The door was locked.
He walked over to the Admin office.
Beryl looked up as he entered.
Her face beamed.
She got up and went to him.
"Gonna dance all night tonight wiv you, I am."
He shook his head and held her at arm's length.
"What's the matter, Danny?"
Danny grimaced.
Beryl looked apprehensive.
"It's like this Beryl…um, well, I'm married. I've got a kiddie, and…well…I need to stay married…so I don't think we should carry on as we are."
Tears appeared instantly.
"Oh Danny. I thought we were both *special* to each other."

She tried to put her head on his chest. He held her away.
They looked straight into each other's eyes.
"If I wasn't married, things would be different. I don't want to hurt you, I really don't, but I don't want to risk my marriage."
Beryl bit her lip as tears ran down her cheeks. She gave a big sigh.
"We could still be together Danny. Your wife don't need to know. We could keep goin' as we are."
Danny shook his head.
"No. It wouldn't be right. It's got to end now. Sorry."
She tried to pull him to her.
But he kept her at arm's length.
"Oh Danny. Just do it to me one more time then, just once."
"No."
"I've got the table all ready, blanket on it."
He turned away and took Jone's office key off the key board hook.
"I need to get a monitor."
Beryl sat down and started sobbing. Her head was in her hands.
Danny turned at the door.
"Sorry Beryl. You're a lovely woman, but not for me. Sorry."
He left the office and went to Jone's office.

He felt like Judas.
After entering he noticed the changes, he guessed it was set up for Tuesday.
When Danny returned to the Admin office, Beryl sat staring at her computer, her face a vision of sadness. Her eyes already red.
He hung up Jone's office key and turned as he got to the door.
"Sorry Beryl, I really am. Bye."
He left the office and closed the door.
Beryl, abject misery on her face, tears flowing, threw her pen at the door.

Ollie, Ham, Myriam and Annabel boarded the taxi.
Ham had given Milly a bottle of the red wine that Danny had given him. Insurance.
He wanted her to be well and truly in the 'land of nod' when they returned.
Too cold to go to the shed in the early hours this time of the year.
In the Baston Inn the party was in full swing.
Loud. Music. People talking, shouting. Laughter.
Steve and Danny's wine was working it's magic.
A few cheers as the four walked in.
After seating the ladies Ham and Ollie went to the bar.

"Danny's not here yet," said Ham.
Ollie scanned the room.
"Early yet."
Wally Bishop, the new man, brought in to replace Jim Mortimer came across and introduced himself.
"I needed a job but didn't really want one under the circumstances of it all," said Wally.
"Not your fault. Welcome. We all used to meet up at Alex's café at lunchtime, but Jones' wife took over after Alex died and she wasn't much good at it. The café folded after a couple of weeks, so no chance to meet co-workers now," said Ham.
Wally smiled.
"Thing is, I went and saw Jim in hospital, he's due out next week. I've been a few times now. Apparently, I just missed you Ollie on your last visit, t'other night. He told me about the funeral and how you guys helped him," said Wally.
Ollie liked him.
He had a shock of blonde hair and stood six feet plus. Looked like he could handle himself. His face was rugged. He'd seen trouble in the past.
"I said I'd help him get back into the swing of things when he came out. He'll be kind of disabled for a while. He gave me the keys to 'is flat so I'll spruce it up, get some groceries

in, that sort of thing. When I went to see 'im yesterday. Alex's Mum was there."

"Oh, that's great. *So* pleased to hear that," said Ollie.

"Have you got a table, Wally? There's room at ours," said Ham.

"No. I'm fine. Sitting with Bill Dunne and the other digger driver. Mad as hatters, the pair of them."

They chatted for a few minutes then excused themselves to take the drinks to their table.

Ham nudged Ollie.

"See Emperor Jones over yonder with the café princess and Mr Personality Plus."

Ollie looked across the room and, in an alcove, sat Jones, Doreen and Nigel Infine.

Sullen, unspeaking. Looking.

"Not much talking or Christmas spirit in *that* neck of the woods," observed Ollie.

"Husband to be, don't be so *catty*," said Annabel.

"Yes," said Myriam, "Leave that to us, the *experts*."

"Was you sick then?" said Infine.

Doreen looked at her husband and replied quickly.

"Yeah. Him was. Flu."

Jones wore a grey suit and a light blue shirt. No tie.

Infine wore black trousers and a matching zip up cardigan.

He had arrived after the Jones', and stood admiring Doreen's low cut, red dress before Jones told him to sit down.

Doreen was glad he looked excited at her cleavage.

She took out a roll up cigarette from a small tin she kept in her tiny carry bag and leaned forward towards Infine.

"Has you got a light, Nigel?"

Nigel's face was aflame.

"No, but I'm goin' to get a drink so I'll bring matches back. Wanna drink Mr Jones, and you, Doreen?"

They gave him their order and he hurried to the bar.

'Fuck! 'er is hot lookin'. Weren't like that in the café, *never*. Never made up and she always wore a scruffy old overall."

He took the drinks back and lit Doreen's cigarette with a match taken out of the free book he'd lifted from the bar counter.

She took a while to ignite the cigarette to give him a good look at her bosoms again as she lit up, then squeezed his leg.

"Thank's Nigel."

The landlord strolled over.
"Sorry, but you can't smoke in 'ere lady. There's a covered bit outside for smokers."
Doreen frowned and nipped the end off of the cigarette.
Jones was oblivious. His worried eyes scanned the room.
"Stewle is coming. Gotta keep an eye out for the bastard."
A female singer joined the band and started to sing Adele songs.
A few couples got up to dance, Ollie and Annabel were amongst them.
Infine, Doreen and Jones drank their free bottles of wine quickly.
Jones and Doreen had poured theirs into half pint mugs.
When the wine was done, Jones went to the bar for more alcohol.
"Bernard tells me you's knew that tart what got killed," said Doreen.
Infine jumped. His face paled.
"Weren't me what done 'er in!"
Doreen squeezed his leg, this time higher up.
"Nigel, don't get so *touchy*. I never said you's did."
Infine sighed.
He liked her hand on him.

"Bernard tells me you's told 'im she liked it in different places."
Infine gulped.
"Well. I… thing is…"
She squeezed his leg again.
"Don't worry, shan't say nothin'. I'm a bit like that meself. Can't beat a bit of variety, can you's?"
His face reddened.
'She were a hot fugger, an' no mistake.'
Doreen removed her hand as Jones returned with their drinks.
They drank quickly and Infine got refills.
As he sat down Doreen started singing along with the lady singer.
"Shut up you daft cow! People is starin', you can't fuggin' sing, you dopey bitch!"
Doreen looked angrily at her husband.
She stood up.
"C'mon Nigel, let's 'ave a dance."
Infine swallowed hard.
"Well…I ain't a lotta cop at the old dancin' lark…"
She grabbed him and pulled him out of his seat.
"Come *on!* I'll lead you's."
He followed her lamely to join the other dancers.
She pulled him close.

"I'll just move you's around with the music," she said.

She manoeuvred him into the middle of the people dancing.

"You is a good dancer you is, Nigel. You's got good rhythm you 'as."

She pressed herself into him.

He pushed his pelvis back against her.

"Do that feel nice, Nigel?"

He swallowed hard.

"Yeah. It feels lovely. Wish I were Jonesy."

They danced close for another few moments and she gyrated against him.

The song came to an end.

She led the walk back to the table.

Jones was at the bar talking to Stewle.

"Whiskey for me," said Stewle.

"Right you are, sir."

When they had been served, Jones asked Stewle if there was any chance of a move to another site, maybe up north.

"Why would you want to move? You're at a good site, be there for years."

"Just fancy a move sir."

Stewle looked around the hall.

"Nothing available yet. If there is I'll think about it."

Jones nodded.

"Don't s'pose there's somewhere I could fill in, say next week or that."
Stewle frowned.
"Next week? Why on earth would you want a move that quick? Police not after you are they, or is it girlfriend trouble?"
"No. No, nothin' like that. Just fancied a quick move is all."
Stewle drained his whiskey.
"Right. You'd better take me round to say hello to the troops and their ladies."
Doreen and Infine sat down after their dance.
She looked at him, a slight smile on her face.
"If Bernard ever leaves, I think that you might want to take care of me. Would you like that?"
Nigel was nervous. Excited. Confused.
"Well, yeah. But he ain't going to leave you's is 'e?"
Doreen ran her hand gently up the inside of his leg and left it so he could feel it.
"He might, soon. I might need a man to look after me. Give it to me the way I like. Would you like to be my man if Bernard ain't around? Do whatever you's like to me? Would you like that, Nigel?"
He looked at her cleavage, felt her hand by his groin.
His face was now aflamed.
"Shit, yes! I would, Doreen. Love that I would."

They saw Jones walking around the hall, introducing Stewle.

Jones was fawning, grinning inanely at some of the workers who hated him.

They finished the circuit and Jones escorted Stewle to the door.

"I haven't had Thursday or today's figures. Why?"

"Not 'ad them? It's that silly girl Ansley, sir. I'll go in tomorrow an' make sure you 'as them, sir. No mistake. Sir."

"Make sure you do."

"Goodnight Sir. Thank you for coming."

"By the way, Bentley started back today. I told him personally he could."

Jones, although shocked, put out his hand.

Stewle ignored it and walked out into the darkness to his car where his wife was waiting.

Jones watched him go.

'Wish I 'ad a fuggin' gun, I'd blow his fuggin' brains in, I would. Bastard! Fuggin' Bentley, wish 'e'd died in the nick. Now I 'as to fuggin' get done for it.'

Jones trudged back to Doreen and Infine.

He slumped down into his seat. Disconsolate. Beaten.

Doreen looked at him, questions on her mind.

Jones shrugged.

"Bastard never said *nothin'*, 'cept about fuggin' Bentley startin' back."
A huge cheer went up. They looked around.
As if on cue. Danny and Vee came in.
They walked hand in hand to Steve and Sylvia's table which was next to Ollie's.
Danny waved to the cheerers. They all started to applaud, with the notable exception of Jone's table.
Ollie stood up and Sylvia hugged him.
"Thanks Ollie."
Annabel sat observing.
When Ollie sat down Annabel leant across to him.
"Why did she say 'thanks'?"
Ham butted in.
"Cos, he supplied the lawyer who got Danny off. The DNA was wrong."
Annabel turned to Ollie.
"Did you? You really are Mister Nice Marvel man. I'm glad I picked you to keep me in luxury."
Ollie laughed and squeezed her hand.
"I knew it couldn't have been him."
The night wore on and the laughter continued. Helped by Danny and Steve's homemade wine.
Jones and Infine sank pint after pint of the strong cider interspersed with glasses of wine.

Doreen got Infine up to dance a number of times and they continued their close liaison.
Just after midnight Jones told his wife it was time to go.
Infine tottered with them to their car.
"Goodnight Mr Jones."
Jones nodded and got into his car. Grumpy.
Doreen kissed Infine. It was a brief kiss, unseen by Jones who revved the car engine. She put her tongue in his month and ran her hand over him.
"G'night Nigel."
He stood excited as she got into the car and the pair drove off into the night.
"Fuggin' 'ell!"
He lurched back to the party.
'Wonder if that Beryl bitch is randy.'
He made a beeline for the bar and bought a cider.
Ham stood nearby waiting for his order to be filled.
"'lo Ham, hows you goin'?"
"Fine thank you Nigel. What about you?"
Infine swayed towards him and half whispered into his ear.
"Gonna fuck that bitch Anstey in a minute."
Ham took a step back.
"Does she know yet?"

Infine's eyes got heavier, and his speech more and more slurred.

"Dunno. Can't see her."

Ham nodded.

"That's because she's not here. She never came."

"Oh, fuggin' 'ell, what a shiters bitch she is and all."

Ham put his hand on Infine's shoulder.

"If I were you Nigel, I'd get myself home. It's nearly closing time anyway. Do you want me to call a cab for you?"

Infine shook his head.

"Nah. Fuggit. Gonna walk."

"But Nigel, you live in Wymondham, don't you?"

"Yah. Fuggit."

He took a large slurp of a half-filled glass of beer that lay on the bar. Who it belonged to, he neither knew nor cared.

"You're best getting a cab, mate."

Ham left him and carried his tray of drinks back to the table.

"Infine is rat-arsed," said Ham.

Ollie looked around. Nigel was still standing at the bar but not too steady on his feet.

"He should go home," said Ollie.

The four watched him as he swayed.

Bill Dunne came to the bar with two glasses in his hand.

He nodded to Nigel, placed the glasses down and ordered.

Nigel staggered and fell against him.

"Watch out laddie! You've had too much."

"Fugg off!"

Bill took a step back, grabbed Infine by the scruff of his neck and half lifted, half pushed him across the bar to the entrance.

Outside three taxis sat waiting for fares.

Bill knew the lead taxi driver.

"Evenin' Horace. Do you mind takin' this idiot home. He's 'ad too much."

"Long as 'e don't honk up in the back of my cab, Bill."

"He'll bloody pay if 'e do."

"In more ways than one, he will."

Bill opened the rear door and pushed Nigel in.

Nigel sat slumped and muttering incoherently.

"He lives in Wymondham, mate. Near the British Legion."

Bill leaned into the cab. His mouth close to Infine's ear.

"If you're sick in this cab pal, this driver will muller you. Understand?"

Nigel, half asleep, nodded.

Bill slammed the door.

The taxi drove off.

In the Baston Inn the band played on, and as midnight approached the music slowed.
It didn't stop all the loud laughter, but some danced close to their partners in time to love songs.
"Well, HTB, I've had a lovely evening. Made a bit of money as well as enjoying good nosh and wine for free."
Ollie looked perplexed.
"HTB? What's HTB when it's at home."
"Work it out, lead head."
He looked into Annabel's eyes.
She was lovely. His heart welled up.
Then he frowned.
"What d'you mean, you've made some money."
"Not exactly *today*, but as soon as I get to the pawnbrokers and flog this ring I'll be minted."
Ollie laughed.
"Since my grandpa got it out of a cracker many years ago, you might get a bob or two as a sort of novelty antique. Anyway, what's HTB?"

Doreen closed the front door.
She heard a tell-tale hiss from the kitchen.
Jones came into the lounge, a can of strong cider in his hand.
"Jesus! Ain't you's 'ad enough tonight?"

"Nope. My fuggin' life ennit? What do you's care?"

He slumped down into a chair.

"Why don't you's leave tomorra? Or the next day, before Tuesday, anyroad? Go to London or some where's. Get a job an' a house, an' then we's can start livin' again. Copper's won't know. I won't tell them or nothin'. Just say you's 'as done a runner."

He took a long draught of his cider.

"Be better goin' to Spain. In London or where ever, they'll want me National fuggin' whatsit number, afore I's can get me a job. In Spain I's don't need it."

"Well, do that then. You's can tell me when you's is set up an' I'll come over with the kid."

He emptied the can.

"Maybe. Get me another."

He handed the can to her, she went into the kitchen.

She pondered.

Either way, arrest or scarperin', she was determined to get Nigel into the house when Jones had gone, even if that meant taking it up her jacksie once or twice. Maybe he could get Jone's job.'

She knew she would need someone to pay the bills when Bernard pissed off. They were already a month behind with the mortgage.

Jones said he was going to pay it up to date with the digger money, but never did.
Maybe she could get some money from them welfare people after Jones had gone, as well.
She took the can into him.
He was asleep in the chair.
Head back, mouth open.
'Ugly bastard. No good at *nothin'*, him ain't.'
She put the can by the side of the chair and went upstairs to bed.

"Oi mate! We're 'ere!"
The driver shouted over his shoulder.
Nigel looked blearily around him.
"Where is we?"
"Wymondham, mate. British Legion."
Nigel started to get out.
"Fifty-five quid, mate."
Nigel rubbed his eyes.
"Did you's say *fifty*-five quid?"
"Yeah. That's cheap at this time a night. Cos you's know Bill is why."
Nigel blinked. He checked his wallet.
'Forty pounds.'
"I's only got forty. Sorry."
The driver got out of his cab and opened Nigel's door.
He looked down threateningly.
"Got yer bank card, mate?"

Horace accompanied Nigel to Lloyd's ATM machine a few yards away.
After payment the cabbie drove off.
Nigel cursed him before walking with a list to his flat.
As he lay on the top of his bed fully clothed, he thought of Doreen.

Ham laughed.
"It's 'husband to be' you numb nut. She said that earlier."
Ollie grinned.
The ladies came back to the table having visited the powder room.
"Right then you two hulks. Take us home," said Myriam.
They departed Swaffham in two separate taxis.
The magic potion that Ham had given Milly had been duly drunk and Myriam listened at her Mum's door to the gentle snoring.
She told Ham.
Ham licked his lips.
"Shed or bed?"
He got the right answer.

Ollie didn't have to ask any questions at his bungalow, twenty minutes later.

TWENTY-THREE

Wally Bishop helped Jim Mortimer onto his wheelchair.
Jim had earlier thanked the nurses for all their wonderful care and expertise. Doctor Ranjid was on a day off so Jim wrote him a note of grateful thanks.
The ambulance driver helped getting the wheelchair up the ramp and into the vehicle.
"You know, I never really appreciated our National Health Service until this happened. How on earth could I have coped financially as well as spiritually without its wonderful help?"
Wally patted his arm.
"Yup, and some want us to have a USA type medical Insurance system. Don't like that idea much."
Jim nodded.
"Ollie said as much at work not so long ago."
"That Ollie's a good lad."

When they arrived at Jim's apartment building, the ambulance driver and Wally made short work of getting Jim to his front door in his wheelchair.

As Wally opened the door Jim immediately saw the flowers.

The flat had been transformed by Wally into a colourful, welcoming residence.

There were flowers everywhere and the gas imitation log fire gave the room a cosy glow.

The flat was spotless.

Jim wheeled into the lounge.

"Wow! You've been busy. It's lovely. Thank you *so* much Wally."

"Shall I make you a cup of tea or coffee. Or would you prefer something stronger?"

"Coffee would be great, thanks."

"Your daily care person should pop in soon. She'll sort certain things out, but I'll make sure I do anything that she might miss."

Wally helped him from the wheelchair into an easy chair.

"Would you like the tv on?"

"Not right now thanks."

He handed Jim the tuner.

"Just in case you change your mind."

He looked around his lounge. Beautiful flowers everywhere. He thought the arrangements were stunning. It must have cost Wally a lot to buy all those.

A few minutes later Wally brought in the coffees and dainty cakes.

He made Jim sample one.

"Hmm, these are very good, Wally. What shop?"

"*I* made 'em. Used to, for me mum, before she died last year."

They sat chatting for over an hour, until Jim started flagging.

Wally made sure he was comfortable and left, with a promise to come back later to prepare a meal.

Danny and Vee cuddled up in the back of Steve's Peugeot.

"Lovely night. Our wine went down well, Steve."

Steve smiled. The only sober person in the car.

"Yeah. Not a drop left. I took eight orders, one was from the landlord."

Danny squeezed Vee's leg.

"Next year Stevie, we'll be millionaires!"

Vee snuggled up to him.

"Just make sure you don't get arrested again."

Danny whispered in her ear.

"No chance. Unless it's for loving you too much."
Vee kissed him.
Steve noticed in the rear view.
"Get a bloody room you two."
Sylvia laughed.
"Ex-cons 'ave to make up for lost times, don't they Dan?"
Danny smirked.
"Too bloody right. 'ere Steve, pull into the next layby, no one's around."
"Don't you dare, Steven Skipmore. Get us home. Old ladies like me need our creature comforts," said Vee.
"What's it like bein' an ex-con then Danny? Is it true about other inmates who've been in a while try to…you know, each other?" said Steve.
Danny was almost asleep.
"Yeah. But after a while, kissin' a bloke wiv a beard don't seem so bad."
Vee punched him on the thigh.
"Don't be disgusting Danny Bentley. You was only in for a short while, no one touched you," said Vee.
"True. Good ol' Ollie. Me mate for life, 'e is."

Bernard Jones woke up.
He peered at the clock on the mantlepiece.

Eyes felt stuck together.
Three o'clock. No sign of Doreen.
Felt sick. Hastily unlocked the back door and threw up over the pathway to the front.
Tuesday. Doomsday was on his mind. Needed a plan.
He picked the can up off of the floor. Refreshed his mouth.
After an hour and two more cans of cider, he hatched a plan.
Jones fell asleep again in the chair, where Doreen found him at eight o'clock.
Doreen had a plan too.

Jones drove slowly to the pub.
He hoped Penny and Ronan Brady would be in.
He knew they especially liked a drink on a Saturday lunch time, before placing bets. He prayed they'd be there today.
As he entered the pub, to his relief, he saw Ronan and Penny sitting in their usual places by the window in a corner of the bar reading a racing paper.
He bought a pint of beer and walked over to them.
"What's *you's* wantin'? said Penny.
God! He hated that snooty ugly Irish bitch.
Jones smiled. Friendly.

"Needs a bit of help."
Ronan sipped his cider and looked up at him.
"How much?"
"No. No. Nothing like that."
"Okay. Such as?"
"Sometime, early next week I 'as to disappear, an' I wondered if you'd 'elp me."
Penny laughed.
"What? You's wantin' us to do you's in, d'ya mean?"
Jones shook his head.
Fuggin' bitch!
"No, not that. I's need a safe haven."
There was silence for a few moments.
"Coppers after you's?" said Ronan.
Jones nodded.
"Maybe. I just don't want the bastards to see me."
"Whatcha done, boyo?" said Penny.
"Nothin'. I just don't like the way everythin' is stackin' up against me," said Jones.
Ronan sighed.
"Get to it boy. What do the coppers *suspect* you's of, then?"
"They *may* think I 'ad somethin' to do with a prossie getting killed. But I never."
Ronan looked at Penny, then back at Jones.
"Wasn't that prossie what they found on your work site, was it?"

Jones nodded, his eyes lowered.

"Weren't me. Never met the woman," he said lamely.

Penny looked angry.

"Ronan, tell this arsehole to fuck off, *right now*. We're not getting' mixed up with this *shite*."

Ronan smiled.

"You heard the lady. Now fuck off!"

Jone's face reddened. He spoke quickly.

"If they take me in, it might slip out about the digger an' that. I's wouldn't mean to say nothin', but it might just slip out, that's why I's need to disappear."

It was Ronan's turn to look angry.

"You shite-head. I ought to rip yer fuggin' head off, right this fuggin' minute."

Jones held his hands up.

"I would never *want* to say nothin'. I just need to get away is all."

Penny shook her head.

"Alright, slime-ball, where would you's like to fugg off to?"

"Well, I knows you've got a place in Spain. I wonder if you's could let me stay there, maybe? Just for a couple of weeks, 'til I sorts meself out like.""

"How will you get there? The coppers will be watchin' the airports an' ferries, if they suspect you done a murder."

Jones felt inwardly elated. Light in the tunnel.
"Nothin' can happen afore Wednesday. So, if I cleared off before then, no problem."
"Leave us alone for a few minutes. We needs to discuss this," said Penny. Angry. Venom in her voice.
Jones stood up, pint in hand.
"Right you's are. I'll be at the bar."
They waited until Jones was well away from them.
"Fuggin' murderin' bastard! He mutilated the poor wee thing," said Penny.
Ronan agreed.
"Yup. Trouble is, the gobshite is right. If he blabs to the law, they'll visit us, they might just sniff around an' find the fuggin' digger in our lean to."
Penny now looked concerned.
Silence.
Ronan took a long draught of his cider.
"I'd like to rip his fuggin' 'ead off, so I would."
Penny sighed.
"I know, but you's can't do that."
"What shall I do, then."
"Let him have the villa for a fortnight. No one will know. Phone Leonard to make sure the bastard is gone after two weeks. That's plenty of time for him to fuck off somewhere else."
Ronan thought about it. Then smiled.

Jones was watching them out of the corner of his eye.

They beckoned him over.

"Right boyo. We've decided that you *can* stay in our villa. When will you fly? I'll get my villa watcher to meet you at the airport."

Jones was almost in tears.

"Oh, thank you's both. You'll never regret it, I promise."

Ronan thought he wouldn't, but that bastard Jones would.

They lay in each other's arms in Ollie's bungalow.

"Lovely night. I laughed a lot, but then again, when I look at you, I always laugh a lot."

"Thank you, wife to be, or not, as the case may be."

They had decided earlier that they would live in Ollie's bungalow, and Annabel would rent her flat out. The honeymoon location was another matter. Ollie thought Spain or Portugal was far enough. Annabel liked Bali. They did agree on a white wedding at St Mary's in Attleborough.

Ollie thought this was a good idea as they could all just cross the road after the service and catch the number 475 bus to the burger take-away in Wymondham for the reception.

Annabel smiled. Shook her head.
"You should get a response back from the school next week regarding your ap. I just know you'll get interviewed. I gave the head a tenner."
Ollie turned and kissed her.
A long kiss, that led to other things.
At breakfast they discussed the date of their nuptials. Summer was Ollie's choice, but Annabel wanted May.
"May is *early* summer, really, isn't it?"
"You mean like January is early spring?"
My mother was a May bride, and so was my Nan."
"Wasn't a joint wedding, was it?"
Annabel almost choked on her toast.
"I spoke to my Mum and Dad about it. They said anytime, anywhere, as long as the bride was you."
"Sweeties."
After breakfast they took Bess for a walk.
She interlocked her arm in his.
"I don't think I have ever been so happy," said Annabel.
Her arm squeezed his.
"Why would that be, then?"
She smiled.
"I just saw Bess have a big poo by that front gate, and you've got the 'poo-bags."

When they arrived back, they drew cards for the wedding arrangements.
Spain won the day, in May, with a proviso that they visit for a long weekend beforehand to pick a villa or apartment that they both liked. Annabel didn't trust photographs.

Jones arrived back at home.
Cock a hoop. Things were looking brighter.
Easy to get a job, no questions asked in Spain.
Them timeshare sellers were always recruiting.
Bar work would be okay too if needs be.
English and Irish bars all over. Cash in hand.
No P60 shit.
Doreen was sitting watching television.
Cigarette on the go.
He sat down opposite her.
"I needs to get away for a bit, Dor."
She looked across at him. No light in her eyes for him.
"Where? When? What about me?"
He shuffled uncomfortably.
Face turning red. Averted her eyes.
"Well, thing is……er……I needs to clear off on me own. I'll send you's money every couple of weeks, soon as I 'as a job. When…..when…..I

'as a job an' a nice place, you's can come over."

"Over? What you's mean, *over*? Where? Where you goin'?"

He knew she'd ask him that.

"Up north. Got a mate in Newcastle. He'll put me up at the start."

"How long afore you gets me to Newcastle then?"

He was relieved, she believed him. She always was thick.

"Soon as possible. Couple of weeks max. No problem."

She relit her roll up. Blew out the smoke.

Thought for a few moments.

"As you got any money, now? Tide me over."

"A little. Fifty quid. I'll give you more afore I goes."

"As we got money in our bank?"

"Yer, course. I'll draw it out afore I goes and give it all to you's. I don't need much for meself."

He took his money wallet out and handed her fifty pounds.

She looked at the money then up at him as he stood in front of her.

"I'll need regular money to look after me an' the kid, an' pay the mortgage."

"Yeah. I know. I won't leave you's short, no way."
There was no trust, either way.
He left and drove to Kings Lynn.
After the bank he visited the travel agent and bought a one-way flight to Malaga, leaving tomorrow at seven pm.
Ronan had given him details of the address.
His man Leonard would meet him at the airport.
He phoned Ronan from a pay phone and gave him his flight details.
The car was his only problem. Until it dawned on him that he had two options. One was to just leave it at the airport. The second was to get Nigel to take it off his hands, returning it to Doreen after dropping him off at Stansted.
He drove to Sagittarius End to get Nigel's address.

Nigel looked shocked at his visitor.
"'lo Mr Jones. What's up?"
"Need a favour doing."
They discussed his request and Nigel agreed to take him to the airport.
He said he was meeting a friend there off a flight from France and would come back home with them in their car. He was taking Monday off, part of his holiday allowance.

It was returning the car back to Doreen that clinched it.

As he drove home he decided to pay a final visit to Sagittarius End.

Nobody would be around on a late Saturday evening.

Leave them all a nice going away present, especially that bastard Stewle.

TWENTY-FOUR

He turned the main intake valves to seventy five percent, and grinned.//
This little party should be just about starting as he touched down in Malaga.//
In the Admin office he went through all the drawers and files.//
Anything that might possibly be important was shredded, especially historic readings from all the sites.//
In the main fuse boxes for the site he removed all the fuses. He intended to throw those in the hedgerows as he drove home for the last time.//
He ripped out the phones and cut the wires. Every bulb in his old office and the Admin office were removed and smashed in a dustbin along with the spares held in Beryl's cupboard//
After unplugging the photocopier, he opened it up and urinated in it.//
He laughed out loud.//
He always wanted to screw Beryl, and this was one way of doing it.//
As he was about to leave he heard a noise across the site.//
He stood still and quiet.//
Sounded like his office area.//
He peeped out the window.//
Gordon Bayfield, one of the new watchmen, stood looking at his car.

"Fuggin' 'ell," he said out loud.

He watched as the watchman tried the handle on Jone's office. Locked, of course.

Gordon started to walk towards the Admin office.

Jones hid behind a filing cabinet. He heard the handle being tried. Locked.

He waited five minutes then peeped out. No sign of the watchman.

After waiting a further fifteen minutes he ventured out.

He could see, in the distance, a figure with a fluorescent yellow jacket on trudging up the hill towards C Site.

"Here you are, Doreen. 'ere's two 'undred. Should keep you's goin', 'til I get more to you's."

"Ta. This'll not last long. What about the mortgage thing?"

"Money goes in on Thursday. Plenty there for the mortgage direct debit."

Doreen counted it and put it in her handbag.

"When are you's leavin'?"

"Tomorrow around one o'clock. Nigel's comin' with me to Cambridge. My mate is meetin' me there an' then Nigel is bringin' the car back to you. You'll 'ave to drop 'im at home. He only lives in Wymondham."

Doreen brightened up at this news. Helped her plan.
The two drank a lot that day.
He to celebrate leaving.
Her to celebrate a coming romance with a younger man who would secure her financial future.
She allowed Jones to have his way with her that night.
Tomorrow was another day. With Nigel.
In Sagittarius End the pressures were slowly building.

Nigel looked at himself in the bathroom mirror again.
He'd taken a bath earlier. He decided to apply aftershave after he'd dropped Jones off at Stansted. Nice and smelly for Doreen.
"Right Nigel. Here's me address to drop the car off for Doreen. Have you ever been to Stansted?"
He handed a piece of paper to Nigel.
"No, never."
"Right. Do you know the way there?"
"No."
Jones bit his tongue. Fuggin' moron.
"Right. We go on the A11 all the way. Stansted is signposted off the A11."
"Okay. Is it far?"

He wanted to smash this boy idiot.
"'Bout two hours, give or take."
It had not been a good parting with Doreen. She told him that if money wasn't forthcoming the police would have to be told what she knew.
He always knew Doreen was a self-centered bitch.
"Where you goin', Jonesy?"
"Don't call me fuggin' Jonesy."
"Sorry. Where you goin', Mr Jones?"
"I told you. Goin' to Stansted to meet a mate from Germany an' then we's goin' to his house in Newcastle."
"I thought you said France? He was from France."
Jones. Angry.
"Never fuggin' mind where he's *from*, we's goin' to fuggin' Newcastle."
Infine nodded.
"Right. An' you're back on Tuesday then."
Jones started to get agitated.
"What the fuck! Why all these fuggin' *questions*? You a copper suddenly, or what?"
Nigel looked surprised then sulky.
"No. Just *askin'*."
Quiet.
"Yeah, well, I am back on fuggin' Tuesday, as it 'appens."

"Right. We've gotta 'ave our NAD doing then, *again*. It weren't Bentley what done it."
Jones, angry again.
"It's fuggin' DNA not NAD. Anyways, I *still* think it were Bentley. Probably payin' off the bloody rossers. Putting the blame on innocent people like you an' me. Tosser, he is."
They journeyed on in silence.
The miles sped by.
At Stansted Airport Infine took the keys and Jones disappeared into the terminal.
'Shithouse. Never even said 'go'bye, or thanks.'
Nigel got into the car and promptly got lost in the network of highways around the Stansted turnoff of the A11.
Eventually he progressed onto the right A11 and smiled to himself as he thought of Doreen.
'Goin' 'ome first. Put the old after shave on and then get to Doreen.'
He was ready for her. More than ready.
He remembered Friday night.

Jones sat on Ryanair 4545.
He'd drunk five pints of cider in the terminal, was ready for more as soon as the plane levelled, and the seat belt signs went off.

His seating neighbours were an old couple from Dereham. No conversation to or from them. Good. He just wanted a couple more drinks and landing, free, in Malaga.

After the aircraft touched down he got his bag and went through Immigration.

He breathed a sigh of relief when the half asleep, bored Guardia Civil man waved him on.

It was warm. Warmer than Stansted.

He bought a large coffee out of a machine. Tasted good.

He cast his eyes over the waiting expectant throng as he came through the exit doors.

A tall thin man holding a sign up caught his eye.

'JONES'

"Leonard?"

"Yes gov. That's me. Mate of Ronan and Penny I am."

London accent.

They shook hands.

Leonard had long shoulder length hair, a dirty blond colour. His stubble was grey. Dressed in jeans, white tee shirt and wearing white trainers.

"Good to meet you's," said Jones.

Leonard smiled as he led him to the car park. He had some gold teeth.

'You might not think that when you see what I've got in store for you.'

They drove along the carriageway towards Benalmadena, then turned off into the hills.

The Mercedes purred along.

Jones wound his window down a couple of inches and sipped his coffee.

"Does Ronan 'ave a place in the country, then?"

Leonard applied the car lighter to his cigarette. Big drag. Smoke in the car.

"Yup. Sort of. Not far now."

They drove off the tarmac road down a dusty dirt track.

The sun was starting to fall beneath the horizon.

"Just pulling in here. Need a piss."

He pulled into a flat piece of shrubland and got out.

Leonard went to the rear of the car and 'popped' the boot.

Jones felt a bit uneasy. The keys were still in the ignition. He wavered

He could see the man along one side of the car after he had closed the boot.

'He's not had a piss yet. Something not right here'.

Then he saw it.

A pistol with a long silencer attached.

Leonard stood opposite the car door.
The gun pointed through the window at Jones.
"Get out."
Jones squirmed in his seat. Terrified.
"Oh please, no. I won't say nuffin' bout Ronan and the digger, promise. Please don't."
"Get out, you fuckin' moron, this is the end of the fuckin' road for you. Ronan's orders," shouted Leonard.
Jones slowly got out of the car.
Leonard took a step back.
Jones acted.
The coffee splashed into Leonard's face. He took another step back and Jones kicked out as hard as he could.
The kick caught Leonard in the groin and he doubled up, grunting.
Jones kicked him again, this time to the bowed head and he was about to flee when he realized the tall man was still. Unconscious.
He picked up the gun that lay a couple of yards away from the prostrated Leonard.
Holding the gun to the man's head he relieved him of his wallet.
As the fallen man groaned and started to come to, Jones jumped into the car and drove off.
A swirl of dust behind the speeding car.
Leonard standing bowed over, in the distance.

The sweet-smelling Nigel left his flat and started driving to the Jone's house.
He was excited, nervous.
He knew one thing, in a few minutes he would have her.
The car cruised to a halt outside the Jones ex council house.
There were lights on.
Nigel rang the bell.
Nothing.
'Shit. Hope she ain't gone shoppin'.'
He knocked on the door.
He heard an inner door open.
He waited expectantly.
The front door creaked open.
A young child stood.
Jam or similar around his mouth. Scruffy. Hair askew.
"What'ya want? Me Dad ain't 'ere and me ma's in the bogs."
"I've brought the car back."
"Give us the keys an' I'll tell Ma."
"Just tell your Mother that Nigel's 'ere with the car."
The door closed.
'Little bastard'.
He waited.
Five minutes later the door opened.
Doreen.

Wearing the same dress as at the party.
She smiled at him. A big smile.
"Nigel, Come in."
She took his hand and pulled him across the threshold.
After closing the door, she turned to him.
"Just sent the kid to bed. Come through."
She took his hand again and led him into the lounge.
"Sit down. Wanna drink?"
Nigel sat on the couch.
Nervous. A little sweaty.
"Yeah. What you's got?"
"Cider."
He smiled at her.
"Cider is great."
She went into the kitchen.
Nigel could smell her perfume.
He hoped his after shave had reached her. God knows, he'd put enough on.
"'ere you are, my dear. You don't need a glass do you's?"
"Nah. I like it straight from the can. Ta."
"A *real* man always drinks it from the can."
She had a glass of red wine in her hand.
"Right. This is nice an' cosy, ennit? "
"Yeah. Nice an' cosy."
They each took a drink.
"So, where did you's drop Bernard off, then?"

"At Stansted. Thought you knew?"
She momentarily let the mask slip.
"Stansted? Not Cambridge?"
"No, it were Stansted. The airport, it were."
She recovered. Smiled.
"Oh yeah. Of course. Stansted."
Nigel took another swig of cider.
"He said he were meetin' a mate from France or Germany or somewhere, an' then goin' somewhere else. Back on Tuesday for the new NAD thing we all 'as to 'ave, again."
"He won't be back on Tuesday," Doreen said. Quietly. Solemnly.
Infine looked surprised.
"He won't?"
Doreen shrugged.
Recovered herself again.
"Well, his business might take another day, is what I means."
She noticed he was observing her cleavage.
Doreen put her hand on his knee and moved closer to him.
"You's can kiss me if you wants Nigel."
He needed no further urging.
'Kissin', real kissin'. Even tongues. Better than Rosie, an' no payment required.'
After a few minutes of kissing and above clothes caressing, she stood up.

After turning the lights off she unzipped her dress.

Nigel's sought-after, yearned for moments, had arrived.

Jones drove for more than five miles along the dirt road, shaking, shivering.

He had wet himself.

No matter. He was *alive*.

He kept looking in the rear view.

That bastard Ronan had ordered Leonard to actually *kill* him.

Kill him. For what? He'd never done owt to warrant that.

But what the hell to do now?

He had no idea where he was. And no one to turn to.

He had five hundred pounds.

The dial said the car had three quarters of a tank of diesel.

But, where to go. It needed to be away from this area.

Leonard would probably have plenty of seekers looking for him. He'd taken his car *and* his gun.

He pulled over.

He'd kept a watchful eye behind him for any sign of telltale dust.

Jones stretched his legs, then searched the car.

There was a shovel in the boot. He shuddered as he thought he could imagine what that had been intended for.

There was also a blue boiler suit with 'Electricidad', written across the back.

He found a box of San Miguel beer on the floor behind the driver's seat. A book of maps was in the glove compartment plus sixty Marlboro cigarettes.

In the compartment on the driver's door was Leonard's mobile phone and a set of house keys with a tag that said 'Ronan. Villa Dunlin. Benalmadena.'

He looked through the maps and thought he should put as much mileage as he could between him and Leonard.

He decided to head for Benidorm and maybe then by bus, or train, to a little town further on called Javea. He'd heard of it, he thought.

The car would need to be dumped. Preferably where it wasn't found.

Maybe in a river or down a deep ravine.

Leonard had to walk six miles back to the main road before he could hail a taxi.

He had a bad stomach ache. His head pounded and there was blood on his shirt.

'If ever I catch up with that bastard, I'll kill him, slowly. In the barn.

I'll hammer nails into his body like I did to Alfonso last year. Took him four hours before he croaked.'

The taxi driver was skeptical about taking him because of his appearance but when Leonard produced five twenty Euro notes he calmed.

"I fell off my motor bike", he explained to the driver.

"Muy peligroso," the driver replied.

The taxi dropped him off.

He limped to Ronan's property, climbed very gingerly over the wall and retrieved the spare villa keys from the pool pump room.

"It's me."

"Have you sorted him?"

"You'll never believe this, but the bastard knocked me out, stole the car and fucked off with my gun and my phone. I think he's ruptured me. I'm in pain *and* he broke my bloody nose."

"Jesus!"

"God knows where the runt is now. I'll tell the Guardia that me cars been nicked, maybe they'll get him for us."

"No. He'll grass about a little bit of business we did together recently, then *I'm* in shit street. Just put your feelers out. I'm catchin' the next flight over. Outside in the wall opposite the barbecue there's a big loose stone. Behind that is a Glock, an' the keys to the Range Rover."

"It's okay. I've got another gun in *my* house. You'll need to give me your flight details. I'll stock the fridge up, as usual."

"Right. Be in touch. Keep me up to speed if anything breaks."

"Yeah."

He stood up and kicked the chair back under the table.

"Bastard little runt."

TWENTY-FIVE

Ollie and Annabel invited Ham, Myriam, her mum Milly, and Ollie's parents round for Sunday lunch.
It was a joint effort. Ollie bought the joint and Annabel put in most of the effort.
They laughed, hugged and kissed in the kitchen as the morning and cooking progressed.
The radio played love songs and Annabel serenaded her HTB.
Bess sat patiently.
Watching.
She knew that with all those wonderful smells, a treat was coming. Maybe later, but it *was* coming.
At two o'clock Ollie's Mum and Dad arrived. They brought two good bottles of red to go with the lamb and a 'chewy' for Bess.
Lots of chatter about the wedding. Dad spoofing that he loved Spain and what about

all four of them getting a villa together for the honeymoon, sharing the cost? Mother told him to stop embarrassing everyone.
At two thirty Ham, Myriam and Milly pitched up.
More bottles of wine and hearty greetings.
Just after three, lunch was served.

The phone was ringing.
'Why didn't that idiot kid answer the bloody thing?'
It stopped ringing and drunk Doreen fell back to sleep.

Stewle cursed.
'Where the hell was that useless imbecile Jones, when needed?'
He looked through his telephone index again.
Just Jones and Anstey B. Who the hell was Anstey B.?
He phoned the number.
Beryl was sitting with her mother and daughter watching the afternoon film. Full of Sunday lunch. Beryl's mother nodding off.
The phone rang.
Beryl jumped up to get it.
"Hello."
"Who's that?"
She recognized Stewle's voice.

"It's me, Mr Stewle, Beryl?"

Stewle frowned, then his memory recalled her. The woman in the office.

"Yes, now look. There is an emergency at Sagittarius End. One of the fields is on fire after an explosion. I need someone to get there, the fire service is nearly there but they have no idea how to deal with it, or the high pressures that our remote figures show. I can't get hold of Jones. Who's his deputy? Have you got a number? We need someone there *quickly*."

"I'm sorry I ain't got no names, nor anything on me."

Stupid bitch!

Stewle sighed.

"Right, well, you'll need to get in your car and drive to the site. Phone me when you've got a name with a number. Any of the site monitors will do."

'Flamin' cheek! On a Sunday lunchtime. I don't *think so*.'

"Sorry Mr Stewle. I'm not well. Laid up in bed. Can't move. Me back's done in."

'Jesus!

Stewle closed his eyes. Big sigh.

"Right. Do you know the names of *anyone* and the town, or city, where they live?"

Silence.

"Hello? You still there, Beryl?"
"I'm tryin' to think. Oh yeah. I know Ollie's number 'cause I had to tell him the final numbers for the 'do'."
"Who's Ollie? Is he a monitor?"
By now, Stewle's voice had gone up a few octaves.
He had perspiration under his armpits, dampening his shirt and a bead or two on his forehead.
"Yeah. He is. Ollie Wilson. Probably more switched on than Jones. Jones is thick."
'Shut up you stupid bitch!'
"Okay. Give me his details please. Quickly."
"Just a mo."
She took her time. God this was fun. Explosion then a fire and Jones not around. Beautiful.
"Hello, Mr Stewle?"
"Yes!"
She slowly read off Ollie's number.
Stewle hung up.
'Pig! Never said thanks nor nothin'."

"And Grandpa said, the other four hundred is from your grandma."
The joke was good, and just about Sunday lunch clean.
Ollie had heard it before, but he laughed along with the others.

The phone rang.
Ollie got up and answered it.
Stewle told Ollie what had happened.
"Okay. Ham Veene is here with me. We'll leave now. Here's Danny Bentley's number. Tell him to get Steve and meet us there."
Ollie explained the problem and he and Ham ran to Ollie's car.
"Sounds bad," said Ham.
Ollie nodded.
"Yup. If the next explosion is big enough it could rupture the rest and blow the whole field, plus fracture the national grid link. My main worry is the storage tank. If *that* blows everything within two miles is history."
"Wow!"
Ollie put his headlights and flashers on. Foot to the floor, where he could.

One of the new night watchman, Roy Hunter, who lived nearby heard and saw the explosion, called the police and fire brigade. His terms of reference contained no company number or person apart from Stewle, who didn't seem to know what to do.
Roy stood at the gate and waved them through.

"Boy, am I glad to see you. You can feel tremors under foot once you leave these lower roads."

Ollie ran to Jones' office and kicked in the door. He came out with two monitoring machines.

He told Roy to direct the fire brigade to the hill on fire and to get the police to evacuate everyone from the village to three miles away. Danny and Steve were to get their monitors and go to sites not yet on fire, or as close as is safe and lower any pressures they could.

The hill of Site A was on fire. Sporadic smaller booms, followed by blue fire bursts shot skywards.

There was a boom and a huge fireball shot up into the sky from Site B. The ground shuddered.

"Ham if you hurry to your site, site D, I'll do B, then go on to C."

Ham ran off towards his site.

Ollie turned to Roy.

"When Danny and Steve get here, tell them to hurry to C and D, you leg it then and make sure the coppers have moved the villagers away to at least three miles out. Okay?"

"Yes, thanks, Ollie."

Grey smoke started wafting across the sites.

It felt almost as if the air itself was on fire.

"I *know* it's Sunday Reggie, you don't have to bloody well tell me. I need Barron here *now*, otherwise we may have a catastrophe on our hands, if that oxyparalemtic storage tank goes up."

Deep sigh from Reggie. A good golf day ruined.

"Okay. I'll get Barron and send him to the site in the chopper."

Stewle hung up.

He left Norwich on the A47, driving his Bentley like a bat out of hell.

Lights on.

Sweat on his brow.

Wanted to piss.

No time.

Jones drove along the A92.

Agitated. Frightened.

Eyes continuously looking at the rear vision mirror.

He drank the six cans of beer that were behind the driver's seat but wanted more.

The Mercedes ate up the miles.

He pulled in at a service station and loaded up with San Miguel beer, biscuits and crisps.

He also bought a map on the way out.

By the door was a Spanish/English translation book on a revolving bookcase. The little book fitted neatly into his pocket as the shopkeeper served another motorist.

He couldn't see a river so decided to ditch the car in a ravine or similar.

He estimated he had about sixty miles to run before he'd get rid of the Mercedes. Not too far then to hitch it to Benidorm.

He worried about getting stopped by the cops as a search of the car would yield up the gun and certain arrest.

He wanted to ditch the gun but needed it. Insurance.

He knew he couldn't keep the car for much longer. Police might be onto it.

The car radio was on an English-speaking station and the news didn't have any report on his episode.

He drank three of the cans quickly and tossed the empties out of the open passenger window.

Next came two bags of crisps and the chain smoking of three cigarettes.

Not much traffic.

No blue lights.

Getting dark.

Needed to ditch the car.

He pulled into a lay by and read up the Spanish word for 'ravine'. 'Barranco'.

Ten miles further on the magic words appeared 'Los Herias profundo barranco 1km'. 'Los Herias deep ravine'.

He pulled off the A92.

The road to Los Herias was not much more than a dirt track. Bumpy and dusty.

Warning signs told him the ravine was 200 metres ahead on the left.

He stopped the car and walked forward. He squinted in the failing light.

The dirt track skirted a very deep ravine.

He got back in and drove as close as he dared to the ravine edge, stopped and got out. The hand brake was off.

The Mercedes was in 'Drive'.

He removed his gear and stowed it by the track.

Jones picked up a stick and leant through the window.

He gently touched the accelerator.

He jumped back as the car moved forward, landing on his back.

Jones scrambled to his feet.

Stood back, hands on hips, heart pounding as he watched the vehicle edge very slowly up to and over the edge.

Clattering down, it gathered speed on the slope, then disappeared.
He listened to it banging and scraping on its downward path, then silence for quite a few seconds before a loud bang resonated around the immediate area.
He couldn't see anything but guessed it had reached its final resting place.
No flames, no explosion. Just quiet.
He stood in the dark and finished off the beers.
Time to start walking.

Ollie ran to B Site. He started turning the junction valves to zero. The ground underneath him trembled. Three hundred metres above him a loud bang and a burst of blue flame shot skywards. It made him stop in his tracks.
"Jesus!"
He looked across at A Site.
It was totally on fire and bursts of blue/green flames intermittently shot up into the air.
He looked across at D Site and saw Ham running to the next junction valve. No explosions there. Yet.
Ollie ran quickly from valve to valve to turn off as many as possible.
He saw Danny and Steve running to C site.

His pocket vibrated. Couldn't hear the calling sound. Too much noise all around.

"Yes!" he shouted into his mobile.

"Ollie, Stewle here. Is it contained?"

An explosion knocked him off his feet.

He rolled downhill, away from the source.

"Hello?"

A tremendous explosion rocked C Site.

Ollie stood up. Danny and Steve were running back down the hill. They stopped halfway and started turning off the valves. Above them the hill was on fire.

"Stewle, it's Ollie. Don't think we can contain the bloody thing. It's pretty much out of control."

"Shit!"

Stewle looked at the hills before him. Three of the four sites were burning and exploding. Only D was clear.

"Ollie. What can we do?"

"I'm calling the boys back. Need to turn off the valves in the Storage tank. Can you do that?"

Stewle looked perplexed.

He shook his head.

"Don't know how to do that. Do you?"

Ollie called Ham.

"Leave it Ham. Get back to the entrance gate, *now*!"

"Okay."

Danny and Steve were already running down the hill.

They looked across and saw Ham and Ollie running back too.

A massive explosion blew Ollie off his feet. A blast of heat swept over him, singing his hair.

He got up and ran as fast as he could towards the Storage tank.

Stewle stood near his car, open mouthed at the scenes unfolding before him.

The grey black smoke now covered the site hills and intermittent explosions echoed around the area's.

Ham was just behind Ollie, Danny and Steve as they arrived out of breath at the office site.

"There is an engineer coming by chopper, but he's twenty-five minutes away."

"It'll all be gone by then, I reckon," said Ollie.

Stewle looked terrified. Helpless. Hapless.

Ollie took control.

"Right you four. Get in your cars and bugger off. Make sure all the people around here are three miles or more away from this place."

What about you?" Said Ham.

"I'm going to try to turn the main valves off in the Storage tank."

Stewle looked at Ollie. Mouth open.

"Do you know the sequence? Which valves?"

Ollie shrugged.

"Nope. Just going to try. That's all."
Explosions rocked the sites again. This time from D Site.
Ollie pointed to the exit gate.
"Get moving. I'll join you in a few minutes."
Stewle, Danny and Steve ran toward the parked cars.
As they did so two vans arrived. BBC TV and ITV.
Ollie shook his head. He shouted.
"Tell those pratts to fuck off, pronto!"
He turned to Ham.
"Clear off Ham. No sense you being here, too."
Ham shook his head.
"I'm staying with you. Let's do it."
They ran to the Storage tank building.
No keys.
Ham ran to Jones' office and came back, panting, key in hand.
Ollie unlocked the iron doors.
"You should bugger off, Ham."
"Nope."
Inside alarms were ringing loudly. Lights flashing.
"Shit! Where do we start?" said Ham.
Ollie stood looking at the different gauges and dials.
He sighed. Gulped.

Ollie turned off one gauge. Nothing. Alarms rang, and lights still flashed.

"Bollocks! Here's hoping."

Ollie turned off two valves. No change.

"Ollie. We need to fuck off. This place is going to blow any minute."

"You leg it. I'll follow in a couple of minutes."

Two of the pipes started vibrating.

He turned off another valve.

"C'mon Ollie. Let's go!" Shouted Ham.

"You go. Two minutes."

Ham ran out the door.

Ollies car was close to Jone's office.

He started the vehicle.

Back in the Storage building Ollie cursed.

"Come on you bastard! One of these has *got* to work."

He turned off the last gauge.

No change.

He ran out of the building. Ham was waiting. Passenger door open.

Ollie dived in.

"*Go!* It's going to blow!"

Two miles away, on a rise on the landscape where the Sagittarius End site could be seen, stood the site workmen, Stewle, policemen, and firemen.

Their vehicles stood in line on the country road.

All eyes were looking in the direction of the site. Every so often small explosions could be heard and plumes of smoke drifted across towards them.

Ollie's car came screeching to a halt alongside the group.

Stewle looked anxiously at Ollie and Ham as they approached.

Eyes pleading for good news.

They both shook their heads.

Stewle's shoulders slumped.

A helicopter flew over them.

Stewle waved to it.

"I think that must be the engineer. Too bloody *late*," said Stewle.

The TV crews panned around the assembled men.

"So, you couldn't stop it then?" said Stewle.

The camera's panned in on Ollie.

Ollie shook his head.

"Don't think so. I turned the valves in what I thought might be the right way, but the pipes still vibrated. We had to leave. All the alarms were screaming and the dials going backwards and forwards."

A TV cameraman recorded the conversation, then interviewed Ollie.

"Weren't you worried, when you were trying to stop it?"

"Didn't have time to be too worried when I was turning the valves. When I saw that nothing worked, we ran, *then* I was worried."

"You've singed your hair Ollie," said Steve.

Ollie ran his hand over his scalp.

"Yeah. New style."

Stewle looked at his phone.

He didn't recognize the number.

"Ain'tcha goin' to answer it?" said Danny.

Stewle turned away.

A police Sergeant and the team leader Fireman came over to Ollie.

"Excuse me sir, could you tell us what the state of play is now."

Ollie pointed to Stewle.

"He's the boss of it all. Better ask him."

The policeman shook his head.

"We have done. He doesn't know."

Ollie nodded.

"Right. The pressures that we lowered had no effect on the individual sites. They all blew and set the hills on fire as you can see, even from here. I expect the gas storage tank facility to blow any minute. That will, I believe devastate an area of about a two to three-mile radius. I did ask that everyone within that radius be evacuated."

"Yeah, the watchman told us what you said. Everyone's out of those houses, we think."
The Fire Chief stepped forward.
"I've asked for back up. Should be here soon."
"Just got to wait now," said Ollie.
"Better phone the girls, Ollie. Let 'em know we're okay," said Ham.
Ollie phoned home. Annabel answered.
"Are you alright? It's on the television."
Ollie sighed.
"Yeah. We're both okay but we couldn't save the Sagittarius End site. We're just waiting for the final explosion. It should come any minute, I think."
"Bugger that place. As long as you, and the others, are alright. That's all that matters."
Just then the helicopter arrived overhead. It circled twice then landed in the field beside the road where they all stood.
Barron, the engineer came across the field and straddled the fence.
He came directly to Stewle.
"Bloody mess that site is, Malcolm."
"When will it blow?" said Stewle.
The TV cameras panned onto the group.
"Blow? It won't blow. Your man turned the storage feeds off. Nothing for me to do."
Steve patted Ollie on the back.
"Well *done*, Ollie. You did it!"

"Thank God!" said Stewle.

The Policeman Sergeant and the Fire Chief shook hands with Ollie.

"It wasn't just me. Ham here was with me."

They shook Ham's hand.

The engineer addressed them all.

"The individual sites may continue to blow a little for a couple more hours, but it should all die down by tea time today. It looks like some bastard has turned the override master switch and the valves for each site to 75%, and that's what has caused it all."

Stewle frowned.

"What? Like sabotage, you mean?"

The engineer nodded.

"They don't turn *themselves* on to 'Full', Malcolm. *Someone*, who knew what they were doing, turned them on."

The policeman addressed Stewle.

"Who, in your knowledge, had the know how to do that, Sir?"

"Only the engineer here, oh yes, and Jones, the site manager. Where *is* Jones? Anyone seen him?"

They all shook their heads.

The Fire Chief turned to Stewle.

"Bit daft isn't it? Only *one* person knew how to avert a disaster, like this? If it weren't for your two switched on brave lads here, God know what the outcome might have been."

Ollie looked across at the group of people moved from their homes.

"Is it safe for those people to go home now?" said Ollie.

Barron, the engineer nodded.

"Yup. There'll be some very small localized explosions for another hour or two, but nothing to affect them. The smoke will be about for a few days yet, so I'd tell them to keep their windows closed."

The Police Sergeant walked over to the group of residents.

Stewle and Barron talked together for nearly an hour.

Nigel lay beside Doreen.

'God that were good'.

First time that way for him. She had wailed a bit but took it.

"Nigel."

He turned on his side to face her.

"That 'urts me that do. Doing it there."

"Wha'dya mean?"

'God, this idiot is thicker than what Bernard is, sometimes.'

"When you's bugger me. You's need to get some grease or summat."

"Oh right."
He loved this talk. Excited him.
She saw his erection.
She pulled the sheet down to expose her breasts.
"Nigel. I needs some money to tide me over. Can you's help me a little?"
Her hand wandered. She grasped him.
He groaned.
"Ahhh……. Yeah….long as it ain't too much."
An hour later, just before she drove him home, he gave her thirty pounds.

TWENTY-SIX

"Benidorm?"
"Yes. Si. Benidorm, please senor."
He threw his bag in and climbed up into the truck.
The driver wore scruffy jeans, a white tee shirt but had no shoes. Barefoot. He hadn't shaved for a couple of days. His hair was grey and tussled.
The cab stunk of cigarettes.
"You Inglis?"
"Um. Yes. Si. English."
"El coche no bien?"
"Sorry. What?"
"You car issa no bien? No dinero para autobus?"
"Yes. Si."
He hoped he'd got that right.
The driver talked in Spanish for a few minutes then gave up.

Two hours later Jones was dropped off at a toll station.
The driver pointed to a side road.
"Benidorm."
Jones walked along the CV20 road that led to Benidorm.
Many cars passed him.
He smoked. Took pee breaks behind bushes and swore at vehicles that ignored him.
Tired now. Fed up. Angry.
Just wanted a few drinks and a lie down, somewhere soft.
A Seat Ibiza pulled up. Two young Spanish men inside.
They spoke in Spanish. He shook his head.
"Inglis?"
"Yes. Si. Benidorm please."
"Get in back," said the driver.
He got on the back seat. They drove away.
"Where you live?" said the Spanish passenger.
"Benidorm," said Jones.
He felt uneasy, but his hand on the gun gave him reassurance.
"We go Benidorm for girls. Inglis girls, Danish girls, Holland girls. We like to fuck."
The two laughed.
They had a bottle of whiskey and passed it between them.
The passenger passed it to Jones.

He took a long swig. Nectar.
"You like girls?"
Jones nodded.
Another swig.
"Yes. Si."
"Good. We go club. Plenty girls there. Benny's club. You want come with us?"
Jones smiled.
"I am Pablo, him is Roberto."
"Hello, my name is Bernard. I need to take my bag home first. I'll come later, okay?"
"Si. No pasa nada."
They drove on in silence, passing the bottle until it was empty.
The passenger threw the bottle out of the window. It broke on the hard rocky ground.
As they pulled into Benidorm, Jones saw a bus stop.
He leant forward.
"Here please. My house is here."
The Seat pulled to a halt and Jones got out.
The passenger put his head out of the window.
"See you. Benny's later."
Jones waved.
The car sped off.
He walked to the bus shelter.
The whiskey had lifted his spirits.

The timetable was difficult to read but he worked out that there would be no buses to anywhere until the next day.
He wanted to leave Benidorm as soon as he could.
If the car was found, the police would reason that Benidorm was the destination of the felon.
The first bus to Javea was at eight fifteen am, arriving at nine forty-five.
The cost was six Euros, which pleased him.
He walked around in the back streets for half an hour, undecided as to what to do.

Annabel stood at the front door to welcome him.
"My hero. My HTB is a TV star."
He smiled as he took her in his arms.
"This is how a TV star kisses his women."
After the long kiss Annabel asked him if she could be his agent, now that he was a hero *and* a TV star.
"Yes, you can be my agent. Ever heard of the 'casting couch'?"
"Later, darling, later."
They walked, arms around each other, through to the lounge.
Bess followed, tail wagging.
They sat on the settee.
"So, what happens now?"

"Stewle says the site will be closed as a national grid provider until everything is repaired and the safety certificate is given. We all have to attend a meeting on Tuesday *before* the cops have done the DNA thing. We've got Monday off."
Annabel lifted his hand and kissed it.
"You and Ham looked so handsome on the television. Funny how it distorts things isn't it?"
"Cheeky monkey."
"What caused it? The fires."
"The chief engineer thinks it was sabotaged by someone who knew what he, or she, was doing. They had put the regulators on to too high a setting. As it was a weekend, none of us were around to regulate the thing so it started to blow."
"God. Who do they suspect?"
Ollie shrugged.
"The finger may be pointing at Jones. He seems to have disappeared. Stewle spoke to his wife and she said he'd gone to Newcastle. She didn't know why, or when he'd be back."
"Do you want to see the Look East coverage? I recorded it for you, and to show your children what a hero you are."
She played the recording back.
Fields on fire, one or two eruptions.
Ollie shouting orders.

The finale was when the engineer announced that Ollie had saved the day, and he said Ham had stayed with him throughout and helped.
The camera panned in on both of them. Pats on the back and smiles all round.
They spent what was left of the day discussing the wedding and their honeymoon. Annabel had booked two flights and accommodation for them plus Ham and Myriam to go to the Costa Del Sol the coming weekend for a couple of days to have a look at Villas. They were flying Friday after work and coming back late on Sunday.
Annabel wanted to make sure that their honeymoon accommodation was on the right side of brilliant.
"When we come back you've got your teaching job interview. I just know you're going to get it."
Ollie nodded.
"Yes, but what about the job?"

Nigel took Doreen to the Legion in Wymondham on Sunday night.
He had designs on her spending the night at his flat. He knew the kid was with her mother for a couple of nights.
As they drove she questioned him about the troubles at Sagittarius End.

"What could make thems explosions things what were on the telly."
Nigel had his hand on Doreen's thigh.
"Probably a fault of some kind. I don't know, really."
His hand slid higher. She put her hand on his and stopped it moving.
He took her hand and placed it between his legs. She left her hand there but didn't respond.
"Will Bernard get in a row 'cause he weren't there?"
"Maybe. When is he coming back?"
"Dunno."
"'e's got to be back for Tuesday to 'ave 'is NAD done, like the rest of us."
Doreen looked across at him. Her tone was sharp.
"'e *won't* be back, I can tell you's that *now*. No *way* will 'e be back!"
Nigel frowned.
"*Why*? What makes you so sure. Him's *got* to be back, otherwise coppers will charge 'im."
Silence for a few moments.
"'e done it."
Nigel looked across at her. His eyes wide. Shocked.
"Wadya mean? The explosions?"
"That dead bint. 'e done it. 'e done 'er in."

"Does you's mean about the girl, the prossie, Rosie?"
Doreen crossed her arms.
"Yep. 'im done 'er in. 'e told me. Said she was breakin' in the office, or somethin', but I knows that were bullshit. Admitted it, 'im did. Straight to me face."
"Jesus! Do the coppers know? 'as you told 'em?"
She shook her head.
"Nope. Not goin' to, neither. Nothin' to do with me, like."
Nigel puffed out his lips.
"Jesus! If Jones ain't there Tuesday, they'll guess it were 'im."
Doreen put her hand on his man hood and squeezed.
"Don't care. Me 'as you now, Nigel. Likes what you does, I do. Does you's like me?"
She squeezed again.
He smiled.
"I do. Love it, I does."
Nigel parked up.
He wanted something there and then.
She wouldn't have it.
"Later. Better on a bed."
They went into the Legion bar, arm in arm.
Four pints later he took her back to his flat.
He'd bought some Vaseline.

Jones had been walking for half an hour.
Tired now. Long day. Stress. Worry.
'Not fuggin' fair. She were only a fuggin' prossie. If she had let me do straightaway what I wanted instead of fightin' me, she'd be 'ere now. Who'll miss the fuggin' bitch? No one. Nobody owns up to havin' a dirty prossie in their family.'
As he turned the corner he noticed a taxi, engine running, sitting outside a small villa. Villa Martinez.
He stopped. Moved backwards into the shadow of a tree.
There were four villas' in a line. Tidy, probably expensive in this part of Benidorm.
"Come on kids, hurry up. We'll miss the flight."
A tall man, tanned, wearing shorts and a tee shirt came onto the road.
Two suitcases. One in each hand.
He shouted over his shoulder.
"C'mon Gina. Time we were off!"
His blond lady ran down the drive past a 5 series BMW, carrying a soft bag. It looked heavy. She was followed by two children, both carrying smaller bags.
They threw their bags into the taxi's boot and got into the vehicle.
The taxi drove off into the night.

Jones stood silently in the shadows for ten minutes, just in case they'd forgotten something.

All was quiet, so he walked past the villa, looking, listening.

He turned back, undid the gate catch and walked quickly past the BMW and around the back of the villa.

A large swimming pool, six recliners, portable BBQ and an oblong metal table greeted him.

He had no interest in any of these and made his way to the back door.

He scouted around the villa. No burglar alarm box, not even motion sensing lights.

'Just need to break in, and *wallah*!'

Using one of the BBQ tools, he levered up one of the double back doors and it popped open.

Piece of cake, no noise, nothing.

Kitchen. Nice. Modern. Big upright freezer, similar 'fridge beside it.

He opened the fridge.

Eureka!

4 bottles of white wine and a dozen large cans of Stella Artois beer. Cheese too, but not much else.

In a cupboard he found a tin of dry biscuits.

He sat at the kitchen table in the dark and finished off the cheese accompanied by a few biscuits.

A bottle of white wine went down well, so he opened another and drank from the bottle as he wandered around the three bedroomed property.

Nothing much took his interest except a mobile phone in one of the smaller bedrooms.

The large double bed in the en-suite looked inviting.

He woke up next morning, around six am.

Jones crawled along the floor so as not to be seen and went into the kitchen.

In one of the cabinets were four bunches of keys and a tin with sixty Euro's in notes and a little change in it.

How very considerate of them, especially as one of the keys had a BMW fob attached.

At seven o'clock he had left Benidorm and was driving at a moderate speed along the N332 to Javea.

The BMW was almost new.

It was still dark, and very little traffic was on the road.

He had taken the wine and beer from the 'fridge in Villa Martinez but was hungry, so an early opening café was his first port of call.

Bacon, eggs, fresh bread rolls, lots of butter and coffee.

Half an hour later he was back on the road.

He felt good. Everything had gone his way thus far.

The car had half a tank of diesel, so he wouldn't need to spend money on fuel, and the signpost said 'Javea 15 miles'.

He knew that before long he'd need to get rid of the car.

He looked attentively for a 'barranco or a rio', but none came into view.

Maybe drive it *through* Javea as if going to Valencia. Ditching it then somewhere close to the highway and the police would think he was headed away from Javea.

He'd double back and find a bed and breakfast, or small hotel.

Jones came to Javea and followed the road as if going to Valencia.

He pulled off near the first bus stop.

Four hundred metres further on was a narrow lane with a sign that said, 'Basura'.

Driving along the lane for a short distance he came to a yard that had a hundred or so big rubbish skips in it. The place stunk. There were a few mangy cats running around. They backed off when the vehicle drew near.

He drove around the back of the yard and pulled into the middle of some scrub.

A half hour later Jones got off the bus outside Hotel Xabia.

Tuesday arrived and the monitoring team, pipe layers and the rest of the employees, including Beryl, all assembled outside Jone's office.
Stewle turned up in his Bentley.
The DNA team had set up the office again.
Stewle spoke to all the employees before the DNA gathering started.
"There has been quite a bit of vandalism in the offices. You can all see that the field is a mess. The engineers tell me it will be safe beyond all doubt by tomorrow. The Health and Safety people will inspect it on Thursday. If we get a clean bill of health, work will resume on Friday. It will take the pipe layers and the engineers two to three weeks, working flat out, to get it all back to the way it was. All the monitors will assist the pipe layers until then.
I want to thank Wilson, Veene, Bentley and Skipmore for their sterling efforts on Sunday. They kept the destruction down to a minimum by the work they did. Well done."
The congregation all applauded.
"As soon as you've all had your DNA done please come back out here and the pipe layers foreman will allocate the work that's needed. One last thing does anyone know the whereabouts of Bernard Jones?"
Many shook their heads, others shrugged.

One whispered rather loudly, "Who the fuck cares about that heap of shite."
"No? Right, that's it. After you've given your DNA, you can have the rest of today and all tomorrow off, except for the safety engineers. Don't worry, on *full* pay. Back in on Friday. Thank you."
A policeman, standing by Jone's battered door, shouted out they'd call everyone in one by one.
Infine smiled.
'Great. Soon as I'm done, off to Doreen's I go.'
Ollie walked over to him.
"Nigel, you're friendly with Jones. Any idea's?"
Infine looked nervous, guilty almost.
"No. He never told me owt."
Danny was one of the first in.
He came out smiling.
"Hey, Ollie. If I give any more DNA samples, they'll 'ave to put DNA after me name."
The Forensic team got through the gathering fairly quickly.
The only name outstanding was Jones.
Ham, Ollie, Danny and Steve walked to the car park.
Beryl was getting into her car, she showed a lot of thigh.
"'Lo Danny."
"Hi Beryl," said Danny.

His three workmates all smiled.

"There's got to be a reason he's legged it. I smell a rat," said DS Baker.
Chief Constable Greenberg nodded.
"Yep. Looks like it."
"His missus says she thinks he's gone to Newcastle looking for a job. Doesn't know exactly where he's gone, or when he's coming home. Not been in contact with him. Never told his boss."
"Mmmm. Best put out an apprehend notice on him, John."
"Will do, sir. I'll get Pondie on it."
"Good man."
Greenberg returned to his office.
Jack Pond, a retired policeman, worked in the main office at Wymondham as a police civilian IT assistant.
On instructions from Baker he sent a routine message to all ports, docks, airports, railways and Interpol.
Pond received a response quicker than he thought he would.
He relayed it immediately to Baker.
"He left Stansted on Sunday evening on a flight to Malaga. No return ticket booked, Sarge," said Pond.

"Thanks, Pondie. Can you alert the Guardia Civil in Malaga, please? Put questioning on suspicion of murder of Elizabeth Patricia Holmes, on or around the eighteenth of December this year."
"Will do."

TWENTY-SEVEN

The happy four arrived at Stansted.
Ollie parked the car and they raced each other to the terminal.
Ham won.
Straight through security and into Wetherspoon's Windmill bar.
Chatting, laughing, two drinks apiece and onto the aircraft.
A little turbulence after take-off into the climb but nothing to speak of.
Landed at Malaga, picked up bags and into the taxi.
It was a short journey to the Arroyo and the two bedroomed flat that Annabel had booked.
They had a quick look around, unpacked and then into the night for drinks and food.
Three hours later, after some food and too much wine, the laughing four returned to their accommodation, looking forward to meeting up

with the local estate agent, who also handled villa rentals, the next day.

At ten o'clock they shook hands with Pepe Drevero. Five feet four, bald, fat and wearing glasses.

"I have six villas' for rent out minimum two weeks, maximum four months. All here in Javea or here, just outside Javea."

He showed them an album on his computer screen.

They decided on three.

Pepe had a seat six Nissan Titan, and they toured around Javea looking at the three available properties.

They all agreed on particularly liking a three-bed villa, with en suites and a pool. It wasn't overlooked and came in at £1000 for two weeks in May, all inclusive.

Ollie paid Pepe a £200 deposit.

At lunch they looked at the brochure of the villa that Pepe had given them.

All agreed it was lovely and a very good spot to have a honeymoon.

After a lot of smutty jokes about honeymoon couples, they decided, as it was bright and sunny, to beach it for the rest of the day.

Jones decided not to take a room at Hotel Xabia.

Too expensive.

He toured rental estate agents, and the cheapest he could get was a tiny studio apartment at three hundred Euros a month.

Three hundred dented his stash, so now a job beckoned. Urgently.

The estate agent told him that some bars were closed for the winter, so jobs in those were limited. There were three timeshare selling decks that he knew of. They all operated out of resorts, the nearest one was at Super Sun Resort just down the road from the Javea beach.

He had a couple of drinks from a bar close to Super Sun and then walked in to the resort's reception.

An Irish girl took his details and told him to take a seat and she'd call up one of the managers.

Martin Streets was a tall man in his forties, who hailed from Bradford. His hair was now sparse, and although it was winter he had a good tan.

He shook hands with Jones and sat down.

"The job is self-employed. You're responsible for paying your own tax and social security. Thee has to show me your P60 to prove you're legit."

Jones gulped.

"Ain't you got one?"
Jones shook his head.
"Good job you've just shown me it then, eh?"
"No, no, I ain't got one."
Streets smiled.
"That's what I said. Good job thee just showed it to me. Fancy a beer? I'm paying."
The manager led the way into the bar area that looked out onto the sea.
They took their beers to a table where they could see the other tables.
"When the sellers get a sale, they bring the punters in here to keep them sweet. Don't want the *darlings* to have second thoughts or nothing."
They sat in silence for a while watching proceedings.
"What did thee do afore you came to Spain, Bernie?"
'God! He hated people callin' him 'Bernie'.'
"Nothin' much. Bit of Insurance sellin'."
"Insurance eh? Life or cars, what?"
Jones was ruffled.
"Em, bit of both really."
Streets looked suspicious.
"You ain't on the run are thee?
Jones shook his head. His face reddened.
"God no! Nothin' like that. Just broke up wiv me missus like."

Streets smiled.

"Join the fuggin' club, lad. Lot of folk like thee over 'ere, me included."

Streets explained to him briefly how the sales team worked and what the commission only pay was.

Jones was amazed at the money he could make.

They had another beer and Jones was told to come in on Wednesday for a day of training.

"Make sure you're neat and tidy. No need for a tie, but nicely ironed trews an' shirt. Shoes cleaned. That sort of thing. Don't stink of booze neither. Get some peppermints if you had a bender night before. Don't want you breathin' death on the clients."

He handed Jones a brochure.

Jones went back to his apartment building with a spring in his step.

Got away from the cops. Got a flat. Got a job. Very happy.

He sat down at the bar below his flat, ordered a beer and started to look through the brochure.

John Baker went to see Doreen again.
Although it was eleven in the morning, she still had a dressing gown on.
She let him in but wasn't happy.

Nervous. Fidgetty.

"I told you's all I know's about Bernard. He's gone."

"You sound as if you think he's not coming back."

Doreen shrugged.

"Don't matter to me if him don't."

Just then Infine opened the door and came in. Jeans. No socks or top on.

He looked shocked to see the policeman.

Baker got the picture.

"Well, *hello*. Mr Infine, isn't it?"

Doreen looked angry.

Infine blanched.

"Yyyes."

Face turning red. Guilty.

"I don't suppose you know the whereabouts of Mr Bernard Jones, do you, Mr Infine?"

Infine, eyes wide.

Doreen, waving her hand and shaking her head Unseen by Baker.

"No. No. I…..I just dropped 'im off at Stansted."

"Did you now? And what day and time *was* that?"

Infine looked from the policeman to Doreen and back again.

"It were…er…Oh yes, it were Sunday. Late afternoon. He were meetin' a mate."

Doreen looked at Nigel then up at the ceiling.

"Did he say who this *mate* was?"

Infine shook his head.

"Nah. I just dropped 'im at the terminal an' drove back 'ere to get the car to Doreen."

"Would you say he was happy at work?"

"Dunno. He was the boss. 'e liked me but none of the others. 'e thought I were manager material, 'e did."

"I see."

Doreen butted in.

"He thought *Stewle* was a prat. Always 'angin' up on 'im, stuff like that. Higgerant, he said 'e was," said Doreen.

"Mmm. Never said he'd like to blow the site up, or anything like that?"

"No, never," said Doreen.

"No," said Infine.

Baker brought out a 'photo. Held it up.

"Ever seen this young lady before?"

Nigel thought his head would explode.

"Nope. Is she the tart what's dead?" said Doreen.

"Yes, murdered."

"No," said Nigel.

Sweating now'. Hands jittery in his lap.

Baker noticed.

He looked straight at Infine. Eyes met. Nigel lowered his.

"You *do* know her, don't you, Nigel?"

Infine looked up at the Detective. Pleading almost.

"Yes."

Long silence.

"She's Rosie. I know 'er. She were a prossie. I seen 'er a couple of times in Rose Lane."

"Did Bernard Jones *know* her?"

Nigel nodded. Crestfallen. Staring at the carpet.

Baker stood up.

"Mr Infine. I think you and I had better take a little ride down to Wymondham. Before I go, Mrs Jones, can I use your bathroom please."

"Yyyes. There's one off the kitchen, or one at the top of the stairs."

He went up the stairs.

In the bathroom he picked up a comb that had hairs in it.

Downstairs again, he asked Doreen if the comb belonged to Jones.

"Yeah. It do. Why?"

He looked at Infine.

"You haven't used it have you, Mr Infine?"

"No."

Baker pointed to a framed photograph on the mantlepiece.

"Could I have that photo for a couple of days, Mrs Jones. I'll make sure you get it back."

She gave him the photograph.

"Keep it, for all me cares."

The four stood on the promenade shaking sand off their limbs and clothing.
It had been a lovely day. Booked the villa for the honeymoon. Sun shining, not too hot, cool wine and beer, lots of laughs.
They stopped at a promenade bar and had drinks for about an hour. People watching.
On their way back to the apartment they passed a restaurant that looked inviting. They decided to eat there later.
Close to their own apartment they passed a little bar beneath an apartment block when Ham suddenly grabbed Ollie's arm.
"Ollie! Look there! Isn't that Jonesy?"
Ollie turned.
Ham pointed at a man leaving who had his back to them.
"Dunno, to be honest. Looked a bit like him but I only saw his back."
Ham looked determined.
"I was bloody *sure* it was him."
Myriam looked doubtful.
"Why would he come here? Probably someone just like him."
Ham began to doubt himself.
"Yes. You're probably right. Dead ringer though."

Ollie smiled.

"Your problem is, you've got Sagittarius End withdrawal symptoms. Missing Jones obviously. May require a visit to the doctor's."

Annabel laughed.

"You don't think he's *turned*, do you?

Myriam pulled a face.

"Well. He has been walking kinda funny just lately."

The four walked on.

Jones stood around the corner, panic stricken.

He looked back.

He watched them laughing then walking on.

"Jeez, that were fuggin' close!"

He hurried to the lift that took him up to his apartment.

Looking out over his small balcony he saw the four entering the Delize apartment building, some five hundred yards or so on the opposite side of the walkway.

"Shit!"

Jones had seen the four approaching him and recognition on the face of Ham.

He had dashed off around the corner.

He walked on shaky legs up the stairs to his apartment.

Wine out of the fridge, top removed.

He drank half the bottle without pausing for breath.

He sat on the settee. Mind in a whirl.
What if Ham told the coppers?
Should he run? Should he stay?
Everything had been going so well. Fuck Ollie and his bints!
'No. They had all been laughing. If they had seen him they would have looked interested, concerned, even dumbstruck, but not laughing.'
He stayed in all next day. Still on tenterhooks.
Every so often a peek out the window onto the walkway.
A beeping horn made him look out of the French doors and over the verandah.
A beautiful sight heartened him.
Four people putting their cases in the boot of a vehicle and then the taxi driving off.
The four were bound for Malaga Airport.
Returning home. Mission accomplished.

On Wednesday Jones walked into the Super Sun Resort to start his first day as a Timeshare salesman.
He was good at it.
All he had to do was lie through his teeth.
He watched, as an observer, the first and second couples at the presentation refuse to sign up for eight thousand pounds. The rep played it straight.

Streets took him to one side at lunch break and asked him about the two deals that 'walked'.

"'e were a prat that rep. Punters asked 'im if they could sell the timeshare when they'd had enough, rep said they could try but no real resale value. Maybe get nine hundred for it. The other rep was a prat too. Told 'em in August probably wouldn't get what they wanted. They had young kids."

Streets smiled at him.

"You see already, that a few little porkies goes a long way, don't it?"

"Yep, it does."

"Good man."

He was allowed on his own the third day and never looked back. Five percent on each deal meant an average of four hundred pounds on a successful sale, and he had two shots a day. He considered it was like taking sweets from a baby, and he was buggered if he was going to offer up anything for income tax. Couldn't anyway.

On Sunday evenings the reps and the three managers always had drinks in a local bar to round the week off.

Jones had three deals to his name, so he was happy.

He sat next to a man who was going back to the UK in a few days as he'd had enough of timeshare selling and Spain without money was tough, if not impossible.

"What you's doin' with your car, Adrian?"

"Flogging it. It's in good nick."

After a short description and an inspection by Jones, the old Citroen C4 exchanged hands for three hundred pounds. Jones now had some paperwork with his new name on it if stopped by the Guardia. Adrian John Mirren.

He had promised Adrian that he would make sure the paperwork was sent off to effect change of ownership.

That promise was never kept.

Whilst not back to its previous high output Sagittarius End was improving.

Engineers and pipe layers worked flat out to repair all the damage.

Stewle had asked Ollie to take over Jones' job as chargehand.

He offered an uplift in wages and Ollie said he'd think about it.

He said he'd need the Friday morning after Christmas off due to a family commitment.

Christmas Day was an all-day party and lunch at Ollie's.

Ham, Myriam, Milly and Ollie's parents came.

Annabel was astounded to find that Ollie really *could* cook.
He was a star at it, right down to the gravy.
Even his Christmas pudding was excellent.
He didn't mention that it came from M and S.
Ollie bought Annabel a very expensive fake fur collared coat. She bought him a Tag Heuer Formula 1 watch.
Bess got a chewy toy that was gone before ten am.
Everyone stayed overnight except Ollie's Mum and Dad.
They went home very happy via the same taxi firm that had delivered them.
"Oh, they do look *so* happy."
"Aye. She's a fine girl, that one."
"I knew she was the one as soon as I saw them together."
"Aye. Sometimes prayers do get answered."
On Friday Ollie had his interview with a panel of three for the teacher's vacancy.
Three weeks later he was asked to come forward for a second interview, after which he was offered the job.

Baker was extremely optimistic when Radford, one of the forensic scientists, knocked on his office door.
"Well?"

"We have a match."

"Brilliant. Thanks."

He told Chief Constable Greenberg of the match.

"That's great, John. Get it on the Interpol Ap1 list straightaway. I'll send another message to the Guardia, confirming he's the chief suspect now and for them to hold him. Get me his photo."

"Right you are, Sir. I've got his photo. I'll ask Bailey to drop it in to you in a few minutes."

Baker was pleased and busy for the next hour. His team knew.

He also told Stewle.

"Bless my soul, Malcolm. You've had all sorts on that damned site of yours. Plenty of theft and sabotage, now you've got a bloody murder. You do see life, that's for sure."

Stewle couldn't disagree.

"Yes. Glad to see the back of that Jones idiot. Copper told me they believe he's in Spain. Interpol are on the case. We've had nothing but trouble since he's been in charge. Wouldn't be surprised if he wasn't the thief behind all the stuff we've lost."

"Maybe. Could well be. Mind you, he'd have needed help with that digger. S'pose you'll advertise for a foreman now?"

Stewle stood up. Walked to the drinks cabinet. Poured himself a large one.

"No. I've offered the job to that Wilson fellow. As you know, he saved the site. Risked his life into the bargain, him and that black fellow. If the storage gas had gone up….well, you know what *that* would have done.

"Indeed."

"Used to be a teacher, so he's no bam pot, unlike Jones. That's another thing, Jones could well have been the shite house that put all the settings up the Swannee and vandalised stuff in the offices, as a parting shot."

"Yup, I suspect it was him. You could do worse than giving the job to that Wilson guy."

Stewle sipped his Scotch.

"Engineers tell me if the pipe layers work their socks off, we should be fully back on stream late-January."

"That's music to my ears. Yours too, I imagine."

"Sure is."

At the end of January four of the young men that killed Alex were sentenced to life imprisonment with a tariff of a minimum fourteen years before consideration for parole.

The other two were jailed for five years each for assault occasioning grievous bodily harm.

Five Months Later

TWENTY-EIGHT

"Are you nervous?"
Ollie turned.
"About what?"
Annabel grabbed his hair.
"You know what."
"Ow. Okay, okay, yes."
"Good. So am I."
"Yes, it's not every day a man and a woman proclaim to fifty odd people that they are going to have it off together in bed that night."
"Is Ham nervous?"
Ollie frowned.
"He's not going to be in the bed as well, is he?"
Annabel grabbed his hair again.
"Ow. Ow. *Yes*, he's a little bit nervous. Mostly about his speech. Said he's been rehearsing it for weeks."
Annabel leant over and kissed him on the cheek.
"What about your Dad?"

"Oh, he's alright. Glad to know that his son is going to stop offering women in Attleborough money for sex on Saturday nights."

They had dropped Bess off at Ollie's parent's house that afternoon in preparation for the wedding next day and their flight to Spain.

The couple watched television and just before ten Ollie drove Annabel to her flat in Hingham. They had agreed not to share a bed that night. They kissed goodnight. Looked into each other's eyes. Annabel had tears in hers.

"You're special," she said.

"Thank you."

"Yes, they have special schools and homes for people like you."

He drove back to Attleborough happy.

Glad he'd met her.

Truth be known, *she* was the special one. He felt so lucky.

Ham had gone over his speech for the fourth time that day.

He sat in the kitchen.

Tomorrow he would be word perfect with it.

Myriam came in.

"You're not *still* going over that *again* are you?"

"Need it to be good. No mistakes."

"Ye Gods! *I've* read it *three* times for you. *You've* rehearsed it a dozen times. You *must* be au fait with it *now*, surely to God?"
Ham sipped from a can of orange.
"Yes. I just want it right."
She sat on his lap.
"It's perfect. I'd have told you, had it not been."
Milly came in.
"Oops! Not interrupting anything am I?"
Myriam got up.
"No Ma. He's just having his eighteenth nervous breakdown over his Best Man's speech."
"Nice cup of tea will sooth him. Won't it, Ham?"
"A treble scotch in it might help."
"I must say I'm looking forward to it. Not as much as I'm looking forward to *yours*, *whenever* that may be, of course," said Milly.
"Soon as we've saved enough, Ma."
Milly smiled.
"Well, the pay rise, that Ollie got you, should help."
Myriam agreed.
"Yes, but it's still a smelly and boring job, isn't it Ham?"
"Yup. Ollie said he'll not be there by the end of the year. Me either if I can help it."
Milly poured the hot water into the pot.

"Strange that he stayed on. He got the teacher's job, if he'd wanted it," said Milly.

"I know. Annabel wanted him to leave and take the job," said Myriam.

"I told you before. He stayed because he was offered the job by Stewle and he said he'd take it only if we all got a pay rise *and* if the company installed showers for the staff. If he'd left, none of that would have happened."

"It certainly made a difference to the pong factor, that's for sure, and our monthly savings," said Myriam.

Myriam put his cup before him.

"Funny they never caught that bloke what killed that girl. You'd think nowadays with all them European coppers working together, they'd have nabbed him."

Ollie woke at half past four.
The bedside clock told him he was awake far too early.
He turned off the alarm.
Laid there. Thought of Annabel.
In a few hours they'd be Mr and Mrs Wilson.
He smiled.
Jumped out of bed, into the kitchen.
No Bess.
He remembered. At his Mum and Dad's place.
Kettle on. Telly on. Bread in the toaster.

His suit in the hall way looked the same as the previous twenty odd times he'd looked at it, hanging up. Pretty damned good. Made to measure.

Ham said he'd be round at twelve and to have the glass of Scotch and the valium ready.

He thought his Dad would be nervous, but glad his wife wouldn't be there on the way to the reception to continuously tell him to remember not to tell any 'smutty' stories.

The job was now going well.

Apart from the two off sites, he rotated the team around the different sites at Sagittarius End daily so that the horrible D site was shared equally. He had been very surprised when Stewle had agreed immediately to his three conditions for taking the job of foreman. Pay up to ten pounds an hour for the men and he got fifteen. The biggest surprise was the agreement on setting up proper shower units, so they could shower and change clothes before going home at night.

He'd also agreed to paying someone to run the café again.

Ollie approached Archie Binns, from the Bricklayers pub, who sourced a young lady barmaid that had worked for him on occasion and who was looking for just such an

opportunity, and this suited her well as she lived nearby.
Annabel was disappointed that he turned down the teaching position, but he assured her that before the year was out he'd resign and apply for other teaching positions in the area.
She understood.

Jones stood naked in front of the bathroom mirror.
He'd grown a beard. His hair was cut quite short. He dyed both beard and hair blond, every week, without fail.
He wore clear vision glasses, slightly tinted. An important part of the disguise, just in case.
He thought he looked good. Sun tanned.
Gloria Wallace lay in bed. Still tired.
Couldn't wait for Monday to come, two whole days off.
She'd left her husband in the UK *and* their two children.
Let *him* see what it was like to have no fun. No good times. Just counting pennies. Washing. Ironing. Cleaning. Cooking. Just be a fuggin' drudge for the rest of your days. No thank you.
Like Jones, she dyed her hair blond and sunbathed every available minute she could. She always dressed in black and showed plenty of cleavage.

Gloria could take her alcohol with the best of them and had become partial to cocaine and marijuana.

Jones was okay. Bit of a prick but she could handle him. She'd had worse. She accepted what he wanted.

He paid the bills.

Her bank balance was beginning to look very healthy.

On their first night out together, after lots of drink, he'd taken her to his flat, stripped her naked, turned her over and had his way.

It had been painful, but she was drunk, that helped.

He came in the bedroom.

Dripping. Wet. Towel around his waist.

"Ah. She's awake. The coke 'ead is conscious."

She smiled at him. Dreamy eyed.

"Great last night, weren't it? Fuggin' blast. Smithy were mullered. *And* the silly bastard drove home."

Jones took his towel off his hips and rubbed his hair with it.

Gloria looked him up and down.

He looked a lot better with clothes *on*.

She sat up.

"Time is it?"

"Half nine."

She walked past him. Touched his penis. Kept walking.
He shook his head.
"If I had time you'd be fuggin' for it."
She went into the bathroom and sat on the loo.
In an hour or two everything would have worn off.
She'd feel like shit.
Luckily, they had toilets at the sales deck and she had a stash of coke to lift her spirits. It would get her through the day.
Now that Jones was a team leader, he had to be in before ten am to take part in the manager's morning meetings.
Each manager had five rep's to oversee.
Bit of chat from the boss, Adrian Reynolds. He was short, bald, red faced and rotund. He considered the female sales staff his harem.
Last days figures. Scolding for any no sales. The fear of the sack was always prevalent.
Coffee and give the crews their starting list.
Round of applause for those that were successful on the previous day.
He'd soon got the hang of it as a rep.
Lie, lie and lie again.
Punters were invited off the street for a two-hour timeshare presentation and in return they got a free holiday for two. Except it wasn't really free, as they found out much later.

After four months they made him a team manager. He was a good liar at that too.

His main job was to come onto any table, where the rep sat with two punters, and smooth out a sale at the end of the presentation.

He'd been very successful and the rep's liked to call him onto their tables if they had difficult clients.

However, he always had a dread of being recognized.

As of now he hadn't seen anyone, on or off the resort, who he thought looked familiar, apart from those bastards from Sagittarius End, and that was months ago.

He thought his new look would help if anyone from his neck of the UK passed a glance at him.

Jones always scoured the punters through the one-way window of the manager's office, before going out amongst the tables. Just in case.

He carried the gun with him everywhere he went. Except on the sales floor, it was secreted in his locker in the office set aside for managers.

Gloria didn't like him much, but he had a flat, paid for the meals they had out, and she kept

her mouth shut when she knew he was going to a brothel, which he did often.
She was enjoying her life and if the price was his kinky ways, she could stand that. Someone better would surely come along one day.
The gun worried her.
Especially when he was angry, drunk or high.

Myriam and Milly drove along the country roads to drop off Ham and then to pick up Ollie's Mum.
Ham sat quietly next to Myriam. Milly sat in the back.
She called out to her daughter.
"What are they doin' when the reception is finished?"
"They're going to the Maids Head Hotel, staying there overnight, then flying to Spain from Norwich tomorrow morning. *Late* tomorrow morning."
"Maids Head, eh. That must cost."
"It's a special time, Ma. Weddings are really a day to remember. Aren't they?"
Milly pulled a face.
"Me an' your father just had a day out at Yarmouth on the Sunday. He was back at work Monday."
"Yes, but things are different now."
Milly looked out of the car window. Far away.

"We was saving for furniture, for when we got a council house."
Myriam looked at Ham. They smiled.
They'd heard this story a dozen times.

She was ready when they came. Had been for over an hour. Fidgeting, nervous.
Inspecting her husband took fifteen minutes.
He stood on parade in the lounge near the patio doors, so she could see him better.
"Now Henry, just remember…"
He sighed.
"I know, Edith. No smutty jokes."
"Yes."
Ollie's father waved the four of them off.
He had over an hour before the limo came for him.
Just time for a wee snifter.

Annabel looked at herself in the long mirror.
White bra and pants. White stockings and suspenders.
She hoped Ollie didn't have a heart attack!
Her wedding dress lay on the bed.
The hairdresser had finished half an hour ago.
Brenda Oxford from 'The Day' in Norwich was coming to help her get all her finery on.
They'd been pals for years.

Brenda had been a teacher but left to start the Norwich shop. It had been a big success.
'Fifteen minutes and she'll be here,'
She was so happy and just a little nervous.
The weather was kind. Not a cloud in the sky.
She'd been to the loo six times. Nervous pee's.
Housecoat on.
At last Brenda came. All reassuring and professional.
The two bridesmaids and a page boy also arrived a little later in their limo.
They were children of two close friends.
She sat them in the kitchen with the driver plus a few biscuits and orange juice.
When ready they would go in tandem.
Henry would make sure they all arrived ten minutes late.
Just as it should be.

Ollie and Ham stood in front of the altar.
The vicar nodded to them and whispered.
"Not long now, gentlemen."
The church was packed to the rafters.
Outside, nearly a thousand onlookers stood, in good spirits, waiting for the bride to make her entrance.
The Groom was a local hero, after all. Been on TV.

There were cheers as two black 1950 Bentleys made their way slowly through the throng.
Many people shouted, 'Good luck'.
Billy Oxford, the local film maker and Brenda's hubby, was shooting the whole thing.
The page boy and bridesmaids got out first and stood with Myriam as the second car bearing Annabel and Henry pulled up.
A very loud cheer echoed around St Mary's as Annabel was helped from the limousine by Henry.
Ollie and Ham heard it and turned to the partially open doors.
The two men, nervous now, more than ever.
The doors parted.
Annabel and Henry walked slowly in.
The bride was stunningly beautiful in her elegant wedding dress, followed by her entourage.
Henry said later that she looked so lovely he had thought about driving her up to Gretna Green.
As she walked down the aisle, the wedding music was playing.
Annabel, with proud Henry beside her.
She nodded and smiled as her friends and relations mouthed 'Beautiful' to her.
Ollie was all for kissing her there and then.
He beamed at his bride.

They looked at each other. Both sure.
The ceremony progressed, and was over too quick, or so it seemed.
Man and wife.
Church bells ringing. Crowd cheers. Whistles. Applause. Confetti everywhere.
They posed for photographs outside the church.
Perfect.
The Bride and Groom drove slowly through the crowd and away to the reception at Barnham Broom Golf and Country Club.
"Thank god we've got photographs and a film of all that. It went so quickly," said Annabel.
"Yeah. A blur really. But you, you look so beautiful in that wedding dress."
"That's as maybe. I'm still not washing up tonight after supper."
Ollie smiled at her.
"There must have been over a thousand there, inside and out. I noticed a lot of Sagittarius workers there, with their ladies, too."
"How was my Dad?" said Ollie.
"Brilliant. Think he'd had a couple beforehand, though."
"I did too, and Ham."
"The vicar did too. I smelt it on his breath."
"Bunch of bloody alkies."

TWENTY-NINE

They drove to the main reception at Barnham and were met by the Resort Manager.

He showed them the large ballroom where the reception would be held, and then a booked suite where they could change and freshen up if they wanted to.

The ballroom was set up for two hundred and fifty guests.

It looked the picture of elegance with flowers everywhere. Tables dressed to perfection. The resort staff were professionals.

The Manager told them he would advise the couple when all the guests were in situ in the ball room. In the meantime, the mini bar was fully stocked, as arranged, and if they required anything else, to just lift the phone.

As the manager left, Ollie scooped Annabel to him.

He kissed her.

It was a long kiss. No longer HTB.

Later they came into the ballroom to great cheers and applause.
Ham's speech was a triumph.
Henry remembered. No smutty jokes.
The Bride and Groom took to the floor first.
Handsome. Beautiful. Elegant. Perfect.

The aircraft touched down in Malaga.
Twenty-five minutes later they were in a taxi headed for the Hotel Xabia.
The next six days were spent mostly laying on the beach, eating, drinking, and making love.
It was a Saturday. One they will never forget.
They went down to breakfast around ten.
Sun streaming through the windows. One or two swimmers already in the pool.
They decided to visit the castle in Fuengirola.
Taxi. Walk round. Bought a couple of souvenirs. Had lunch at a local café and returned to the Hotel Xabia for an afternoon nap.
After their nap they decided to swim in the sea.

Jones and Gloria lay in bed after snorting a line of coke.
He lit up a joint and passed it to her. Breakfast.
"Only one fuggin' wave today. At eleven. Be in the bar by one, us will be," said Jones
He went into the bathroom to shower.

She opened his bedside drawer. Usually he'd throw his wallet and other money in there last thing before he got into bed.

Happiness. Two twenty Euro notes and three fives. She took one of each. Stuffed them in the lining of her hand bag.

A towel covered something.

She lifted the towel.

Shit!

His pistol. Walther 22.

He had spent nearly an hour taking off the silencer to make it smaller. Fitted nicely into his pocket.

It frightened her.

He was dim enough and sometimes angry enough to pull the trigger.

Gloria dropped the towel back over the gun and closed the drawer.

She finished off the spliff and laid back on the bed.

At ten past one the last punter left.

Jones and Gloria changed clothes in the apartment and, clad in shorts and tee shirts, made haste to one of their regular haunts, 'Ronnies', a bar adjoining Javea beach.

They drank a lot in a short space of time and then laid on the golden beach.

"Ah, this is the fuggin' life."

Gloria fell asleep.

Jones smoked and eyed the women.
He'd looked down at Gloria.
If she wasn't careful she'd burn.
'Fuggit. Her lookout.'
After half an hour he was back at 'Ronnies'.
A good vantage point for watching talent go by was the raised part of the bar at the front. It was here he positioned himself.
Pedro brought him two San Miguels.
Regular order. Good customer, this one and his girlfriend.
Jones nodded as the barman pulled the caps off and placed the beers before him.
"No working, today, Adrian?"
Jones swigged from the bottle.
"Nah."

She ducked him under.
He lay prone, head down in the sea.
Unmoving.
She stood watching him.
He didn't move.
She knew he was play acting.
Wasn't he?
She grabbed his shoulders to lift him up.
He stood up and splashed water at her.
"So, try to drown me, would you?"
They embraced. Kissed. Hugged.
"Want a drink?"

"Have you got money?"
He unfolded a very wet twenty euro note from out of his swimsuit's little pocket.
"Ever the boy scout."
They walked hand in hand through the beach to the nearest bar. Ronnies.

Jones was finishing his second bottle when he saw them.
Both were wet. Ollies hair was a mess, but he knew it was him.
"Jesus!"
He jumped down off the bar platform.
Ollie saw him.
Puzzled.
Someone he knew but couldn't figure.
Jones ran around the back of the bar and across the road to his apartment.
He slammed the door, breathing heavily.
"Shit! That was close!"

Ollie and Annabel sat on the plastic chairs skirting the bar.
"I recognised that bloke."
"What bloke?"
"The one who jumped down off that high bar."
He pointed to the raised bar seating area.
"Who was it?"
He shook his head.

"Dunno. But his face was sort of familiar, somehow."
The barman came to take their order.
They ordered two small beers.
"Do you know who that man was, that was at the high table?"
Pedro nodded.
"Si. Him is Adrian. He come here all the time."
The name Adrian didn't ring any bells.
"No?" said Annabel.
"No. Adrian means nothing."
"Too much sea water floating around your brain."
Gloria came in. Bleary eyed.
"Pedro. Seen Adrian?"
Pedro nodded.
"He *was* here but him ran away. He no pay neither."
"Tosser," said Gloria.
She walked past Annabel and Ollie and sat at the bar.
Pedro knew her style.
The vodka he served was a *very* large one.
Ollie was going to ask Gloria about 'Adrian', but decided against it.
They finished their beers and walked hand in hand back to the Hotel.

It always gave him a kick to go to the Hotel reception and ask for 'Mr and Mrs' Wilson's key please, room 305.'
They showered together.
Dried each other
Loved each other.

Jones had snorted some coke by the time Gloria came in.
"Where did you piss off to?"
Jones shrugged.
"Needed a dump. You's was asleep."
"Could've woke me."
"Nah. Had to race here. Just made it."
"I paid Pedro."
"Okay. You's want a line?"
She perked up.
"Oh, yes please."
He grinned.
"It'll cost you's."
She paid the price.
They both got high.

Nigel told Baker *everything*.
It felt good when he'd finished.
Baker thanked him after he had signed his statement.
Nigel drove back to Sagittarius End a happy man.

He'd got all the shit that Jones had put in his head out and away.

The only drawback to his happiness was that Wilson had got the job that he had expected to get.

Oh yes, things were better at Sagittarius End now, what with the showers, better pay, the cafe and the rota system, but he thought when Jones had gone he would be the main man.

'That bastard Wilson. Now he's away for two weeks. Fancy makin' that nigger a boss when him away. Not right, me being white, *an'* English.'

He got to Sagittarius End around two.

'Three hours then me is going to pork 'er'.

His relationship with Doreen was okay apart from a couple of issues.

'That fuggin' kid. He were always interruptin' things'

'The other was she were always askin' me for money. As soon as she let me have her, she always went on about him givin' her some fuggin' dosh.'

Before he started work he wanted a drink and a roll.

'Bollocks to the nigger boss.'

He went into the reopened café.

'She were not a bad lookin' wench that one. Wonder if she'd…'

"Yes dear. What can I get you?"
"Tea an' a 'am roll, ta."
He got his tea and roll and sat down.
The only other customer was one of the engineers who was on his last day at Sagittarius before heading back to Head Office. His inspection gave the site a ten out of ten. He was checking his route home to the North.
Nigel went to the counter again.
She looked up at him and smiled.
"Choccy bar. Umm, Snickers, ta."
She handed him the chocolate bar.
"Ta."
"You're welcome."
He turned away.
Angry with himself.
'Fuggit! Should've spoken to 'er. Idjit!'
He sat down again.
'Quarter to three. Better get movin'. Only another two hours an' she'd be getting' it. Need to get rid of that fuggin' kid. P'raps if I buy 'im a make-it-yerself aeroplane kit, send 'im up to bed early to make it.'
Five o'clock and he was gone.
Burning rubber along the A47 to Doreen's house.
He stopped at the village shop.

No model aeroplanes but there was a magazine on aircraft, with a simple DIY balsa plane to make up. He took it to the counter.
"Eight forty, please. Sir."
Shocked. Stunned.
"Eight what? Did you's say eight pounds?"
The man nodded.
"Eight pounds forty."
Nigel coughed.
Face red.
"Sorry. Got the wrong one. Me brother said, 'is one were two quids."
The man shook his head.
"Most of this type of magazine are all around the eight to ten pounds area."
Face beetroot.
"I…um…well, don't wannit then."
Plan A shelved.
He arrived at Jone's house.
Not happy, but she could change all that.
He had a key.
Went straight in.
Doreen on couch in dressing gown.
Sound asleep. Snoring. Empty wine bottle standing by the settee.
No sign of the kid.
He gently lifted one side of her gown.
Exposed left breast and thigh.
Pulled the other half of the gown to one side.

She wrinkled her nose.
He bent over and licked her nipple.
She woke up with a start.
"What the…..!"
She sat up.
"You're early."
"Not really. Came straight from work. Wanted you's. Been wantin' you's all day."
She sighed. A fed-up sigh.
She unzipped him.
"Where's the kid?"
"Running an errand."

An hour later as they sat on the couch drinking strong cider, the kid came home.
"Auntie Jean said I can stay with 'er an' Reggie Sunday night."
She sent him into the kitchen to eat some crisps and a bar of chocolate.
Nigel thought it was little wonder he was a big, greasy, fat slob. Fancy eating chocolate for your tea. Pie an' chips yeah, but chocolate, never.
"Shall I stay tonight, or what?"
He ran his hand up the inside of her thigh.
She closed her legs.
"Maybe. We'll see. I need a bit of money for some grub."
She looked up at him.

Demure. Licked her lips slowly.
He smiled sweetly at her.
"I've got twenty quid for a little lady who'll let me do it the way I like."
"I don't see why not. Long as you's takes it easy. Not go fuggin' mad like last time."
He grinned.
"I will. Gentle as a lamb I'll be."
He stayed the night and she was gone from the bed when he woke.
He went into the kitchen to get something to drink. The kid sat eating chocolate weeties from a very large bowl.
"Where's your Mum?"
"Shoppin'."
Saturday morning. Thought he'd go home, change and down the Legion.
On his car, behind the windscreen wiper, was a note from Doreen.
'We won't not do that no more an' whers the 20 quids'.
He went back into the house.
Left her a scribbled message saying he'd be back Sunday afternoon and a begrudged twenty-pound note lay beside it.
He put both on the mantlepiece.
"I left summat on the mantle for you's mum. Don't touch it or I'll bash you."
The kid frowned.

He unlocked the door to his flat.
Home.
Doreen's place is better, if it wasn't for the kid.
He remembered that Wilson was getting married today, in Attleborough.
'Bastard never invited me.'
His mobile phone rang.
The caption said Jones, but it was Doreen calling from her home.
"Thanks for the money Nigel. So, you're coming tomorrow afternoon are you's?"
He smiled.
"Yeah."
"Well, the kid is at 'is aunties' for the night so you can stay over, but no more buggerin' me Nigel. You 'urt me again last night. No more of that. Bring some wine."
"Okay, see you's tomorrow."
"Afore you go, I was thinking, you spendin' so much time 'ere, an' me an' you is sort of a couple now ain't we? You could sort of, well, move in and we could be a couple like *properly*."
Wow! Bit of a shock, but he rather liked the idea of having it on tap whenever he wanted it.
"Okay. Yeah. Sounds alright."
His mind was running overtime. Sell his flat or rent it out. Only pay half for electric, water, rates. Might be a hell of a lot cheaper, *and* she

was available whenever he wanted it. She could cook, wash and iron his stuff.

"We can talk about it tomorrow. What about Jonesy though?"

"He won't be coming back. If the coppers get 'im he'll do fourteen years minimum. Murder an' all."

"Right. Okay. See you tomorrow. Bring a couple of bottles."

"Okay."

He spent most of the day between the Legion and the bookies. The more he drank the more he betted and the more he betted the more he lost.

He woke up Sunday morning with a hangover.

He totted up how much he had lost at the bookies.

Three hundred and fifty quid! Shit!

At two o'clock he started the drive to Doreens'.

He stopped to get two bottles of wine at the Burrows' off-licence.

He picked up the cheapest he could find.

Two elderly ladies trying to find the right money at the till.

Nigel jittery.

Taking their bloody time.

Fuggit!

He slipped out the door, a bottle in each hand.

Ran like the wind to Merton's Alley.

Shout from behind.

"Stop him!"

Off duty policeman had just parked up.

Nigel ran past him.

Mr Burrows hot on his heels.

"He's …stolen …from me shop!"

Policeman sprinted and grabbed Nigel.

Pinned him against Nigel's car.

Nigel swung a bottle at the policeman's head.

Smashed. Opened deep cut.

The policeman fell back. Blood flowing.

Mr Burrows, out of breath.

Punched Nigel, hard.

He bounced off his car.

Policeman, with a handkerchief to his head and Mr Burrows, stopped him from going anywhere.

"You're nicked."

Many hours later Nigel was released from Wymondham Police Station.

Charged with assaulting a police officer, resisting arrest, causing grievous bodily harm and theft.

Nigel never made it to Doreen's that day.

THIRTY

Jones sat in the bar 'Amigos', well back from the beach.
'Ronnies' was too close to where Wilson might be for his liking.
He thought he must be here for a holiday. But what if he wasn't?
What if he was working here? Maybe on the offshore rig just being constructed out at sea. He knew there were many rig workers living in Javea.
Jones hated the idea of having to move on.
He had it made here.
Good job, good flat, lots of money. A woman who said 'yes' to everything.
He worked out his options.
Find out if that bastard Wilson was on holiday or not.
How to do that?
Bingo!

Go to Hotel Xabia and check the duration of his stay.
If he was only there for a couple of weeks, great. No need to move, just lay low until he'd gone.
He drank two beers in quick succession and went to his apartment.
Gloria was in the shower.
He collected his Walther and left.

Ollie looked down at his bride.
Even in the morning with her bed hair all over the place, she was still so beautiful.
He felt that he could swallow her whole.
Lovely.
Proud to have her as his bride.
He slipped out of bed, visited the loo then stood on the balcony.
Bright and sunny day again.
People setting up on the beach.
It was Sunday and the Spanish were enjoying Javea sea side in May.
Last chance before the hordes of holiday makers descended for four months.
It was an idyllic place.
He looked down at the people passing by the hotel.
Suddenly he saw that man again.
Now who the hell did he remind him of?

The man went out of view for a few seconds as he passed some trees.
Came into view again.
Yes! Got it! It looked like Jones!
Had a beard and his hair was all short and blond, and even with those tinted glasses it definitely looked like Jones.
He shouted out.
"Jonesy!"
Jones heard his name.
Looked up in a panic.
"Fuck!"
Hurried into the hotel.
Straight to the concierge.
"Can I help…"
"What room is Wilson in?"
The Concierge didn't like being spoken to in such an abrupt manner.
"Are you a friend of Mr Wilson, sir?"
Jones, eyes bulging, pulled the gun out of his pocket.
He pointed it at the Concierge.
"Just fuggin' tell me what fuggin' room? You dago bastard!"
The Spaniard took a step backwards. Hands held up.
"Please sir, I…."
Jones' face was beetroot red. His eyes blazed in anger.

"What fuggin' room?"
"Jonesy!"
A shout from the stairs.
Ollie.
Jones wheeled round.
"Why did you 'ave to be 'ere? You've fuggin' spoiled it, you fugger!"
He pointed the gun at Ollie.
"Jonesy. Don't be silly, I.."
The gun fired.
Well over his head. Smacked against the bannister rail.
Ollie turned. Ran up the stairs.
Bang.
The second shot fizzed past his head and ricocheted off a stair metal bar.
Ollie continued up and dodged down around the top of the stairs.
Jones was pursuing him. Shouting.
He ran up the second and third stairwells. Unlocked his door.
Slammed it shut.
Heart pounding. Anger mounting.
'That shitty bugger actually tried to *kill* me'.
Annabel came out of the bedroom.
Bleary eyed. Smiling.
"Hello darling. I missed you, I…"
Ollie's face told her something was very wrong.

"What is it? What's happened?"

Jones slipped on the stairs. Cursed.
He ran back down.
The Concierge was calling the Guardia.
Jones ran across to him.
"What number? Come on you's fugger! What fuggin' number?"
"I….please….I."
The gun was pointed at his head.
The Concierge. Afraid. Shaking.
"305…305."
Jones hurried across to the lifts.
Pressed the 'Up' buttons on both lifts.
Cursing.
"Hurry up you's shithouses. Hurry up!"
One of the lifts 'pinged'.
Two elderly ladies stood as the sliding door opened.
"Get out the fuggin' way."
Jones grabbed one lady by the arm and hauled her out.
She screamed.
"You're hurting me!"
She fell over onto the tiled floor.
He turned to the other and pushed her away.
She, too, fell over.
"Get the fug out of it!"
He pressed 3 on the lift control panel.

Pressed it and pressed it. Rapidly.
The door closed.
It stopped at the second floor and a man and a woman were going to get in.
He shouted at them. Waved his gun at them.
"No!"
They both looked terrified and stood back.
Jones pressed 3. He rapidly hit the button a number of times before the door closed.
'Fuggin' Wilson. Spoilin' everythin'.
The lift 'pinged' and the doors slid open on the third floor.
He raced along the corridor until he came to '305'.

"It *was* Jones I saw the other day. He's in the hotel, with a gun. He's gone loopy. Shot at me."
Annabel bit her lip.
"Oh my god!"
He pulled her to him.
"I just hope the Concierge has called the police."
"Bloody hell! So do I. What shall we do?"
He kissed her forehead.
"We sit tight. Wait until downstairs tell us everything has been resolved."
There was a knocking on the door.
They looked at each other. Both scared.

He pushed her towards the bathroom.
Go in there and lock the door.
"But what about you?"
"I'm going to try to talk some sense into the idiot, through the door. The more time we buy, the better the chances of the coppers arriving. Now go."
She looked at him.
"No. I'm staying with you."
He looked sternly at her.
"Now look. You….."
Banging on the door again. Louder and longer this time.
Ollie stood to the side of the door. Annabel stood behind him.
Nervous, shaking.
"What do you want?"
Bang!
A shot came through the door and crashed into their far wall.
"Jesus!"
Ollie pulled Annabel along with him to the bathroom.
"Get in there. If he won't bugger off, I'll join you."
She nodded. Fearful. Trembling.
He went back to the door.

Three shots rang out in quick succession and the door lock spun off the door and fell to the floor.
"Go!" said Ollie.
"No!" said Annabel.
The door slowly opened.
A hand came through, clutching the Walther.
Ollie grabbed it and pulled. It fired.
The shot hit the far wall with a loud zing as it ricocheted away.
He kept hold of Jones' hand and twisted it.
Jones kicked him and pulled away.
He pointed the gun at Ollie.
Annabel screamed.
It startled Jones and he looked at her.
Ollie punched him. Hard.
Jones fell back and banged into the open door.
Before he could recover Ollie kicked out at him.
It found the meaty part of his stomach.
Jones doubled up.
Ollie grabbed the gun barrel and pulled.
Jones let go.
Ollie hit him with the gun butt.
He fell back. The cut over his eye bleeding.
Ollie straddled him on the floor.
He shoved the gun barrel hard, really hard, into Jones' mouth, it broke his two front teeth.

Ollie pulled the trigger.
Click.
Jones eyes squinted.
Ollie pulled the trigger a number of times in quick succession.
All he got was a series of clicks.
It all went quiet.
He withdrew the barrel, threw the gun away and punched Jones as hard as he could, square on the nose.
"That's for spoiling our day, arsehole!"
Jones started sobbing as the blood oozed out of his broken nose.
A shout came from the corridor.
"Policia! Senor! Policia! Put down the weapon. *Now!*"
Two Guardia Civil officers squatted. Their guns pointed at the two.

Three hours later, Ollie, Annabel and the Concierge were allowed to leave the police station.
There was a posse of cameramen, TV reporters and newspaper hacks as they left, and even more at the hotel.
The two went straight into the hotel bar escorted by the Concierge who had also signed his statement.
He sat with them.

They ordered strong drinks and the waiter served them quickly.
Everyone knew what had happened.
Back in their room. Annabel let it all out.
She clung to Ollie and sobbed.
Later, she asked him about the fight with Jones.
"You put the gun in his mouth and pulled the trigger. I heard the gun click. Did you really want to kill him?"
Ollie shook his head.
"Dunno. It's all a haze now. I know I was *very* angry. Hated the pig for trying to kill me and spoiling our honeymoon. Whether I wanted to actually kill him? I guess at that moment I must have."
There was quiet for a few moments.
Annabel reached out and covered his hand with hers.
"He *didn't* spoil our honeymoon. It *was* getting a bit boring."

The next morning's UK newspapers front pages were full of the story, portraying Ollie as the hero of the day.
Pictures of Ollie and Annabel were prominent.
The BBC News on television and radio reported the story in depth.

Ollie and Annabel were virtual prisoners in the hotel.

They had breakfast sent up to their room to avoid publicity gawpers.

British newspapers were on the tray.

They looked at them. Amazed it was them the story was about.

"Just my bloody luck. My daft husband has to be a hero, *twice!*"

Ollie smiled across the table at her.

"I'm so glad I married you."

She nodded.

"I should think so. Who else would put up with a husband practicing dentistry with a pistol on their honeymoon."

His mobile beeped.

Ham had texted him to tell him Infine had his court appearance set by Norwich Magistrates for the end of June. He ended it by asking if he could still be a friend to a major national celebrity?

The Hotel arranged for them to spend the rest of their honeymoon in a sister hotel further up the coast in Oliva.

They left by the kitchen entrance late at night.

They were given the Bridal Guest Suite in Oliva, the rest of their honeymoon was uneventful, apart from the fact that Annabel returned to the UK with a little lodger in her tummy.

THIRTY-ONE

The happy couple arrived back at Norwich Airport in the late afternoon.
Ham and Myriam were there to greet them, along with a large group of cameramen, including ITV and BBC TV.
As they pulled into their road in Attleborough a posse of friends, family and onlookers greeted them with cheers and applause.
Balloons were tied to the fence and front gate.
Edith Wilson clutched Annabel to her and cried and cried.
"You're safe. You're both safe."
Henry Wilson had brought in stocks of alcohol and the cheerful group partied until one am.
Ham and Myriam had to stay the night on the floor in the lounge.
Edith and Henry took the spare room.
Ollie had to help his Dad up the stairs.
Edith would have given him a tongue lashing but was just too happy.

On June the 29th Nigel Infine was sentenced to 24 months in prison.

In August, Bernard Jones at Norwich Crown Court was sentenced to Life Imprisonment, with a tariff of fifteen years.

On January the 10th Annabel presented Ollie with a 7-pound son. They named him Henry Hammond.

Ollie started his new job as a teacher on the 28th of January.

Almost a year to the day that Danny was arrested, he received £15,000 compensation from the police for wrongful arrest.

OTHER BOOKS BY JOSEPH DICKERSON:

OPERATION THURSDAY

THE TUESDAY EMPIRE

THE WEDNESDAY WOMEN

IN PURSUIT OF POWER

THE TENNER

All available on Kindle and in paperback at Amazon

Printed in Great Britain
by Amazon